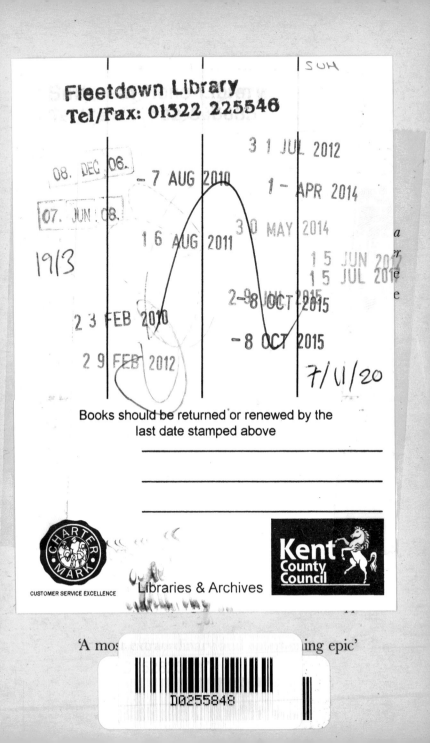

'A most extraordinary and astonishing epic'

D0255848

Books by Val Rutt

THE RACE FOR THE LOST KEYSTONE

THE MYSTERY OF THE DARKSTONE

Val Rutt

The MYSTERY of the Darkstone

PUFFIN

PUFFIN BOOKS

Published by the Penguin Group
Penguin Books Ltd, 80 Strand, London WC2R ORL, England
Penguin Group (USA) Inc., 375 Hudson Street, New York, New York 10014, USA
Penguin Group (Canada), 90 Eglinton Avenue East, Suite 700, Toronto, Ontario,
Canada M4P 2Y3 (a division of Pearson Penguin Canada Inc.)
Penguin Ireland, 25 St Stephen's Green, Dublin 2, Ireland
(a division of Penguin Books Ltd)
Penguin Group (Australia), 250 Camberwell Road, Camberwell, Victoria 3124,
Australia (a division of Pearson Australia Group Pty Ltd)
Penguin Books India Pvt Ltd, 11 Community Centre, Panchsheel Park,
New Delhi – 110 017, India
Penguin Group (NZ), cnr Airborne and Rosedale Roads, Albany,
Auckland 1310, New Zealand (a division of Pearson New Zealand Ltd)
Penguin Books (South Africa) (Pty) Ltd, 24 Sturdee Avenue,
Rosebank, Johannesburg 2196, South Africa

Penguin Books Ltd, Registered Offices: 80 Strand, London WC2R ORL, England

www.penguin.com

First published 2006

1

Text copyright © Val Rutt, 2006
All rights reserved

The moral right of the author has been asserted

Set in Monotype Baskerville
Typeset by Palimpsest Book Production Limited, Polmont, Stirlingshire
Made and printed in England by Clays Ltd, St Ives plc

British Library Cataloguing in Publication Data
A CIP catalogue record for this book is available from the British Library

ISBN-13: 978-0-141-31748-9
ISBN-10: 0-141-31748-5

For Madison with love

Acknowledgements

It was reading about Africa that made me want to go there, and writing this story enabled me to do so. I am grateful to Kendall Lee, MBE, and Arnold School in Blackpool, England, and to Kenneth Mwamampalila and Majenda Mhutila in Buigiri, Tanzania, for making it possible. My thanks to Judy Bould, Sandra Cardiff and Ginny Clee for being there – *asante, sisters.*

Thank you to Apaisaria Doyle for Swahili lessons.
Asante sana.

My thanks, too, to Zachary Bergman, Phil Graham, Graham Puddifoot, the Roald Dahl Museum and Story Centre and Yerbury Primary School.

Love and thanks to Annie Graham:
artist, guardian of Fearless and
great-niece to the woman herself.

Author's Note

For the purposes of this story I have described buildings in the Udzungwa mountains where none exist and taken liberties with the geography of that area.

A note about heartstones

Heartstones have various uses and powers. Owning a heartstone will enable you to develop extraordinary skills and abilities. The longer you wear your heartstone, the more powerful it will become and the more you will be able to achieve. Some heartstones are not suitable for wearing but make excellent sources of energy for powering machines. These are called minnyons and sakers. Some heartstones have very particular powers; one, for example, is used to time travel and is known as a keystone.

A heartstone that has been unworn and unclaimed will make a bond with the first suitable person who touches it. Unfortunately, not everyone has an affinity with the heartstones; for most people there is no reaction and the stones are useless. But, in the right hands, the bond is instant and powerful and must not be broken. A heartstone may be willingly passed on to another but it cannot be stolen. Of the thirty-four heartstones known to exist, only one has ever been forcibly removed from its owner. This heartstone's energy became trapped. It became heavy and black and is called a darkstone.

Contents

The Race

Fridays are almost always good days, but Phil Reynolds had a feeling that this particular Friday something wonderful was going to happen. He ran across the park in long loping strides, every so often taking a leap so high that his return to earth flung his untidy hair skywards and lifted his school bag from his back. When he reached the south side of the park he ignored the gate in favour of the railings, which he vaulted with ease.

After checking for traffic, Phil sprinted diagonally across Morven Road and darted through Mrs Parker's front garden before slinging his bag down on his front door-step and leaning on the doorbell. He bent down to peer through the letter box, his breath leaving a film of condensation on the brass.

Michael Reynolds came out of his office and a look of exasperation quickly replaced the quizzical expression he had been wearing.

'Key? . . . Key?' he yelled at the gaping hole that framed his son's eyes. 'Will you ever remember to use your key?'

As Michael opened the door, Phil threw his school bag inside and rushed upstairs to the bathroom, yanking off his tie as he went and shrugging himself out of his blazer, which he let fall halfway up the stairs.

'And hang that up please!' his father cried. 'What's the big hurry anyway?'

A moment later Phil reappeared wearing jeans and a T-shirt. As he ran downstairs, he snatched up the discarded blazer. 'It's the end of term,' he panted, stuffing it over the banister. 'And I've got to meet Kate and race her home.' He gave his father a glancing grin as he rushed past. 'I'm gonna win this time!' he added, disappearing through the front door and slamming it behind him.

Michael Reynolds shook his head and sighed as he stooped to retrieve his son's blazer, which was in a heap on the floor once more.

Ten minutes later, Phil was standing on the corner of Harpenden Road, watching the south end of the high street for Kate's bus. He checked his watch; she should be along any moment. Although he had reminded her about it at least three times that morning, he didn't entirely trust her not to forget. He glanced behind him at the alley between the Thai supermarket and the dry-cleaner's and when he looked back the bus was coming. *Right*, he thought, *this is it. Time to concentrate.*

Kate spotted Phil as she got off the bus but she took a moment to wave to her friends. Then, as she turned

towards her brother, the smile vanished from her face and her flecked eyes narrowed.

'You are a complete pain in the bum. Can't you just give up?' she asked.

'No, because today I'm going to beat you,' Phil replied cheerfully, 'and then, once I've beaten you, I'll give up.'

Kate raised her eyebrows and shook her head, as if she pitied him.

'You only think you're better than me because you're older and because you got your heartstone first,' Phil fired at her.

'Oh no, not that again!' Kate groaned.

Standing there, squabbling by the bus stop, they looked like an ordinary enough brother and sister, but, as they knew only too well, appearances can be deceptive. Three summers previously, when Phil was nine and Kate was twelve, their parents had revealed to them the existence of an elderly great-aunt and, rather surprisingly, this simple fact had turned their ordinary world completely upside down. From that moment on things had become ever more extraordinary and strange. On the eve of their great-aunt's arrival, suddenly and without warning, their pet cat, Barking, had begun to speak. Then the next day, when Great-Aunt Elizabeth roared up on her gleaming Harley-Davidson, her golden retriever, Fearless, had bounded out of a glass-domed sidecar and, like Barking, he too was able to talk. And when Great-Aunt Elizabeth climbed off her motorbike, Kate and Phil realized that the woman standing before them was, without a doubt, the most extraordinary person they had ever seen. She towered over other adults, men and women alike, spoke and laughed in a voice loud enough to shatter glass and was so strong she could lift grown men from the ground with one hand. Her motorbike was equipped with technology that seemed to defy the laws of physics and, as Kate and Phil soon discovered, her home in New York was a curious combination of antiques and dazzling super-technology invented by her scatty but ingenious assistant, Harold Baker. Great-Aunt Elizabeth was opinionated, forthright and formidable but she was also enormous fun and very loyal and her great-niece and great-nephew became extremely fond of her.

The key to her unique abilities and the strange events that began to unfold from that day onwards could be attributed to the heartstone that Great-Aunt Elizabeth wore round her neck. It emanated a strange energy and radiated a peculiar red glow. Even before their adventures began, Kate inherited a heartstone from her mother and very soon she learnt it was a curiously powerful object which, when worn close to the skin, enabled her to achieve amazing things. Kate immediately began to change and Phil had watched, not without envy, as his sister became far stronger and cleverer than would normally be thought possible for a twelve-year-old girl.

Kate eyed Phil up and down.

'No bag?' she asked.

'I've already been home,' Phil replied.

'Obviously. You have an unfair advantage.'

'Give your bag to me, then, I'll take it.'

'No, it's OK. I was only teasing.'

'No, I know you – if I do win you'll say it was only cos you had a bag and I didn't.' Phil pulled the rucksack from Kate's back and swung it on to his own. 'And you can have a head start,' he added.

'Ha, now you're being silly!'

'No, I mean it. I'll count to ten.'

Kate considered his determined expression for a moment or two. He had grown nearly as tall as her and, now she came to look at him closely, he looked much stronger than he used to. For the first time she experienced a tiny flicker of doubt as to whether she would, in fact, beat him home on this occasion, but she quickly stamped it out.

'I'll tell Mum and Dad that you'll be along in a minute, shall I?' she asked casually.

Phil ignored her, took a deep breath and began to count.

'One . . . Two . . .'

'OK, then.' Kate sighed, pulled her mass of thick hair free from the loose band at the nape of her neck and shook it out before scraping it back into a tight, high ponytail.

'Three . . . Four . . .'

Kate dropped her hands to her sides and shook them a few times, then she bent her knees and stood on tiptoes. She placed her hands on her hips and leant from side to side, stretching her back.

'Five . . . Six . . .'

Kate rocked forward, then drew the upper part of her body backwards, as if she were pulling taut the string of a bow. Suddenly, in a blur of motion, she was off.

Phil forgot to count as he watched her sprint up the road. She was fast. Had he remembered that she was that fast? He had better get going too. He turned towards the alley and disappeared into it at a run.

By the end of that first extraordinary summer with Great-Aunt Elizabeth, Phil was in possession of his own heartstone. The mysterious and much-coveted keystone had been missing for many years, but after a previously unimaginable adventure he and Kate helped to retrieve it and Phil turned out to be its rightful owner. Quickly he began to appreciate the strange bond between a heartstone and its wearer. Whatever he did, his keystone somehow shared and enhanced the experience so that his learning and his physical development became accelerated.

At the end of the alley, Phil climbed up a stack of pallets and heaved himself on to the wall. He ran along it, wavering arms outstretched, then jumped on to the roof of the library. He crawled up its slope and peered over. Several people were standing waiting to cross the road and he knew that a movement from above might attract their attention. He waited until he heard the *beep beep beep* of the crossing before running along the apex of the library roof. He leapt on to the flat roof of the adjacent

supermarket, where a large black cat was sitting beside a ventilation outlet, holding one paw in the air as if interrupted in mid-wash. Dangling from the paw was a stopwatch.

'Two minutes, thirteen seconds,' said the cat. 'You'll need to make up time in the park.'

'Thanks, Barking,' Phil murmured as he sped across the roof and swung himself over the low wall that edged it before dropping five metres on to the cab of an articulated truck in a loading bay below. He jumped on to the body of the truck and ran to the end. The tailgate was open and a man in a forklift was unloading crates of tinned food. Phil didn't hesitate but leapt from the roof of the lorry across the rising stacks of tins that blocked the operator's view and landed lightly on the cab of the forklift truck.

After their lives had been altered so irreversibly, Kate and Phil found it difficult to adjust to ordinary life when they returned from their adventure in America. For Kate it was especially hard to get back in with her friends, who, in her absence, had shared many things – things that they talked about endlessly and that, if she were honest, didn't really interest her. There was little she could tell them about life with Great-Aunt Elizabeth, as most of it was a secret. When she did talk about flying over the Statue of Liberty in a helicopter or horse riding in Central Park, her friends listened quietly, but even to Kate it sounded like bragging.

It was difficult in a different way for Phil. He didn't talk much with his schoolmates, but then he never had – his problems were more practical. He constantly had to restrain himself from winning every tackle, scoring every goal and knowing everything before everyone else. His friends thought of him as a daydreamer, someone who was a bit on the thin side and untidy. Though still prone to scruffiness – or, as Great-Aunt Elizabeth called him, a dirt magnet – Phil had changed physically. His bearing was straighter and stronger than before and his demeanour was less vague and dreamy. He couldn't just slip back into the place he had previously occupied.

And so, for a long time after returning to England, Kate and Phil were happiest in each other's company and gradually they found ways to make life bearable. After dark, brother and sister took to scaling the back of the house and enjoying the freedom of the rooftops. A leap from their back extension took them on to the roof of a row of terraced houses where they played, testing their wits, stamina and strength. Occasionally things went wrong and then life got really interesting. Once, after slipping on the wet tiles and clattering noisily before recovering his balance, Phil had spent half an hour of a moonless night crouched on his neighbour's roof. Disturbed by the sound of him falling, Mrs Parker had come out and swung a torch around, calling, 'Who's there?' The beam of light had passed across his body several times, but thanks to his training in advanced virtual invisibility she had not seen him.

But as the school year passed, Kate shared more and more with her friends and began to spend less and less time with Phil, until eventually she stopped playing on the roof altogether. Phil begged and pleaded, but Kate pronounced the roof boring and told Phil to grow up. Once Kate had made her mind up, that was it. Phil knew this, of course, but he could not help himself and carried on wheedling, 'Why not, Kate? Come on, Kate. Oh, go on, pleeease!' Getting on Kate's nerves was no compensation for the fun they'd had, but for a while it was Phil's main source of family entertainment. Then one day he had a brilliant idea. He called it 'The Philip Reynolds End of Term Challenge'. It was very simple: on the last day of term he would meet his sister at the bus stop at the top of the high street and race her home. Kate agreed on condition that Phil didn't pester her about anything at all ever again. Phil crossed his fingers behind his back and promised. So far, they had had eight of these races and Kate had won every one of them. But this time Phil had chosen a new route and he had been practising. It took him over roofs and necessitated scaling a four-metre wall. It was dangerous in places but it was a shortcut that shaved three and a half minutes off his previous best and, more importantly, three minutes and fifteen seconds off Kate's. He was in with a chance.

As she careered out of Cowper Street, Kate looked behind, expecting to see Phil turning into the end of it, but there was no sign of him. She tore up to the end of Graham

Road and it occurred to her, for the first time, that he might have gone a different way. She rounded the corner but there was still no sign of Phil. She relaxed a little. He couldn't be that far ahead so he must be behind her. And trailing by quite a long way too. Kate allowed herself to slow to a jog, glancing back once or twice as she went. She was just passing the house next door when Mrs Parker popped up from behind the privet.

'My goodness, you in a hurry as well? Just caught your brother diving over my hedge. Took a shortcut across my garden and left footprints in my borders, he did, the cheeky monkey. I says, "Whatever is wrong with your own gate and path, that's what I want to know?" But, you know me, dear, I'm an old softy, me. I couldn't be cross with the poor lad, gasping he was. Thought he was going to collapse, bless him. And I says to him, "Where's the fire?" and then he says, "End of term", just sorts of pants it out as he falls through the front door. I says, "I used to love school when I was a little girl. Ran all the way there, but you'd not catch me running home." Hello, here's another one! Don't tell me he goes to school!'

Kate had stopped halfway up the garden path, recovering her breath while she listened to Mrs Parker, and waited for an opportunity to speak. She simply could not believe that Phil had got home so quickly. Now she turned to see to whom Mrs Parker was referring.

Bolting across the road towards them came a sleek black cat, his ears flat on his head and his tail streaming out behind him. His eyes met Kate's and he opened his

mouth. For an awful moment she thought he was going to speak in front of Mrs Parker.

'Barking!' called Kate. 'You naughty cat, you mustn't run across the road!' Kate inclined her head towards their neighbour so that he would understand why she was talking to him like that. For, although he occupied the body of a large black cat, ate from a bowl on the floor and answered to the name of Barking, this was in fact Billy, Michael Reynolds's younger brother and Kate and Phil's uncle. Billy had become a cat at the age of eleven when he was forced into the Humanitron, a monstrous transformation machine that combined animals with humans. That same day the youngest of Michael Reynolds's brothers, Frank, had been merged with a puppy and had since lived his life as Fearless, Great-Aunt Elizabeth's golden retriever.

At that moment, the front door opened and Charlotte Reynolds came out with a grinning Phil beside her. His red face glistened with sweat and his hair, which usually stuck out in tufts, lay slicked flat to his scalp.

'How did you . . . ?' Kate began, but was cut short by the roar of an approaching engine.

Barking leapt into Charlotte's arms as a shining Harley-Davidson swerved up the drive and came to a halt.

'Oh my, more excitement!' exclaimed Mrs Parker.

The motorcyclist was a statuesque woman clad in black leather and wearing an old-fashioned open-faced crash helmet.

'Great-Aunt Elizabeth!' cried Kate and Phil together, rushing towards the familiar figure.

As she removed her helmet, letting a mass of grey curls escape from a lopsided bun, the dome of the sidecar rolled back and out sprang Fearless. His yellow fur gleamed like gold in the sunshine as he shook his large body from his great head, with its lolling pink tongue, to the tip of his long tail, which was wagging so hard he couldn't walk straight. He squirmed his way towards them and began licking Kate's and Phil's fingers. Great-Aunt Elizabeth dismounted the bike and advanced with her arms open wide. She was magnificent. The afternoon sun bathed her in a warm glow, and her face, though wrinkled with age, was rosy with health. 'My dear ones!' she cried, and swept them all back into the house, leaving Mrs Parker alone in her garden. She leant along her hedge in the hope of catching a last glimpse of them before the front door closed.

A Scientist at Work

Emily Baker reached for the large magnifying glass that hung over her head and switched on the integral light. She pulled it down over the faulty circuit and pushed her glasses up over her forehead, where they held her fine blonde hair away from her small, pale face. Emily grimaced as she took a deep breath. It was a comical frown, her brow deeply furrowed and her lips pushed forward in an exaggerated sulky pout. And then, suddenly, her expression softened into a smile. She had spotted the cause of her problem: a wire soldered to a resistor. It must have happened when she was distracted with Cicely. *Little pest*, she thought, and her smile broadened to a grin. Just then a loud and hearty burp came from the monitor at her side. Emily sighed happily as she clicked off the magnifier's light and pushed it back towards the ceiling. She climbed down from her stool and went upstairs. In the darkened bedroom a small snuffling came from the corner.

'Cicely, are you awake?'

'Mama, my wake up, my done poo, Mama.'

Laughing, Emily drew back the curtains and sunlight

brightened the room. She turned towards the cot where her tiny daughter, her face flushed with sleep, held on to the cot bars, which she had used to pull herself to her feet. Cicely's development was precocious. Despite Emily's passionate desire that her baby would not grow up as quickly as she herself had been forced to, Cicely's progress along a steep learning curve was astonishing. Her intelligence and ability to communicate were far beyond what anyone could expect from a child of fourteen months. Not even from the child of two such brilliant scientists as Harold and Emily Baker.

The afternoon sun lit Cicely's Afro-curls in a golden halo and her honey-brown skin gleamed. Emily lifted her from her cot and kissed her warm cheek. 'Well,' she laughed. 'You may be gorgeous . . . but you smell disgusting!'

'Gusting!' agreed Cicely, wrinkling her nose.

After changing her nappy, Emily carried Cicely downstairs to the lab and placed her behind the little picket fence that divided a playroom – an area of cushions and tunnels, teddies and wooden building blocks – from the laboratory bench with its racks of test tubes, microscopes and specimen slides.

Just then a light flashed on a curved stainless-steel door in the corner of the room and they both looked at it expectantly. A moment later the door rolled back and a tall, thin man, his hair a mass of black curly spikes, stepped into the room. A wide grin lit his brown face.

'Papa!' squealed Cicely, holding her arms up to him.

Harold Baker crossed the lab towards his daughter, kissing Emily as he passed by.

'Oh good, you're home – you can keep an eye on Cicely while I rewire this,' said Emily.

'Ci-Ci!' cried Harold, lifting Cicely over the fence and high into the air. 'We've got to let Mama do some work for Great-Aunt Elizabeth.'

'We go park, shall we, Papa?' Cicely replied happily.

Since Harold had joined a research team conducting experiments in particle collision at the CERN high-energy physics centre outside Geneva, the family had lived in France, close to the Swiss border. The other physicists were impressed with Harold's achievements and ability and were amazed by his commitment to his work. It seemed to them that he was always either in his laboratory or his office, but in fact Harold spent a good deal of his day at home. He had not enlightened his colleagues about the teleporter he used to move from the corner of his living room to his office. They had often seen him walking in and out of his locker but they had attributed this behaviour to eccentricity. After all, Harold wore pyjama tops under Fair Isle vests and mismatched socks with sandals and was renowned for once munching his way through a large Spanish onion as if it were a crispy apple.

'How are you getting on?' Harold asked Emily, peering over her shoulder while Cicely pulled down the springs of his hair and let them go, giggling as they bounced.

'I've finished the Insult Fermenter,' Emily replied, 'and I've designed a prototype compact Night-Vision Scanner,

but I'm really stumped with this other thing she wants. Maybe we can have a look at it together when Kate gets here and looks after Cicely for us?'

'Sure. When does Aunt E want it by?' Harold asked.

'You know, it's funny. She didn't mention it at all the first time she was here, but she popped back the next day and I got the impression that it's really important. She was a bit weird, actually.'

'You mean you hadn't noticed?' Harold laughed, rolling his head from side to side while Cicely attempted to catch hold of his nose.

'No, I mean more weird than usual . . . I don't know – she was in a hurry, I guess.' Emily frowned as she remembered the visit.

'Did she say what she's up to?' Harold asked.

'No. Why? Are you worried?' Emily stopped what she was doing and studied her husband's face.

Harold shrugged. 'Well, she's not wanted an Insult Fermenter since Kate and Phil broke into Lampton Laboratory.'

Cicely pulled her thumb from her mouth. 'Wotsa ninsort mentor?' she asked.

Harold responded by blowing a raspberry down her neck and holding her up at arm's length over his head. 'Never you mind. Come on, let's go to the swings.'

Travel Plans

Unfortunately for Mrs Parker, the Reynolds family went through to the living room at the back of the house and her afternoon's entertainment ended abruptly. Michael Reynolds came out of his office and greeted Fearless with a paw to hand high-five, then bent over and hugged him. Fearless placed a long lick down the side of his brother's face.

'Oh please!' Michael cried, pushing the giant head away from him while wiping the saliva on his shirt sleeve.

'Sorry,' said Fearless. 'That's kind of an irresistible urge for me!'

'I decided it was time for a family get-together,' Great-Aunt Elizabeth was saying as Michael and Fearless joined them, 'and I have some good news for you.'

Everyone looked at her with interest and she savoured the attention a moment while she unwrapped a chocolate and put it into her mouth. 'I have come into some money and I'm going to treat you all!'

'Well, that's great,' said Michael. 'Congratulations!'

Realizing that Phil's moment of triumph was going to pass without him gloating, Kate, who had been avoiding

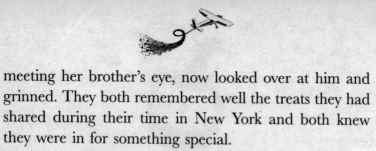

meeting her brother's eye, now looked over at him and grinned. They both remembered well the treats they had shared during their time in New York and both knew they were in for something special.

'That's so kind of you,' Charlotte said. 'What did you have in mind? There's a nice new restaurant –'

'No, dear, not a restaurant. I thought I'd treat you to a holiday. Well, several holidays really.'

The family looked at each other and back at Great-Aunt Elizabeth.

'I am right, am I not? This is the start of your summer holidays, children?'

Great-Aunt Elizabeth reached inside her leather jacket and passed an envelope to Charlotte. Grinning round at her family, Charlotte opened it as if she were about to announce an Oscar winner.

'Flights to . . . oh!' Charlotte's voice became squeaky with excitement. 'Zanzibar! . . . Oh! For . . . Michael and . . . me . . . oh . . . but what about the children?'

Great-Aunt Elizabeth passed a second, bulkier envelope to Kate, who in turn quickly tore it open. Inside was a bundle of euro notes.

'I don't understand,' said Kate.

'Well, my dear, your mother told me about your flair for languages, so I've got you on a summer school French course. My friend Jean-Paul's sister arranged it all for me and you're going to stay with Harold and Emily.' She nodded at the envelope in Kate's hand. 'That's a bit of spending money for you.'

'Thank you, Great-Aunt Elizabeth!' Kate cried, going over and hugging her. She wasn't exactly thrilled about the prospect of school during the holidays but spending time with Harold, Emily and little Cicely more than made up for it.

Great-Aunt Elizabeth turned to Phil. 'So, young man, that leaves you.'

Phil had no idea what to expect and as it now looked as though he was going to be doing whatever it was without the rest of his family he was slightly wary.

'I remember your mother telling me when I phoned one summer that you were rather glum because your best friend had moved away. You were rather close – "like peas in a pod", I remember Charlotte telling me.'

'Mark,' Phil said. 'Yes, but that was years ago.'

'Yes, that's the one. Mark Longbridge. His parents inherited a great fortune or something –'

'They won the lottery,' Phil interjected.

'Yes, well, I got in touch with them and explained that I was arranging a surprise holiday for Charlotte and Michael, and asked if they would kindly have you to stay with them.' Great-Aunt Elizabeth passed Phil a third and final envelope. 'I thought you and he could catch up a bit.'

Phil's envelope contained a first-class rail ticket to the Cornish seaside town where the Longbridges had relocated after their good fortune.

'Have you made any plans for me?' Barking asked from where he perched on the arm of a chair. 'Only, I would

like to go to Zanzibar with Michael and Charlotte if I may.'

'Don't be ridiculous, Barking, Africa's no place for a cat,' Great-Aunt Elizabeth said matter-of-factly.

'I don't know,' said Fearless. 'Africa's full of cats, big cats.'

'Yes, but it's no life for a domesticated cat!' replied Great-Aunt Elizabeth. 'Barking would be a walking meals-on-paws in Africa. He might as well have a best-before date stuck between his ears.'

Barking twitched his tail. 'I'd prefer not to be discussed as if I were something on a supermarket shelf,' he said haughtily.

'Oh, toffee-tarts! Don't take offence,' said Great-Aunt Elizabeth with a dismissive wave of her hand. 'Anyway, I thought you could go to France with Kate and visit Harold, Emily and that sweet little baby of theirs.'

A memory of the Baker family's Easter visit, when baby Cicely had crawled up to Barking while he was asleep and squeezed the breath out of him, flashed through his mind and he flicked his tail again.

Meanwhile, Phil had been quietly studying his rail ticket and thinking about Mark Longbridge. Since Mark had moved away they had kept in touch by email, but as this consisted of forwarding jokes and recommending websites to each other, Phil didn't feel that he really knew Mark any more. In his mind Mark was still a grinning, freckled nine-year-old with messy hair.

The boys had met on their first morning in nursery

class and after a small scuffle in the home corner had resolved their differences and made friends. Soon they were inseparable. They spent afternoons after school and weekends at each other's homes. If you saw one then the other was sure to be close by. They did everything together, from swimming lessons to visits to the barber's, where they had identical haircuts. And the boys had looked remarkably similar, except that Mark was taller and stronger than Phil. Then, at the end of year three, Mark's parents had had a record-breaking lottery win on a triple-rollover week. Just as suddenly as it happened, they moved from their modern terraced house to a millionaire's mansion in Cornwall, and Mark had gone from Brooklands Primary to a posh boarding school, leaving Phil rather bereft.

Phil glanced up to see Great-Aunt Elizabeth looking at him and he smiled. It would be good to see Mark again and, even if it wasn't as glamorous as Africa or France, a house on a cliff sounded all right.

'Good,' Great-Aunt Elizabeth said, looking especially pleased. 'Everything's settled.'

Later that night, after everyone had gone to bed, Charlotte asked Michael to go into the attic and get the suitcases. 'You're out all day tomorrow so I'll make a start with the packing.'

Michael passed down the luggage and then sat on the bed to unlace his shoes. 'That was a surprise – the old girl turning up like that,' he said casually. When Charlotte didn't answer him Michael's suspicions were confirmed.

'OK, come on, Lottie. What's going on? There's no way we're swanning off on holiday if Lorabeth Lampton has come out of hiding.'

Three years ago, when Great-Aunt Elizabeth had unexpectedly burst into their lives, the plan (as far as Michael was concerned) was for the children to go off on holiday with her. As it turned out, Great-Aunt Elizabeth needed the children's help to investigate the cosmetics empire of a woman called Lorabeth Lampton. Initially everything was kept secret from Michael, who had survived a dreadful encounter with Lorabeth Lampton as a child but had been left with no memory of the experience. During the course of that summer, Kate and Phil discovered a number of shocking facts about their family history, including amazing details from Charlotte's startlingly adventurous childhood. But the most shocking and repulsive revelation of all was that the monstrous Lorabeth Lampton was Great-Aunt Elizabeth's sister Margot, Charlotte's mother and so their own grandmother. This close relative, they learnt, was evil and scheming. Under the guise of Lorabeth Lampton, her ambitions had threatened to cause catastrophic devastation to the planet. It was ultimately Kate and Phil who had put a stop to her plans, but their parents were swept up too and Michael had never quite shaken off the feeling that Great-Aunt Elizabeth had unnecessarily put their lives at risk. Lorabeth Lampton had evaded capture and, although as yet there had been no sign of her, Michael feared her reprisal. He had been hugely relieved when

Great-Aunt Elizabeth had insisted that it was too danger-ous for the children to wear their heartstones with her sister still at large. In fact, before they returned to England, she had taken them for safe-keeping.

Charlotte tried to allay her husband's fears. 'Look, Aunt E says that she has been sensing that something is happen-ing but –'

Michael interrupted her with a sudden outburst. 'I knew it! I flipping well knew it!'

'Please listen, Michael. It seems that Margot, Lorabeth – whatever she is calling herself now – *is* active, but Aunt E assures me that all the signals she's picking up are posi-tive.'

'And what's that supposed to mean?'

'Well, you know there is a bond between the heart-stones and particularly when wearers are siblings? You've seen it work for Kate and Phil – how they know things about one another as if by instinct. In the past Aunt E has been alerted to Margot's evil schemes by premoni-tions of danger, but this time it's different. Aunt E says that she has begun to dream about Margot and even to see her suddenly and clearly in her mind's eye as if she were an apparition, but that the accompanying feeling she gets is good. Great-Aunt Elizabeth is convinced that what-ever she is involved in, it won't be illegal or evil this time.'

Michael grimaced and looked askance at his wife. 'Does that sound very likely to you?' he asked. 'Your mother tried to kill me, she kidnapped our children, destabilized

the Earth in a dozen countries and was prepared to slaughter thousands of animals. Yet now, according to Great-Aunt Elizabeth, she's engaged in some nice wholesome activity. Let's see what could that be, Charlotte. Oh, I know, perhaps she is running a little tea shop on the Isle of Wight.'

Charlotte considered this for a moment. 'When I was a little girl, when my father was alive and we lived in Tanzania, she was different then.'

'Define different.'

'Well, we were happy. She and my father were involved in animal conservation. She was sponsoring young people who couldn't afford their education – people like Harold and Emily. She was considered to be a good person in the community. She and I went for long walks in the bush together and we would look at the plants and birds and insects.'

Michael sat quietly trying to imagine it. At last he asked, 'So Great-Aunt Elizabeth thinks we have nothing to worry about? She doesn't need the children?'

'I'm sure that she would tell us if she needed the children, Michael.'

'Would she? Are you sure? I just can't trust her the way you do. I wish I could but I can't. Last time she managed to lose Phil from right under her nose – have you forgotten that?'

Charlotte sighed. 'I understand how you feel, Michael, really I do. But you've got to remember that her heart-stone had been tampered with – she wasn't one hundred

per cent on the ball. But she always, always wins out in the end, and she has the family's best interests at heart. You have to believe that at least, don't you?'

Michael stared down at his feet in his unlaced shoes. 'OK,' he said at last, taking Charlotte's hand and giving it a squeeze. 'For your sake I'll try.'

A Difficult Reunion

As Phil sat on the train, comparing his lot with that of his parents and sister, he couldn't help feeling that they all had a much better deal. It wasn't that he didn't want to see Mark again, but he had a niggling fear that he might not have quite as good a time as everyone else. His mum and dad were about to fly off to an exotic island in the Indian Ocean. The previous day, Great-Aunt Elizabeth had driven Kate and Barking to France to stay with Harold, Emily and Cicely, with whom life was never dull. And here he was on a train to Cornwall.

Phil checked his watch; he was due to arrive in less than an hour. He looked up and stared out through the train window. The countryside streamed by, a blurred procession of greens, and Phil told himself to be positive. After all, he and Mark had been best friends and it would be fun to see him again. A tunnel came and went and Phil paid attention, for the first time, to the man sitting diagonally opposite him. The man was peering down his nose through half-spectacles at a document. Although, for Phil, it was upside down and back to front, he could see that it was a list of names and short biographies beside stamp-sized photographs. What caught his attention was the fact that each photo was of a boy of a similar age to his own, and that the one biography he was able to make out read 'uncooperative and abusive'. Phil's interest was roused and, though he continued to look out of the window, he used the glass to study the man's reflection.

He was tanned and Hollywood-handsome, with a strong jawline. His glossy black hair was highlighted at the temples by a touch of silver. Then Phil became aware of the passenger in the seat beside him. She was a large middle-aged woman who held her handbag on her lap and she too was examining the man's face. She stared with undisguised admiration until the man suddenly looked up and smiled at her, revealing a wide row of perfectly white teeth and large dark brown eyes. The woman blushed and lowered her gaze.

After a while, Phil decided to stretch his legs and apologized to the woman for disturbing her. She had resumed staring and, without seeming to acknowledge Phil's presence, she stood in a distracted dream-like way to let him pass. Phil slid by the table and out into the aisle. The man continued to peruse his document, turning through the pages until he at last stopped at a name and photo that had been circled in red ink. As he passed, Phil glanced down at the page the man was reading. The photo was of a serious-looking boy of twelve, and beneath it the name LONGBRIDGE, MARK JASON was printed in bold capitals. Phil stopped dead and the

man glanced up at him. Phil adjusted his bag, as if its weight had hindered his progress, and passed down the train towards the buffet car. He had had a fraction of a second to see the cover page as the man had turned it over and placed it face down on the table.

It read:

Suitable Candidates

for

Caddington Lodge

In the buffet car, Phil stood in the short queue puzzling over what he had just seen. What could it mean?

Had he remained in his seat, or had the frosted window in the buffet carriage been transparent and not translucent, then Phil would have caught a glimpse of the road where it dipped towards the track and ran parallel to it. And he would have been amazed to see a Harley-Davidson and sidecar speeding alongside the train before veering left with the road and disappearing into the trees.

As the train pulled into the station, Phil saw Mark immediately. He was leaning against the wall beside the ticket barrier and staring lazily ahead of him. Phil could see the resemblance to the soft boyish features he remembered, but Mark's face was more angular and his body was broad and muscular. Phil recognized the man standing a little to one side of Mark, but Mr Longbridge, Mark's father, had aged dramatically in three years. His once-black hair was streaked with grey and he wore it long, cut in neat layers to his shoulders. Phil remembered him as a plump-faced man who was always laughing about something. His face was thin now, lined and deeply tanned, and it appeared to have sagged in a way that, Phil thought, made him look sad. He could not remember anything unusual about what Mr Longbridge had worn when he had last seen him, but now Phil immediately noticed how he was dressed. Darren Longbridge looked somewhat uncomfortable in a fashionable tailored suit – the likes of which a celebrity footballer might wear to a nightclub.

Phil stepped on to the platform and approached the Longbridges. Seeing him, Mark smiled suddenly and pulled himself up straight. Darren Longbridge marched forward with his arm outstretched, but he strode right past, and Phil turned to see him shaking hands with the man from the train. Just then, Mark arrived at his side and landed a hard punch on his arm.

'You've grown!' Mark said, eyeing him up and down.

Phil rubbed his arm and studied Mark's face. 'Ow!' He laughed half-heartedly as he remembered Mark's habit of 'friendly' punching.

Mark turned to move away and gestured for Phil to follow. 'Dad has a meeting with that guy and he might be ages. We can walk home instead of waiting. You don't mind, do you?'

'No, that's fine,' Phil answered. 'Do you know what he does, the guy your dad's meeting?'

'Don't know. Don't care,' Mark replied, then he shouted to his father, 'We're gonna walk. See ya later!'

'How's school?' Phil asked as they moved along the platform, trying to make the question sound casual.

'Don't know. Don't care,' Mark repeated. Then, turning to look into Phil's eyes, he added, 'I've been suspended. Haven't been for a couple of months.'

By now they had crossed the station car park and Mark began to scramble up a craggy slope, weaving his way between gorse bushes as he went.

Phil stood on the gravel and watched him climb. 'What did you do?' he called up.

Mark had reached the top of the slope and turned to stare down at Phil. 'What?'

Mark was standing in front of the afternoon sun and Phil saw only his silhouette, his legs placed wide apart and his arms akimbo.

'What did you do to get suspended?' Phil asked.

'I killed a man – self-defence,' Mark replied in a cowboy drawl, echoing a game they had once played. Then he laughed. 'It doesn't matter – you're here now and that should get my parents off my back. I think they're hoping you'll be a good influence on me.'

Phil shouldered his bag, followed Mark up the hill and was soon standing beside him.

'You're a lot fitter than you used to be,' said Mark, who was still panting from the climb. 'You used to be a bit wimpy.'

Phil raised his eyebrows at this but just said, 'Well, I guess you're right – I've changed.'

They walked together along a path and Phil could feel the sharp salty smell of the sea in his nostrils. He glanced at Mark and noticed that they were now of a similar height and build when once Mark had towered over him. There was an uncomfortable silence between them and Phil was thinking about how to start a conversation when Mark tried to punch him again. He drew his arm back and began a swing aimed just below Phil's shoulder, but Phil sidestepped and ducked. Mark's fist collided with nothing but air and he stumbled and fell on one knee. Mark lunged at Phil's leg, intending to pull him to the ground, but again Phil dodged him and left Mark sprawling. He offered his hand, but Mark ignored him and lay panting on the grass. Phil turned and walked slowly away, following his nose to the sea. After a few minutes he was standing on a grassy bank of dune overlooking the beach, where he waited for the other boy to catch up. When he did he was in a foul mood, his expression thunderous.

Phil turned to face him, wary in case Mark was planning to throw another punch. 'That man on the train. He was reading something about a place called Caddington Lodge. Does that mean anything to you?'

Mark stared at his feet for a while and when he looked up his eyes were wet. 'Dad got a brochure in the post about Caddington Lodge a couple of weeks ago. It's some sort of a camp where I can go and get "sorted out", as my dad puts it. Anyway, I'm not going. Mum is on my side and she pretty much tells my dad what to do.'

'Why didn't you say you were in trouble – or your

mum, why didn't she mention it on the phone when they fixed this trip up?'

'Well, as my mum says, I can't very well go if you're here, can I? Look, forget it. It's not a big deal.'

Phil looked at his watch. His parents would have just boarded their plane. He was silent for a moment, going through the options in his mind. He could call Great-Aunt Elizabeth and ask if he could spend the summer in New York or join Kate in France. He didn't have to stay if things didn't work out, but in the meantime he had better make the best of it. At last he reached over and patted Mark twice on the back.

'Come on, which way?' he asked.

Mark smiled. 'Follow me!' he called, setting off along the coast path, which, at that point, began to curve inland. They headed away from the sea for some minutes before another twist in the path brought them to a steep incline through a forest of rhododendrons. The path continued away to the right but Mark began to push his way through the bushes. 'Shortcut!' he called over his shoulder, and Phil followed him. They soon reached the top and came upon a view of the house. A white balustrade hugged the cliff edge and behind it an acre of beautifully kept lawn swept towards a magnificent stately home. Mark pointed to where the boundary fence ran along an outcrop of cliff. The last fence post was missing and a small triangular gap was discernible against the backdrop of a pale blue sky.

'We have to crawl through there,' said Mark. 'Think you can do it?'

Phil considered the risk. He felt confident of his agility but there was no telling how safe the cliff edge was. Suddenly Mark pushed past him.

'Not chicken, are you?' he asked, moving quickly towards the gap and ducking to crawl through it.

A gull that had been resting in a nook in the cliff face took off into a gust of wind and hung in the air above their heads. Thirty metres below them the sea heaved over giant saw-blades of shale. Mark crawled through the opening and was at the most precipitous point when he turned his head to grin at Phil. Suddenly, Phil saw the smirk on Mark's face turn to terror and he began clawing at the ground and sliding towards the edge. He cried out and then, in a last frantic scrabble, he was gone.

Instantaneously, Phil dropped his bag and sprang forward. Throwing himself flat to the ground and dragging himself through the gap, he peered over the edge and saw Mark clinging to a ledge two metres below.

'Keep still. I'll get you up,' Phil said, and he took hold of the fence post and pulled on it, testing to see if it would hold his weight. He dislodged his bag and let it fall from his shoulder before leaning out from the post and holding a hand down to Mark.

'Reach up and take my hand,' he called.

Mark's eyes widened. 'No way! You won't be able to hold me!'

Ignoring him, Phil hooked his arm around the fence post, bent his knees and began a crouched descent over the cliff edge. He leant down as far as he could and with

his free arm outstretched he was able to make a grab for Mark's wrist. Mark gasped as Phil took hold of his arm and yanked him upwards. Phil groaned with the effort as he dragged himself and then the other boy over the cliff to safety. He collapsed, panting, on the grass.

'H–h–how did you *do* that?' spluttered Mark as he crawled breathlessly away from the edge and sprawled on the lawn.

Phil got to his feet and slipped back though the gap to retrieve his bag. He could feel the muscles in his arms and shoulder burning from the strain.

Beneath him, hidden by a dense gorse bush, a large golden retriever relaxed from a ready-to-spring position and slowly wagged his tail. Almost lost in the depth of yellow curls at his collar, his small heartstone was glowing a vibrant red.

Phil returned through the fence to where Mark was staring expectantly at him and shrugged. 'I don't know. Adrenalin, I guess.'

As they walked towards the house, Mark kept glancing curiously at Phil. Ahead of them the lawn met a terrace and standing in front of open French windows stood Mark's mother, Sally Longbridge. She too had changed from Phil's memory of her. Her clothes were immaculate and there was a film-star glamour in the dazzle of what Phil assumed was very expensive jewellery.

Her voice was shrill as she called out to them. 'Marky! I've told you not to come through the garden. You'll go off that cliff one of these days. And fancy taking Phil

that way! His parents will think we're completely incontinent if we lose him on the first day.'

'Incompetent, Mum, they'll think we're incompetent. Anyway, I did go over the edge and Phil rescued me.'

Sally Longbridge threw her hands in the air and ran down the steps to the lawn. 'I knew it! Are you hurt?' she cried, and turned to Phil, her eyes shiny with tears. 'Oh, thank you, thank you. You always were a lovely boy.'

As they moved into the house, Mark grinned at Phil behind his mother's back and mouthed 'lovely boy'.

They entered a room that was decorated in a style inspired by ancient Egypt. At the far end stood a sarcophagus and two sphinxes adorned the fireplace. Temple cats, over a metre high and made of gold and ebony, stood either side of the door. There were animal-skin rugs strewn across the sofas and the marble-tiled floor. Phil stared about him. The room was painted orange and gold, and a border of black hieroglyphs paraded the walls near the ceiling. Between the sofas the smoked-glass top of a large coffee table rested on the fingertips of a giant upturned bronze hand and in the centre of the palm was an open, all-seeing eye.

'You've just had this room decorated, haven't you, Mum?' said Mark as Phil lowered his bag to the floor and picked up a shiny black ornament – a scarab beetle – from the coffee table. Turning it over, he saw that it was a remote control. Mark reached out and took it from him. On the far wall, what Phil had mistaken for a large photograph of the Valley of the Kings was in fact a plasma screen. Mark aimed the remote control and the pyramids disappeared and were replaced by horse racing from Kempton Park.

Mrs Longbridge satisfied herself that Mark was not badly hurt and brushed at his shoulders to remove any traces of grit.

'Right, you two, watch a bit of TV while I go and speak to Mrs Gardener. We've got an extra for dinner. Dad's phoned to say he's bringing this Mr Tacker home with him.'

Mark turned off the television. 'Mum, don't let Dad bring him here. You promised you wouldn't let him near the house. He's going to make you send me to that lodge place.'

'Don't you worry. He's only staying for dinner, and I'll deal with Mr Tacker. He's not sending my little boy to Africa. Besides, you can't go off now that Phil's here, can you?' She looked past Mark and smiled at Phil. 'I'm so glad my Marky's got you, Phil – you were always such a good friend to him. Now, show Phil to his room, love. He must be exhausted after his journey.'

Sally Longbridge smiled at Phil and he found himself remembering how once, when he was about seven years old, he had fallen over in the Longbridge back garden and grazed his knee. The skin was red and roughed up as if it had been snagged in a cheese grater. It was barely bleeding and yet Mark's mum had made a big fuss of him. She had given him a packet of chocolate buttons

and covered his knee with a gigantic Dennis the Menace plaster.

Phil smiled back at her and followed Mark from the room.

Realizing that he had missed his opportunity to say that he had changed his plans and wouldn't be staying with them after all, Phil climbed the stairs behind Mark, who showed him to a room with a large dormer window and a view across the lawn and out to sea. An old wisteria twisted its way along the sill and, as he looked out, Phil automatically picked out a route for an emergency exit. Not that he could just disappear, more the pity. As he unpacked, Phil allowed himself the luxury of a brief daydream. He imagined cloning himself. That way he could leave his clone visiting with the Longbridges while the 'real' Phil Reynolds went off to France or, better still, New York. It was a brilliant idea and, what was more, Phil was sure that Harold could work out a way of doing it too. He decided he would discuss it with the brilliant scientist as soon as he saw him next. A clone would be useful at school too. He need never go to another assembly.

Suddenly Phil became aware that his mind was wandering and he brought his attention sharply back to the room. He had put his clothes in the chest of drawers and placed his washbag by the sink. He sighed. *One night*, Phil thought. *I'll stay one night. Then I'm off.*

Mark reappeared at the door. 'Come on. I want to show you my room.'

Phil followed him out on to the landing and up a narrow flight of stairs at the top of which was a small door. Hanging from a nail was an enamel sign that read:

DANGER OF DEATH
KEEP OUT

Mark grinned back at Phil as he pushed open the door to reveal a vast attic room that was lit by four large skylights. 'This is the latest state-of-the-art games console,' he said, showing Phil a small cinema screen opposite upholstered leather seats with built-in controls. 'Bet you've never seen anything like this, huh?'

Phil thought of the virtual reality interiors that Harold had developed and how utterly convincing they were – his bedroom in New York had been indistinguishable from a Texan ranch, complete with corral and palomino pony.

'It's great,' Phil said, settling into one of the seats as Mark loaded a game. Together they drove alien mutants from the sewers of New York until Mrs Gardener called them down for supper.

The adults were already seated when the boys arrived. Darren Longbridge, at the head of the table, was engrossed in carving an enormous chicken, the pink tip of his tongue protruding slightly between his lips. Next to him sat his wife and opposite her, across the glassy

smooth walnut table, sat Jim Tacker.

'You should see a Tanzanian dawn, Sally. It's the most beautiful thing in the world – your good self excluded, of course!'

He half stood as the boys entered the room and inclined his head in greeting. His smile was like a beam of warm sunshine and Phil found himself smiling in return.

'Come and sit beside me, Phil,' called Sally Longbridge, keeping her gaze on her handsome dinner guest, 'and Marky, you can sit beside Mr Tacker.'

Jim Tacker turned towards her as if tracking her in a sight finder. He locked his eyes on hers and fired a smile right at her. It was a direct hit and her cheeks flushed pink. 'Please,' he murmured, 'Jim . . . my friends call me Jim.'

Before Phil could do as Mrs Longbridge asked, Mark slipped past him and into the chair beside his mother, leaving Phil to take the seat beside the smooth and smiling American.

Sally Longbridge reached out her hand, took the plate of meat her husband held out to her and passed it to Mark as if under a trance.

Jim Tacker grinned at Mark across the table. 'We were on the same train, I believe,' he said, flashing his Arctic teeth and startling Mrs Longbridge into action.

'Oh, dear me no.' She laughed. 'The boys are very alike. Jim, *this* is Philip Reynolds,' she said, gesturing across the table with a wave of her hand. 'You're my Mark's oldest friend, aren't you, dear?'

Phil smiled politely at Mrs Longbridge before glancing sideways at Jim Tacker. 'I'm Phil. Mark and I used to go to the same school.'

Jim Tacker nodded and smiled, turning his attention to Mark. 'So you're Mark,' Tacker said in his soft American accent. 'How are you doing, young fella?'

Mark had been helping himself to food during this exchange and had just filled his mouth. His reply to this enquiry was a grunt, a shrug and a quick glance up at Jim Tacker.

'Oh, Marky, you behave like a Frankenstein sometimes, you really do!' Sally Longbridge laughed nervously and gave her son a little dig with her elbow.

'Philistine,' corrected Darren Longbridge. 'He behaves like a philistine.'

'Shut up, Dad,' Mark said.

An awkward silence ensued. It was Mr Longbridge who broke it. 'While you boys were getting reacquainted we came up with a plan, didn't we, Jim?'

'A real *Boy's Own* adventure, I'd say, Darren – wouldn't you?' Tacker replied.

Mark began to choke.

'Now, Marky, wait till you hear what Jim has got to say about this lodge. It's a wonderful opportunity.'

'It'll be more like a holiday, son,' Darren Longbridge added.

'And –' Sally Longbridge said, dipping her head and leaning forward in order to peer into Phil's eyes, 'I know you've been looking forward to being here, but I'm sure

you could come again another time. I've called your great-auntie and she says it's fine with her —'

Phil grinned and the thought of the summer in New York was just taking shape in his mind when Sally Longbridge finished her sentence.

'You can go too! Isn't that lovely?'

Phil's knife slipped from his fingers and clattered against his plate before falling to the floor.

A Surprise Visit

Charlotte opened the shutter door and stepped out on to the balcony of their hotel room in Zanzibar's Stonetown. She glanced back to where Michael lay asleep beneath the mosquito net. A short downpour had woken her and she breathed in the fresh pre-dawn air and saw the wet roofs and puddles glisten in moonlight. Across the narrow street, on the stone step of the building opposite, sat two *Maasai* men. They held the red cloth of their garments tightly round their bodies. Charlotte studied them for a while. The *Maasai* belonged on the plains and grasslands of the Tanzanian mainland, she thought. Their horizons should be distant and their livelihood based on hunting and tending their herds of cattle, not the passing interest of tourists. Charlotte sighed. She wondered if they could be happy living like this.

Her thoughts turned to Kate and Phil. What sort of life were *they* meant to lead? Should they be wearing their heartstones and fulfilling some kind of family destiny? Or was it better that they lived ordinary lives as Charlotte herself had chosen to do? When the children first gave up their heartstones and returned from New York to

England, she had watched them carefully. If they had not settled back into school and found their friends again she would have reconsidered. But they did settle down eventually; they were happy and confident, and Charlotte felt sure that, for the time being at least, they had made the best choice. When Kate and Phil reached sixteen they could make their own decision as to whether they wore a heartstone forever or not, and in order to be well informed it was important that they had experience of life both with and without one.

A muezzin began to sing, calling Muslims to prayer, his lilting voice floating across the rooftops. Charlotte closed the shutters and went back to bed.

After the dinner party Phil was unable to sleep. At three in the morning he was still wide awake, listening to the sounds of the house. As soon as he was sure that everyone else was asleep, he got up and opened his door on to the landing. It was dark and quiet. It would be earlier, about ten o'clock, in New York and he tried to picture what Great-Aunt Elizabeth would be doing. An image of her sitting up in bed wearing her old leather jacket, reading a book and eating chocolates flashed into his mind.

Phil moved effortlessly and silently downstairs, took the phone from the hall table and carried it into the kitchen. He had just dialled the first few digits of Great-Aunt Elizabeth's number when he heard a noise. He took the phone away from his ear and held his breath. A moment later he heard what sounded like a sharp object scraping against brick. He clicked off the phone and stood in the dark, staring and listening. There it was again, and it seemed to be coming from beneath him. There must be a cellar, and someone or something was in it. Phil crouched down on the floor and trailed his hand across the marble tiles. He felt a draught against his fingers and he moved silently towards the source, a narrow door in the corner of the kitchen. The panels in the door were vented with holes and Phil guessed it would have once been the larder for the house.

He heard a sudden violent rattle but could not identify what it was. All he knew was that this time it came from just the other side of the door. Slowly and carefully, Phil reached for the handle, and then quickly he yanked the door open.

At the bottom of some steep stone steps, beside an enormous open refrigerator, stood Fearless, his long tail wagging in broad sweeps. Phil ran down the steps and sank to his knees as he put his arms around the dog's neck and hugged him. Fearless's coat felt cool from the night air but Phil buried his fingers deep into the golden curls and found the warmth of the dog's skin.

'What are you doing here?' Phil asked. Then, looking around, he added, 'How did you get in?'

'I removed a few loose air bricks, then squeezed my way in,' Fearless replied, looking back over his shoulder.

Phil followed his gaze to the far side of the cellar, where crumbled plaster, bricks and soil were piled on the floor beneath a gaping hole in the base of the wall.

44

Phil sniffed as he noticed something else. 'Have you been eating?' he asked.

'Ah, yes,' replied Fearless, licking his lips. 'Thought I'd make it look as if foxes had got in and raided the larder. I had to eat the chicken, you know, to make it look authentic.'

'Don't you think they might wonder how a fox could open a fridge, let alone dig its way into the house?' Phil asked, grinning at the empty, greasy plate in the fridge.

'OK. I'll tidy up. You go out to the summerhouse,' whispered Fearless, ending the joke. His damp nose snuffled Phil's ear. 'I'll meet you outside.'

How suddenly things seemed to change in his life, Phil thought happily as he went up the steps to the kitchen and closed the door behind him. He felt excited and as if he might laugh out loud at any moment, but he managed to suppress his exuberance as he searched for the keys to the back door. At last he found them on a hook and quietly let himself out into the night. There was a strong breeze and clouds hurtled across the starry sky and bright moon. The smell of the sea was strong in the air and from somewhere nearby an owl hooted. Phil saw the summerhouse across the lawn and, beside it, Great-Aunt Elizabeth beckoning to him from the shadows of an apple tree. He hurried to her, feeling a rush of relief and amazement wash over him. It was as if he had conjured her up just by his need to speak to her. He took a deep breath as he reached her side, eager to tell her that now he would have to spend the summer with her.

But it was Great-Aunt Elizabeth who spoke first. 'Excellent work, Phil!' she cried, gripping his shoulders in her large hands and giving him a shake before crushing him affectionately against her. For a suffocating moment Phil disappeared into a smell of leather and chocolate, then she released him and held him at arm's length.

'When Mrs Longbridge called to see if it would be all right for you to go to Caddington Lodge you could have spread me with jam and called me a doughnut! I said to Fearless, "He's not even heard my brief yet and he's got an invite into the lodge – just like that!"' Seeing Phil's astounded expression, she added, 'I've had this Caddington Lodge under surveillance for some time, you see.'

Phil opened his mouth and closed it again as words failed him.

Great-Aunt Elizabeth moved into the deeper shadows beneath the apple tree and pulled Phil after her. She was tense with excitement and, as she stared at him, her eyes seemed to him to be capable of piercing his skull.

'The Historograph, Phil!' she cried gleefully, 'I think I might have found it!'

When Lorabeth Lampton had escaped, she had taken Great-Aunt Elizabeth's Historograph with her. A sudden image of this curious object came to Phil's mind. He had thought that it looked like treasure from a Viking burial site when he had first seen it. It was a large metal plate encrusted with small heartstones, each of which could be combined with other heartstones to achieve extraordinary, impossible things. It had enabled Kate and Phil to

look into the past and it could even, so Great-Aunt Elizabeth claimed, allow a person to travel through time.

While memories of the Historograph flickered through his mind, Phil struggled to cope with his feelings. His great-aunt had just said she was delighted he was going to Caddington Lodge; that idea was dominating his thinking and making it almost impossible for him to concentrate on what she was saying.

Great-Aunt Elizabeth clapped her hands together. 'I think that wayward sister of mine has taken the Historograph to Africa!' She nodded enthusiastically at Phil before continuing her rambling explanation. 'After her disgraceful shenanigans posing as Lorabeth Lampton, I've been watching out for any signs that she might be planning something new. I have been keeping an eye on Hildy Martin – she was the woman who swapped places with my sister, allowing her to leave prison.' She scrutinized Phil and at last saw his confusion, though she did not guess the reason for it. 'You didn't know about that? Well, she was. Anyway, this Caddington Lodge that Mr Tacker is promoting – well, my dear, guess who signs the cheques on their business account? Hildy Martin, that's who! And the fact that this lodge is located in Tanzania is just too much of a coincidence –'

Though his face was masked by shadow, Great-Aunt Elizabeth could see that Phil's expression was a mixture of apprehension and doubt. She made herself talk more slowly and lowered her mouth closer to his ear.

'It was in Tanzania that my sister lived under the guise

of Penelope Parton and founded that ghastly Pet Emporium of hers. It makes sense that she would go back there after that Lampton debacle – she would want somewhere remote and inaccessible. I bet she thought she had the perfect hideaway!' Great-Aunt Elizabeth grasped Phil's shoulder. 'This is where you come in, Phil. I need you to have a look inside this Caddington Lodge and report back to me.'

Phil felt overwhelmed by the force of his great-aunt's attention – as though he were a rare specimen pinned down on a dissecting table. While this unpleasant sensation gripped his paralysed body, he struggled with his thoughts, which were all rebelling against the idea of spying on Caddington Lodge. 'But . . . if Lorabeth Lampton is there, she'll recognize me,' he murmured.

Great-Aunt Elizabeth dismissed this possibility briskly. 'I doubt it – it's been three years and you've changed a lot from the little lad you were then. Now, Caddington Lodge is very exclusive and admission is strictly by invitation only. All their clients are loaded, and they need to be too – it costs an absolute fortune! I remembered your mother telling me about your schoolfriend's family winning the jackpot and moving away, so I looked them up. No offence, Phil, but most young people show room for improvement, so I couldn't believe my luck when I discovered that your friend was getting himself into a spot of bother at school. I ordered a Caddington Lodge brochure to be sent to Mr Longbridge. I thought it would appeal to him, as he's finding life rather difficult. They

say money can't buy happiness and that man's a walking testimony to the fact. He doesn't look at all well, does he? Though I dare say he'd get more of a rest if I sent his wife away. Still, never mind.'

During this lengthy speech, Phil had managed to pull himself away a little and think about the implications of her plan. 'Shouldn't you just call the police or the FBI?' he asked at last.

She placed her hand on his shoulder and pulled him back close to her.

'I want the Historograph, Phil, and I need you to get it for me before we involve the authorities. I can't imagine the FBI parting with it if they got their hands on it, can you? There's not a government in the world that I would trust with the Historograph – it makes me shudder just to think of it.' She let go of him then and drew herself up to her full height.

Phil frowned and gazed up to where his great-aunt's head disappeared among the branches. Although only Great-Aunt Elizabeth truly knew how dangerous the Historograph could be if misused, Phil had a vivid imagination and enough knowledge to picture some terrifying scenarios. He was quick to see how someone with evil intent might use it to rewrite history. He felt a knife blade of fear edge down his spine. Beside him Great-Aunt Elizabeth unwrapped a chocolate.

'Is Kate coming with me?' Phil asked.

'What, to a boys' summer camp? Come on, Phil, use your noddle.'

49

'It's just, well, I don't . . . I mean . . . shouldn't we both go? Just in case?'

'Now, Phil, there is nothing to worry about.'

Great-Aunt Elizabeth took a breath and paused for a moment while she tried to consider her great-nephew's point of view. Three years previously, when her intuition had told her that her sister was up to something, she had instinctively known that it would be something bad. But in the last few months she had begun to feel differently. Why, that very morning she had spent nearly an hour lost in memories of a particularly happy day from their childhood when they had lived in Constantinople. And she kept remembering a promise she had made to her mother that, as the eldest, she would look out for her little sister. She couldn't attack Margot without reason, but on the other hand she desperately wanted to get the Historograph back – and had a right to; their mother had left it in her care. She began nodding resolutely as she continued to speak.

'I have reason to believe that she is behaving herself. She did spend several years in Africa running a legitimate business before the Pet Emporium turned nasty. My guess is that she has found a way to make silly people with too much money part with some of it. Now, if that sort of enterprise was a crime, our Mrs Longbridge wouldn't have countless pairs of shoes in her wardrobe.'

Phil continued to look unconvinced and Great-Aunt Elizabeth pressed on in an attempt to reassure him.

'The Historograph is mine, by right, but I can't just

waltz in and take it from her. As you know, the bond between heartstones is strong. When they are in close proximity they flare – it is as if they communicate. The affinity between my sister's heartstone and mine is particularly powerful. As soon as she sensed me in the vicinity she could conceal the Historograph and I would never get it back. I need you to help me, Phil. Your stealth ability is tremendous. You will be able to creep around the lodge unnoticed and find out where she keeps it. Fearless and I will be based nearby and once you have located the Historograph we will work out a way to get it back. If anything were to go wrong we would get you out of there faster than you can say "Uncle Bob's pants are on fire." And don't forget your parents are on holiday in Zanzibar, so they are nice and close if we need backup – which of course we won't.'

Phil did not know what to say. He remembered how a few hours earlier he had felt jealous of Kate and his parents. His summer had promised to be so boring in comparison to theirs. It was amazing how everything could change in just a few moments once Great-Aunt Elizabeth was around.

'We've been to Tanzania to do a recce,' said Fearless. 'I've managed to set up an undercover identity for myself and organized some help from a local pack of dogs. I spread a rumour that I had killed a lion in self-defence.' Fearless lifted a small rucksack in his teeth and dropped it at Phil's feet. 'In here there's a map of the lodge grounds showing where I'll be based. And there's also an Insult

Fermenter and a Night-Vision Scanner for you – just in case.'

Phil picked up the bag. The knowledge that Fearless would be with him in Africa instantly made him feel better.

'The Longbridges have invited me round for coffee in the morning,' said Great-Aunt Elizabeth, 'but I wanted to have a quiet word with you first and give you this.'

Great-Aunt Elizabeth took a wooden box from her pocket and opened it. Inside, Phil's keystone lay nestled in deep-red velvet, where he had placed it three years earlier. She held the box just out of Phil's reach.

'Don't touch it – you mustn't reactivate it yet. If it really is my sister in Tanzania and you turn up with an active heartstone she'll be on to you in a nanosecond. But you must keep it with you and be ready to wear it when you need it.'

Phil smiled at Great-Aunt Elizabeth as he took the box from her and closed it. This made all the difference. With the keystone he could do it. With the keystone he could do anything.

Taking Hold of the Keystone

Above Cynthia Caddington's head an electric fan jerked in squeaky rotations and blades of shadow spiralled across the ceiling. The room was dimly lit by one low-wattage bare bulb. She sat at a table and reached for an old-fashioned Bakelite telephone, her fingers resting on the handset for a moment as she stared into a mirror fixed to the wall beside her. With her other hand she carefully arranged a scarf that covered most of her face like a veil. Her eyes were large and deep-set, and she stared coldly at her reflection. She lifted the receiver and dialled.

'Hildy, I want you to close down the London office.'

She held the phone away from her ear as Hildy's shrill, wavering voice rattled down the line.

'I don't care how many shipping magnates with delinquent sons you've sent out brochures to, Hildy. You're to close the office and leave London immediately.'

She took her ear from the phone.

'Hildy, be quiet . . . It isn't what we planned, but plans change. I know the lodge isn't full, but I may need to move the boys quickly. I can't risk having new boys being uncooperative and rebellious.'

She held the phone at arm's length as plaintive gibbering buzzed through the earpiece.

'Hildy, you're not to call me that any more – it's Mrs Caddington. Now shut up and listen. I'm going to send Bardolph and Frimley to France tomorrow. I cannot wait any longer. I shall tell Tacker that the Longbridge boy will have to be the last one. You're to leave London and go to Bogotá and wait for that idiot Frimley to arrive when their job in France is done . . . Oh, for God's sake – I've made you a rich woman. You can live out your life in luxury . . . Just shut up and do as you're told, Hildy!'

The disembodied voice of Hildy Martin was instantly silenced as the veiled woman slammed down the phone. She pulled the ancient leather bag that she wore slung across her back round on to her lap and cradled it against her thin body.

Phil stepped quietly through the back door into the kitchen and closed it silently behind him. The only light came from the moon shining through the window and a digital clock on the cooker displaying 03.45. As he climbed the stairs to his bedroom he opened the lid of the box and stared down at his keystone. He had to resist the urge to take it in his fingers and experience the wonderful surge of confidence and power that he knew would energize every cell in his body the moment he touched it. Continuing to look down as he crossed the landing, he did not notice that his bedroom door was slightly more ajar than he had left it. Phil pushed the door open with his foot and still had his head bowed over the box as he stepped into his room. Mark jumped out from where he had been hiding behind the door and sent the box flying from Phil's hands. The keystone fell out and clattered across the floorboards, bounced off the skirting board and came to rest in a slice of moonlight beside the window. Phil stooped to retrieve it but Mark threw himself on top of it.

'Where were you? What's this?' whispered Mark as he crawled away from Phil, the keystone faintly glowing in his fingers.

'Give it to me. It's mine,' Phil said as calmly as he could.

Mark turned the keystone over in his hands. 'Erhgh, it's warming up. Has it got a battery in it? What does it do?'

Phil came into the room, closed the door behind him and switched on the light. 'Give it back and I'll tell you.'

Mark looked at Phil for the first time and sensed how important the object was. He tightened his grip on it. 'Why don't you come and get it?' he taunted, holding the keystone out of reach.

Phil moved past him and went over to the window and pulled back the curtain. He stared out at the night shadow of the apple tree and wondered whether Fearless and Great-Aunt Elizabeth were still nearby. He couldn't believe it. Five measly minutes after being entrusted with a mission and given back the keystone, he had lost it to an idiot like Mark Longbridge. He swallowed back his anger. He

had to stay calm. He would have to persuade Mark to give him the keystone willingly, and Mark would be more likely to comply if he was polite and didn't let his frustration show.

'OK. Look at it for a while and give it back in a minute.'

Mark held it up to the light and turned it over and around. 'What is it?' he asked impatiently.

'It's just a lucky charm. My Great-Aunt Elizabeth gave it to me. You had better give it back to me, because she's coming round tomorrow and she'll probably ask to see it.'

'You're lying – this isn't just a lucky charm. Tell me what it's for and I'll give it back.'

Phil stared at Mark for a long time.

'Well, if you don't want it I'll just be getting back to bed.' Mark turned towards the door.

'Wait. I'll tell you.'

Phil sat on his bed and thought about what to say to Mark. He didn't dare tell him the truth. How owning a heartstone could make a person stronger and cleverer. How it could sharpen their wits, hone their instincts and speed up their reflexes. Instead he said, 'Like I said, it's a special sort of lucky charm. It helps me do things.'

Mark frowned and shook his head. 'No, there's more to it than that. Look at it – it's glowing. I've never seen anything like it before. And you . . . you're different. You're different because of this stone, aren't you?'

Just then Phil noticed that even though Mark had been

holding the keystone for several minutes and the stone's response had been immediate, it was barely even glowing now. It gave him hope.

'If you have an affinity with the stone it glows –'

'I knew it! It's glowing – look!' interrupted Mark with excitement.

'Yes, but it's very faint,' said Phil. 'When I hold the stone it buzzes with energy and light.'

Mark's lip curled. 'You just don't want me to have it,' he spat. 'I was always stronger and cleverer than you before and you're just scared I will be again.'

'No, Mark, please listen,' said Phil. 'You've got to trust me. It's important. I haven't worn the stone for three years and so it's kind of gone dormant, and by touching it you've reactivated it. Sure, there is a response, but it's not very strong, believe me.'

'Why should I believe you? You don't even like me.'

Phil blushed and hesitated before he spoke. He had not yet understood this himself but it was true – he didn't like Mark. In fact right now he hated him. 'You've just taken something that belongs to me. What do you expect?'

Mark looked at Phil for a moment. 'OK. How about you let me keep it for a little while, just to see if it helps me? Then I promise I'll let you have it back.'

Phil's anger was suddenly too difficult to control and burst from his lips. 'It's mine! Give it to me! I need it!'

Mark moved quickly to the door and took hold of the handle. 'I'll think about it, OK? I'll see you in the morning.'

And with that he was gone.

Not caring if he disturbed anyone, Phil kicked the door shut with a furious swing of his leg.

Cynthia Caddington checked that her office door was locked and returned to her desk. She slackened the drawstring that held the leather bag closed and reached inside, pulling out a large metallic plate and setting it down carefully in the centre of the table.

She ran her hand lovingly across the surface of the plate and the embedded heartstones flickered. She let the fingertip of her index finger linger on the heartstone that corresponded to the one around her neck and it began to glow brightly. Then she opened a drawer and removed a small gas-powered soldering iron. Lifting her heartstone away from her throat, she directed the flame at the stone and it fell from its chain. She placed it on the Historograph and rotated it slowly, causing a beam of red light to sweep round the room. At last the heartstone clicked softly into place and she leant forward into the red glow as if to immerse herself in the strange exchange of energy that passed between the stones. Above the veil, her eyelids drooped so that she stared through half-closed eyes at the surface of the Historograph. While she watched, a low hum pulsed through the room and this seemed to lull her deeper into her trance. Her breath came in short, rasping gasps and she swayed in her seat, her head lolling forward and rolling from side to side. Cynthia Caddington was reliving a day from her childhood.

She let her fingertips hover above the place where her sister's heartstone should lodge. A haze rolled across the surface of the Historograph and she saw herself as a child of six. She held Elizabeth's hand as they sat together on a marble bench inside the aviary at their home in Constantinople. All around them beautiful birds flew and sang while Elizabeth told her their names and the countries they had come from.

Cynthia Caddington's eyes rolled up in her head and she rocked gently. Her lips moved and she began to speak in the thin, high-pitched voice of a small child.

'What's that pretty bird called, Lizbeth? . . . You are so clever, Lizbeth . . . Will you teach me, Lizbeth?'

For a moment, the room was filled with the soft tinkle of a little girl's laughter and then, suddenly, Cynthia sat up straight. Her head flew back and her eyes snapped open. She took a long, desperate, gasping breath and held it. She reached down, removed her heartstone and hurried to replace it at her neck. She was agitated and her fingers shook. She continued to hold her breath as she struggled with sealing the heartstone. When it was finally done, she exhaled and the stale air left her lungs in a rush of anger and disgust. 'My God! What a simpering little wretch I was!' she cried.

She sat for a moment before reaching for the Historograph and hugging it close to her body. 'Happy days, Elizabeth,' she murmured to herself. 'Remember those happy days and stay off my back.'

*

Mrs Gardener's announcement that a visitor had arrived was unnecessary, as the roar from Great-Aunt Elizabeth's motorbike had rattled through the house and brought everyone to the entrance hall. Mrs Gardener opened the door and Great-Aunt Elizabeth, in the process of removing her helmet, ducked through. For a moment which was just short of being rude, no one moved or spoke, but merely gaped as the visitor advanced towards them and introduced herself.

Phil was used to the imposing size and eccentric appearance of Great-Aunt Elizabeth and had no reason to stare, apart from a desperate need to get her attention and speak to her privately. Sally Longbridge, however, watched the massive woman's every move with an expression that wavered between amusement and horror. Mark, meanwhile, followed her at a short distance and assessed her from top to toe, his head moving up and down like a ventriloquist's dummy. As for Darren Longbridge, he had yet to shut his mouth since shaking her hand and leading the enormous leather-clad woman into the sitting room.

Great-Aunt Elizabeth strode into the centre of the room and stood looking around her for a moment or two. Sally Longbridge gave a shocked little yelp as Great-Aunt Elizabeth suddenly marched across to the leather sofa and stood on it in order to get a closer look at the hieroglyphs that adorned the walls.

'Do you have problems with your neighbours?' she enquired at last, climbing down and gazing about her

once more. 'You know, disputes over the boundary hedges, that sort of thing?'

Sally Longbridge's face paled beneath her shiny black hair and she glanced at her husband. 'No. Why, we get on ever so well with everyone, don't we, Darren?'

'You can't actually read that stuff, can you?' he asked, stepping forward and squinting up at the line of figures and symbols that circumnavigated the living room.

Great-Aunt Elizabeth pointed to a symbol, the start of a repeating pattern. 'Rend the body of my enemies, spill blood, lay waste to the kingdom of my foes, gouge eyes and sever limbs.'

'Oh, my gawd, how terrible,' gasped Sally Longbridge, sinking into the nearest chair. 'I'll get it changed.'

'Oh, I don't know, I rather like it,' interjected Darren Longbridge, gazing round the room, his hands on his hips.

'Well, I think it's a bit disturbing now that I know it says that, Darren, and I'm sure my Thing Shooey adviser won't like it one bit.'

'Now, tell me all about the boys' trip to Tanzania,' said Great-Aunt Elizabeth, settling herself on a replica of Tutankhamen's throne. 'It all sounds wonderfully exciting!'

'Go and fetch the prospectus, Marky,' said Sally Longbridge, whose gaze kept returning to the hieroglyphs, 'and ask Mrs Gardener to bring the coffee in.'

'Caddington Lodge seems the perfect solution for Mark,' said Darren Longbridge after his son had reluctantly left the room. 'They promise that boys find direction there, learn respect and how to get along in life. Lots of sports and activities, plenty of discipline – firm but fair – you know. Not a bullying regime at all, just lots of good strong role models, adults the boys can really look up to. Sally wasn't sure about it but soon changed her mind when she met Jim Tacker, didn't you, Sal?'

Sally Longbridge smiled and blushed and held her tiny hands together in her lap like a nervous schoolgirl.

Darren Longbridge continued. 'He was a bit of a rogue himself when he was a lad – showed us the newspaper cuttings – car theft, that sort of thing. He's living proof that it's possible to make good, isn't he, Sal? Quite an inspirational guy, eh?'

Sally Longbridge smiled serenely. 'Yes,' she said, 'he's a wonderful man.'

Phil stood near the door and watched Great-Aunt Elizabeth, considering how to interrupt things and get to speak to her alone. Mark returned with the prospectus and took it over to Great-Aunt Elizabeth before going to sit beside his mother on the sofa – actually a chaise longue with gold clawed feet.

Great-Aunt Elizabeth held the prospectus at arm's length and read, '"Caddington Lodge – where a boy's life changes forever".' She raised an eyebrow and threw a look at Mark. 'Hmm, not necessarily a good thing that, eh?' She resumed, 'Ah, here we have it! "Personalities polished to perfection!" My word, now that is quite a promise!' She leafed through the pages, nodding her approval. 'Swimming pool, gymnasium, squash courts.

Well, it looks impressive, I must say. And it won't be cheap. I'd say you were a lucky young man, Mark.'

Mrs Gardener had appeared and was placing a tray of coffee and tiny pastries on the table beside Sally Longbridge. She raised her eyebrows and gave an undisguised snort at her employer's reply.

'Oh, my Marky's such a good boy he's worth it, aren't you, poppet?' and she ruffled Mark's hair while he leant away from her.

'Forget it,' he growled. 'I'm not going and you can't make me.'

Sally Longbridge smiled at Great-Aunt Elizabeth as if she hadn't heard him and as if a determined show of cheerfulness would ensure that no one else heard him either.

'Terribly generous of you to send my great-nephew along too,' continued Great-Aunt Elizabeth, and she beamed at Phil, who raised his eyebrows and tipped his head in Mark's direction.

'I need to speak to you,' he mouthed.

Great-Aunt Elizabeth gave him a small nod before downing her coffee in two clean gulps and burping into the end of her fist. 'Perhaps the boys would be so kind as to show me the gardens and the view from the cliff,' she said, placing her empty cup back on its saucer. 'And would you mind if I let my golden retriever out for a run? I can't keep him cooped up in the sidecar for long.'

Her height and bearing as she rose from the throne were majestic. Sally Longbridge struggled to her feet and

gave a little half-curtsy as if she were indeed in the presence of royalty.

They left the room by the French windows and Great-Aunt Elizabeth set off round the side of the house. Phil followed and caught her up as she crunched across the gravel towards her Harley, where Fearless stood in the window of the domed sidecar and beamed at them.

Phil hurried beside her and, checking that they were out of earshot, he began to speak in a low voice. 'Mark has the keystone. He took it from me.'

'Skulls and snake skins, Phil, I hope you're not serious?'

As she released Fearless, Great-Aunt Elizabeth shot Phil a sideways glance and he lowered his eyes from her penetrating stare.

'Well, we'll soon see about that!' she said as Fearless jumped up at Phil and licked his face.

They hurried back to where Mark was waiting for them on the terrace.

'Come along, then, boys! Let's see these cliffs!'

Mark scowled and walked along, kicking at the grass. They covered the length of the lawn and stood before the picket fence overlooking the sea.

'Phil tells me you have taken something that belongs to him,' Great-Aunt Elizabeth began.

'I was just *looking* at it. I never said I wouldn't give it back,' Mark replied nervously.

Great-Aunt Elizabeth surveyed Mark gravely. Phil waited for the storm of angry words that would leave Mark quaking and see his keystone returned to him.

'You seem with have some affinity which the keystone but its power is barely perceptible.' Great-Aunt Elizabeth frowned. 'That is interesting.'

'He stole it from me – snatched it and refused to give it back!' Phil exclaimed.

Great-Aunt Elizabeth held up her hand to silence Phil while keeping her eyes on Mark's face. 'This happened before you held the keystone yourself?' The question was directed at Phil.

'You said I shouldn't touch it – just keep it safe,' Phil replied, his voice small.

'Show me,' Great-Aunt Elizabeth snapped at Mark.

Mark slowly pulled the neck of his T-shirt to one side and revealed the keystone. During the time that Phil had worn it, the keystone had changed shape and size and now had the appearance of a flat and misshapen hen's egg. It was mostly a bluish-black, though a faint glint of red pulsed through it every second or so. Great-Aunt Elizabeth looked down at it, then turned and began to walk to and fro along the cliff's edge.

After hesitating for a moment, Phil followed her, breaking into a trot in order to keep at her side. 'Aren't you going to say something to him, Great-Aunt Elizabeth?' he hissed, suppressing the volume but not the distress in his voice.

After pacing several lengths, Great-Aunt Elizabeth came back to where Mark was standing, stopped abruptly and glared down at the boy. 'Much as your behaviour towards my great-nephew displeases me, I think it best if you keep the stone for now.'

65

Mark's face relaxed into a broad grin.

'But,' Phil cried, 'it doesn't even work properly!'

'That, my dear, is precisely the point,' Great-Aunt Elizabeth hissed in Phil's ear. '*You* cannot wear the keystone because it will signal your presence to my sister and she will be on to you before you have time to scratch your bottom. But, I'm certain that this –' she waved a gloved hand vaguely in Mark's direction and raised her voice – 'this piffling damp squib of an excuse for a bond will be far too faint to arouse her interest.'

The smile vanished from Mark's face.

Great-Aunt Elizabeth pulled herself up to her full height and spoke as if to herself. 'After all, *I* did not detect it.'

'I don't understand,' Phil said miserably.

Great-Aunt Elizabeth saw the anguish in his face and her expression softened. 'Now listen, my darling. I know it's disappointing, but it's safer. While your friend here is wearing the keystone no one else can get their hands on it – not unless he willingly gives it up. So, you see, it's safe and secure until you need it, but it won't give you away either.'

Phil was stunned. 'But what about when I *do* need it?' he asked. He could not bring himself to look at Mark.

'Then Mark will hand it over to you.'

Great-Aunt Elizabeth placed one large hand on Mark's shoulder and tipped his chin up with the other. 'Now, you listen to me, young man. It may well be that Phil will have cause to save your life a second time – yes, I saw what happened when you went over the cliff, so don't

look so surprised. You must give Phil the keystone when he wants it. No questions asked. I am going to Africa myself. I shall be there when you arrive and I don't like to be double-crossed. Do you understand?'

Mark gulped and nodded.

Fearless, who had been padding around them, sniffing at the grass and giving a flawless impression of an ordinary golden retriever, now stared at Mark and growled.

'How do you know that you can trust him, Great-Aunt Elizabeth?' Phil asked from close by her side.

'Oh, he will do as he is told. His life will depend on it,' replied Great-Aunt Elizabeth curtly.

Just then Sally Longbridge's high voice called from the terrace. 'Coo-ee! Anyone for a cake before Mrs Gardener clears the table?'

Great-Aunt Elizabeth relaxed her grip on Mark's shoulder and turned towards the house. 'Yes, I could certainly do with a cake,' she murmured before striding off.

Mark looked at Phil and shrugged. 'Look, I'll give it to you, later on – you know, like she said.' He glanced after Great-Aunt Elizabeth as she strode up the garden.

You better had, Mark Longbridge, Phil thought angrily as he turned to follow her. He placed a hand on the top of Fearless's broad curly head in an attempt to console himself as a feeling spawned from a mixture of disappointment, anger and regret swelled into a painful knot in his chest.

Caddington Lodge

Jim Tacker pulled a square of crisply laundered white linen from his pocket and dabbed at Sally Longbridge's tears. She took the handkerchief from him and held it against her cheek while Darren Longbridge helped the cab driver load the luggage. Mark had marched out of the house and climbed into the front of the taxi, slamming the door behind him. He sat with his arms folded and stared straight ahead.

'Bye, Marky!' called Sally Longbridge, blowing kisses at her son.

'Don't you go worrying about him, Sally,' said Jim Tacker. 'I'll make sure he writes. Why, I'll even write to you myself – let you know how he's getting on.'

'You will?' sniffed Sally Longbridge, brightening.

'Sure I will.' He turned to Darren Longbridge and shook his hand. 'You're doing the right thing. He'll come home a different boy.'

As Phil moved past Sally Longbridge on his way to the cab he said goodbye to her and, to his surprise, she embraced him. She was brimming over with emotion and

couldn't stop herself giving him a hug and a kiss before he slid into his seat.

Jim Tacker climbed into the back of the cab beside Phil, who glanced quickly at him before letting his gaze return to the back of Mark's head. *I should be the one who is sulking*, Phil thought. He had no idea what he was getting himself into and no confidence in either of his companions. All in all, Phil was feeling pretty wretched as the cab pulled away from the Longbridges' house and headed up the drive

'Africa here we come! Eh, boys?' Jim Tacker cried cheerily, but neither boy replied.

Great-Aunt Elizabeth had chosen the scenic route to Harold and Emily's house and so Kate's summer had got off to a far better start than her brother's. Another journey in the Harley's sidecar was, in itself, a treat. It had been modified by Harold and included his interior expansion device. From the outside it might impress the casual observer with the originality of its design, but the inside beggared belief. It was improbably spacious and could comfortably accommodate a family of six. Barking had slept as the Harley sped across the country, but Kate, her feet curled under her as she leant on a large cushion, had gazed contentedly through the glass dome at the passing avenues of trees and fields of sunflowers. She loved everything about France – the scenery, the food, the language – and she was overjoyed at the prospect of seeing Cicely, who was now walking and talking.

In a matter of days, Kate settled into a routine of four hours of school in the mornings and relaxed afternoons at home with Emily and the baby. Emily had become part of the extended family since she had helped to destroy the evil Lampton cosmetics empire and subsequently married Harold. Never having had a family of her own, she was delighted to have Kate around; Kate was the younger sister she had always wished for and the perfect babysitter for Cicely. As much as Emily adored her daughter, it was blissful to have some time to herself. And right now she was in desperate need of it because Great-Aunt Elizabeth's most recent commission was a difficult one and she needed to think.

One afternoon, Kate lowered Cicely from her lap and returned her attention to her homework. Cicely toddled off towards a cushion, where Barking was sleeping.

'Watch out, Barking,' Emily warned as Cicely squealed with delight and fell upon the unsuspecting creature, wriggling her busy little fingers into his fur, which stood up like iron filings repulsed by a magnet.

'Get off, ha, no, tee-hee, stop it!' Barking cried, squirming free from the toddler's grip and retreating to a high shelf, where Cicely gazed longingly up at him.

'Det down!' she commanded.

Barking flicked his tail and blinked at Emily, who grinned at him from where she was working at the bench. 'Your daughter is impossible to resist,' he said, and then to Cicely he called, 'Go and get comfy on the sofa, then I'll come and sit on your lap.'

'You shouldn't talk to her, you know. She'll get confused and expect all cats to talk,' Emily said.

'No, she won't. She's clever enough to work it out. In any case, I've told her that I used to be human.'

Emily frowned. 'I'm not sure that was a good idea. She might think all cats were once people – like all butterflies were once caterpillars.'

'I really wouldn't worry about it, Emily,' Kate remarked, tapping the end of her pen against her lip. 'I think Uncle Bill's right. I used to hate the way adults kept secrets from me when I was younger. Cicely will sort it out.'

'Yes, I suppose she will,' Emily replied with a sigh.

'My pose my will, Mama,' echoed Cicely, happily kneading Barking's fur.

'Right,' said Kate, closing her book and putting the lid on her pen. 'Who wants to come to the park with me?'

'Me do!' squealed Cicely, her face lighting up like a sunny morning.

Through the plane window, Phil saw rose-coloured swathes of cloud clinging to the purple mountain peaks. Further off, smaller, pinker streaks of cloud floated above a sea that shone like gold. On the horizon the sun, a gigantic circle of red, rose from the water. Phil was witnessing his first Tanzanian dawn. Below him, beneath the mirrored wing reflecting clouds, he could see a curve of offshore waves breaking on a reef and a small group of dhows, the Arabic fishing boats, with terracotta and yellow ochre sails. Phil glanced at Mark in the seat beside him. He was asleep, his mouth softly open, his hands curled against his chest. He looked younger and more gentle than usual. Since Great-Aunt Elizabeth had permitted him to keep the keystone, he had been showing Phil little kindnesses, such as offering to help him carry his bag and insisting he took the window seat. Jim Tacker had moved to first class. They had last seen him when a doting stewardess upgraded him. She had taken his arm and walked backwards in front of him, smiling and blinking long eyelashes as she led him up the aisle to the front of the plane.

Half an hour later, they landed at Dar es Salaam airport and as Phil shuffled towards the rear exit he felt hot air creep over the shoulders of the woman in front of him and settle on his face. Standing at the top of the aeroplane steps, he hesitated as he took his first deep breath of African air. It was so warm that he felt it passing down his throat and into his lungs. It was not yet seven in the morning and the heat was shimmering on the tarmac. As he went down the stairs he felt his jeans cling to his legs and the fabric immediately felt heavily damp. He remembered the temperature in the Nevada desert, but that had been a dry heat, not cloying and steamy like this.

Jim Tacker found them in the baggage reclaim area. 'So, what do you boys think of Africa? Kind of hits you right between the eyes, don't it?'

The road that left the centre of Dar es Salaam cut a straight course towards a distant horizon. The urban sprawl of buildings began to thin, yet on either side of the road people remained in great numbers. Some were purposeful and at work, like the women sweeping the road or the men and boys carrying cutdown cardboard boxes displaying snacks of sugar cane and nuts which they balanced on their shoulders. Groups of men stood or sat in the shade of a tree or a building, some of them looking tired and world-weary, others laughing and calling out to their neighbours. Phil watched the passing scenery and was fascinated. He saw a boy running beside a moving car and shouting through the open window at the driver, who made no attempt to slow down. They passed an old man who pushed a bicycle that was so heavily laden with a tatty basket of charcoal that it towered above him and was as wide as a car. Barefoot children played by the side of the road and every so often the brightly coloured full-skirted dress of a small girl, no older than Cicely, caught his eye.

After a couple of hours, Phil saw a lone ragged tooth of a mountain on the gum of the horizon. He was amazed at how far he could see; the plains seemed endless. Directly beside the road, in scrub grass and scattered trees, *Maasai* tribesmen stood with their herds of cattle. As they drove onwards, Phil was surprised to see how green it remained and was astonished by the colour of the soil: a deep burnt orange the colour of a rusty nail. At Morogoro, the bus stopped and Jim Tacker bought them cashew nuts, bananas and bottled water. They drove on towards Mikumi, where the road bisected the National Park and they saw giraffes and elephants walking slowly through the long grass by the

side of the road. At one point the driver slowed the bus to a crawl as they passed a family of baboons that were playing in front of the oncoming traffic, forcing all vehicles to one side of the road. After the town of Mikumi they left the main road and began a slow, winding climb over rough terrain into the Udzungwa mountain range. A sign announcing the entrance to Caddington Lodge appeared some two hours later.

For the last kilometre or so of the steep climb, a levelled and gritted road released them from the blinding swirl of dust and bone-rattling jolts. At last two metal gates blocked the road and the bus came to a juddering halt on a steep incline. The driver yanked on the handbrake. A guard came to the gate and opened it, calling a greeting in Swahili to the driver.

'*Hujambo!*'

'*Sijambo!*'

'*Habari yako?*'

'*Nzuri, asante.*'

'*Safari ilikuwaje?*'

'*Nzuri, asante sana.*'

Jim Tacker leant forward and tried to hurry things up, but the cheerful exchange and slow handshake between driver and guard continued for several minutes before the guard slowly dragged the gate open and allowed the bus to pass through.

The lodge had been built on a flat plateau some forty years before by a group of wealthy European businessmen looking to increase their fortunes. In the north of Tanzania a precious gemstone had been discovered and called Tanzanite, and these men hoped for another new and rare find. They had money to risk and had sunk several mineshafts into the belly of the mountain and blown quarries in the rock. While local men, women and children risked their lives in the dark tunnels within the mountain, their bosses had built the lodge at great expense and luxury so that they might oversee the work in some comfort. It consisted of a main building, with small windows and a tiled roof, shady verandas and bedrooms, which all these years on were still comfortable if a little faded. The traditional Tanzanian method of roofing with palm would have kept the buildings cool naturally, but the installation of ceiling fans and, more recently, air-conditioning saw that the job was adequately if expensively done.

Outside there were rugby and football pitches, cricket nets and an athletics track with a central grassed area marked out for field events. A large swimming pool with three diving boards sparkled in the late afternoon sunshine. Beyond the games fields, further buildings had been added, and housed a gymnasium and squash courts.

As they passed the pool a boy stopped swimming and waved at them. 'Hi there, Mr Tacker,' he called. 'Nice to see you back!'

'Why, thank you, son,' Tacker replied. 'About to complete a goal, are you, John?'

The boy continued to tread water. 'It's Don, sir, Don

Church. I'm going for eight kilometres, got two to do!'

'Then you'd better keep swimming!' Tacker laughed.

As they continued towards the building he leant close to Phil and Mark and said, 'He's a great kid now, but his parents were ready to send him to the South Pole when I went and picked him up.'

Phil glanced back at the figure cutting his way through the crystal-clear blue water. *Eight kilometres is quite a swim,* he thought, and decided that Don Church must be an exceptional athlete.

They entered an air-conditioned lobby and stood beside a tank of tropical fish, where Jim Tacker told them to wait. 'I'll be back in a minute to show you to your room. I'd better just let the powers that be know that you've arrived safely.'

'Where is everyone?' Phil asked, surprised not to see anyone around or even hear any signs of life in the building.

Jim Tacker looked at his watch. 'They'll be having their evening meal. You guys hungry?'

Phil and Mark got their first glimpse of the other boys as they passed through the vast dining room. There must have been nearly 400 in the room, aged between ten and fifteen, and they sat six to a bench on either side of refectory tables. This was like no school dining room either boy had ever seen or could have imagined, for the boys ate almost entirely in silence. The occasional low murmur of 'pass the salt' and the gentle clatter

of cutlery on crockery were the only sounds in the room. Phil and Mark exchanged puzzled looks and were about to follow Jim Tacker through the swing doors that led to another corridor when, from the far side of the room, a boy suddenly leapt to his feet, sending his plate crashing to the ground.

'Get away from me! Get that thing off me!' the boy screamed and yanked at his hair.

A guard who had been standing near the kitchen door hurried forward, took hold of the boy's arms and began to pull him away.

'Robert will have forgotten to take his anti-malaria medication,' Jim Tacker murmured in their ears as he steered them from the hall. 'They'll take him to the sickbay and he'll be fine. Not to worry.'

Phil felt the caution and mistrust that had accompanied him since leaving Cornwall magnify into something more urgent. *Something odd is happening here*, he thought. But what it could be, he had no idea.

Jim Tacker showed them to a small bedroom. 'We like everyone to spend their first week or so in this room before moving into the dormitories. Gives you a chance to get properly settled,' he explained, flashing a warm smile at them. His white teeth shone with an almost audible 'gling!'. Then, as if talking to himself, he said, 'Robert Danby was in here last – maybe we were a bit hasty moving him out.'

Suddenly he clapped his hands and rubbed his palms together. 'Right, I'll leave you to make yourselves at home.

Just head back to the dining room when you're ready and I'll ask cook to keep something for you.'

'Did you see that bunch of loons?' Mark asked, after Tacker had left and they had begun to unpack.

Phil had been wondering about the scene in the dining room himself. It was undoubtedly odd. Not just the boy's violent outburst but the good behaviour and mild manners of the rest puzzled him. There was no sign of a strict disciplinary regime, in fact the only guard had been leaning against the door jamb chatting to the cook. The diners appeared to be quiet and well behaved by choice. Phil did not share his thoughts with Mark but instead he pulled a face and pointed at the walls and ceiling, then at his ears.

'What? Do you think the room's bugged?' Mark blurted out, before clapping his hands over his mouth.

Phil ignored him, pushed the last of his clothes into the drawers beside his bed and left the room.

Mark hurriedly followed him. 'Do you have a plan? What are we going to do? Should we escape?'

Phil stopped and turned to face Mark. 'Just try and be normal,' he pleaded before walking away from him. Phil knew this wasn't particularly fair – after all, he didn't feel normal himself, so how could he expect Mark to? *If only I had my keystone*, he thought. *Then I wouldn't have anything to worry about* – except, he reminded himself, the small detail of a psychopathic grandmother.

'We'll be the only normal ones here!' Mark called after

him as Phil turned the corner at the end of the corridor.

The other boys had left the dining room and as Phil peered round the door, Mark joined him. A warm and cheerful voice called to them from the counter at the back of the room. '*Karibu! Karibu!* You are welcome. Come eat your dinner!'

The voice came from a tall woman who was dressed in catering whites from head to toe. Beneath her paper cap almond-shaped eyes shone out from her long brown face. She placed two steaming bowls of vegetables in front of them and indicated that they should help themselves to rice.

'This place may not be perfect,' she told them, 'but you'll get the best food in East Africa. My name is Judy Mbeli and I am the cook.' With that, Mrs Mbeli turned away from them and sang to herself as she cleared the kitchen.

Had there been a choice, neither boy would have taken a bowl of vegetable stew, but both were feeling hungry and as there did not appear to be anything else they began to eat. They were pleasantly surprised. It was delicious – fragrant and spicy and comforting.

As they finished their meal, Jim Tacker arrived to take them on a tour of Caddington Lodge. The other boys filled the pitches and pool and were to be seen wrestling and fencing in the indoor gymnasium. Each of the boys they saw was engrossed in his activity but it was a strange absorption and it made them appear like automata, as if they had been programmed to perform. Jim Tacker moved briskly through the buildings and it seemed to Phil that

he was guiding them away from any other boys they came across, as if he didn't want to give them the chance to speak to anyone.

A bell sounded and Tacker checked his watch. 'Right, the sun goes down soon and we have a camp assembly before showers and bed. No doubt you'll be tired after travelling and we make an early start here. Come on, then. Follow me to the assembly hall. Mrs Caddington doesn't like anyone to be late.'

'Mrs Caddington?' Phil queried.

'Yep, she's the founder of Caddington Lodge – Mrs Cynthia Caddington.' Jim Tacker looked dreamy-eyed for a second and added, 'An extraordinary woman!'

Phil felt nervous as he considered Great-Aunt Elizabeth's suspicions about the true identity of Cynthia Caddington. He would never forget the tall, icily beautiful woman who had run Lampton Laboratory, the sinister cosmetics empire. He shuddered when he remembered her savage cruelty. Despite Great-Aunt Elizabeth's assurances, he was terrified that she might remember him. For the first time he appreciated the fact that it was Mark and not him who was wearing the keystone. He hoped that Great-Aunt Elizabeth was right and Mark's attachment to the keystone was too weak to be detected.

They followed Jim Tacker to the assembly hall and fell in line with other boys on the way. Phil thought about his school and the chaos and noise that erupted in the corridors when everyone was on the move from one class-room to another. These boys were different and Phil tried to figure out what had made them that way. They smiled and chatted, they looked healthy and, he had to admit, they looked reasonably happy too. They just didn't behave in the way large groups of boys would normally behave, but he couldn't quite put his finger on it. When they reached the hall it was already more than half full. The boys who had gathered there stood in silence and the remainder fell silent as they entered.

Jim Tacker ushered them into a row, then made his way to the front and ran up the steps to the stage. 'Good evening, boys!' he called, tossing his smile out to the furthest corners of the hall. He took a sheet of paper from his pocket and unfolded it. 'I'll just read today's summary of excellence before Mrs Caddington says a few words to you.' He cleared his throat. 'OK . . . Justin Hayton and Gideon Mayhew both exceeded their previous best distance throwing the discus today. Well done, those boys. Jack Preston swam two kilometres today. Congratulations, Jack, another personal best for you.'

As Jim Tacker continued to read from his list of names and achievements, Phil looked around him and estimated that there were approximately 400 boys in the hall. What he saw when he looked back at the stage made his gut turn a somersault. A tall, thin woman dressed entirely in black was standing beside Tacker. Around her head and draped across the lower part of her face she wore a veil so that all that could be seen of her were thin wrists and hands and a pair of large deep-set eyes that seemed to Phil to be horribly familiar.

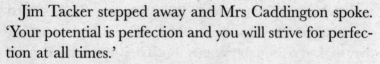

Jim Tacker stepped away and Mrs Caddington spoke. 'Your potential is perfection and you will strive for perfection at all times.'

The boys responded in a brief joyous chorus. 'We aim for perfection! Perfection is our goal!'

Mrs Caddington surveyed the rows until she came to Phil and Mark. Phil forced his thoughts to think of other things – small inconsequential thoughts that induced a state of mind essential to creating virtual invisibility. He did not hear Mrs Caddington welcome him to Caddington Lodge and she did not pay him undue attention.

That night, while Mark slept, Phil lay awake planning how he would get away in the morning and make contact with Fearless. Without the keystone's reassuring presence, he was afraid of losing his nerve. Seeing Cynthia Caddington had given him a shock and he wanted to tell Fearless and Great-Aunt Elizabeth about her as soon as possible. Suddenly, he became aware of a soft hissing noise and he was about to raise himself up on his arm in order to listen more intently, when he found himself unable to resist a powerful urge to fall asleep. The sound faded and his consciousness drifted from him like a stone slowly sinking to the bottomless depths of Lake Tanganyika.

Nikwata

Phil opened his eyes and quickly screwed them tight shut as a searing pain blinded him. Across the room Mark groaned and then whimpered, 'Oh, my head, my throat – I feel terrible.'

Phil slowly opened his eyes again and squinted as they adjusted to the bright sunlight that streamed through the window. He blinked a few times to focus his vision. He had a dull ache at the back of his head and his throat was dry. He reached for the bottle of water beside his bed and emptied it.

Mark staggered to the door and headed down the corridor to the bathroom. 'I'm sick,' he wailed to no one in particular. 'I feel terrible.'

Perhaps alerted by Mark's cry, Jim Tacker appeared from the other direction. 'Everything all right?' he asked cheerfully.

'Mark is ill,' Phil answered. 'He has a headache.'

'And how about you?' Tacker asked peering into Phil's face. 'How are you feeling? It's not uncommon for boys to be a bit poorly when they first arrive. You know, change of climate, maybe picked up a bug or two at the airport.'

Mark returned and collapsed on his bed with a loud groan. 'I think I'm gonna die.'

'Right,' replied Tacker. 'Let's get you two down to the sickbay, have the doc take a look at you.'

Phil shook his head. 'No, it's OK. I just need some breakfast and maybe some fresh air. You look after Mark. I'll be fine.'

Tacker turned down one corner of his smile in a quizzical grimace. 'You sure you're OK?' he asked, and for a moment he seemed reluctant to leave.

Phil nodded. He watched Tacker guide Mark from the room before dressing quickly and heading down the corridor. He didn't like being separated from Mark and he now felt he had more reason than ever to be suspicious of Tacker. The man had seemed almost pleased that Mark was ill and he appeared to be disappointed when Phil had said that he felt well.

Phil was even more determined to get to Fearless now and he pushed all thoughts of Mark and Tacker from his mind as he turned into the dining room, where breakfast was under way. A small group of boys had arrived just before him and Phil stopped to talk to one of them. 'Hi. Have you been here long?' he asked.

The boy was surprised to be spoken to. 'Not long, but I'm nearing my goals,' he said. He spoke quietly and pleasantly but immediately turned away.

Phil stood in the queue and thought about the boy's strange response. *No one, but no one talks like that*, Phil thought to himself, and his need to make contact with Fearless returned with renewed urgency. He looked for an opportunity to get outside as he peered around the dining room, where placid boys were filling the benches and spooning millet porridge with honey into their mouths. At the far end of the room a door stood open, with only a mosquito screen to prevent his exit. The guard was leaning on the end of the canteen counter, chatting away to Mrs Mbeli. Phil was sure that none of the boys was paying him the slightest attention so he took his porridge to the bench nearest the door and ate quickly. After checking that no one was looking his way, he slipped through the screen door into the heat and dazzling sunshine.

Caddington Lodge lay nestled on a plateau 2,000 metres above sea level, beneath the summit of Luhombero in the Udzungwa mountain range. It was less humid than Dar es Salaam had been, but the sun was so hot and fierce Phil could imagine that he really was closer to it than he had ever been before. He pulled his baseball cap down over his eyes and headed across the compound, which was neatly bordered with painted white stones, trying to appear as if he were merely out for a casual stroll. He had memorized Fearless's rendezvous point and he walked slowly and thought small thoughts in order to be inconspicuous. He wandered into the shade between the gymnasium and the squash courts. He could see the fence fifty metres ahead and when he reached the wire mesh he could see the road three metres below, down a steep bank.

Across the road a pack of wild dogs crouched in the sparse shade of a thorn tree. Each dog's thin body showed signs of the trauma and hardship of its life: a torn ear or a limp or bald patches revealing scabby skin and sores. The entire pack was a fuzzy blur of flies and every so often the general lethargy was broken as a head whipped round and snarling teeth snapped at the pests. Phil squinted into the gloomy shade and gave a low whistle. A dog with a tail so bald it looked like a stick of white bone lifted its head and gazed at Phil briefly before lying back in the dust.

Phil glanced nervously over his shoulder. He did not want to consider the possibility that Fearless might not be here to meet him after all. And then, from beside a boulder behind the tree, a large dog stood up. Phil screwed his eyes up and tried to focus. Could this be him?

The dog padded heavily across the road and picked its way carefully up the bank. And Phil could see that it was indeed Fearless, but his glossy golden curls were matted with filth and his usual bouncing lope had been replaced by a slow lumber.

'Are you OK?' Phil asked, shocked by his appearance.

'I told you I'd be undercover,' Fearless replied. 'You don't see dogs up a Tanzanian mountain looking like they've come straight from a pampering in the grooming parlour.'

'You look terrible,' Phil said, affronted by the smell that wafted towards him.

'You look a bit rough yourself.'

Phil nodded. He hadn't yet shaken off the dull ache in his head, and aside from that he was feeling anxious.

'This place is really weird. There's definitely something strange going on.'

Just then the sudden movement of a small lizard captured Phil's attention. It scuttled through the fence and ran up the wall next to him before stopping at his eye level. It was greenish-grey in colour with pale fawn flanks that suggested a yellow belly beneath. Its head was the shape of a spade on a pack of playing cards.

'I want you to meet Nikwata,' Fearless said.

'Tk tk tk tk tk hs hs tk *hujambo!*' The voice was tiny and tinny, as if it had been recorded and was now being played back through a miniature speaker.

Phil frowned at Fearless. Surely he wasn't introducing him to a lizard? He looked back at the tiny creature that was now leaning on its left side, holding two of its suckered little feet in the air and peering with one glassy eye into Phil's. For a split second Phil saw his own reflection in the black beady dome, then a membrane of white skin drew across it.

Fearless spoke. 'When Harold worked for Penelope Parton and built the first Humanitron he used rodents and reptiles as early test specimens. The transformations were primitive and incomplete. Fortunately all the children survived unharmed, but it meant that the animals had far fewer human characteristics. Nikwata's language is limited but he's clever and you will soon understand what he is trying to tell you. Nik's an old friend and, as you can imagine, he's an enemy of the woman who once called herself Penelope Parton. He's agreed to help us.'

'Tk tk tk tk pocket? Tk tk tk!' A tiny tongue flickered from the side of his rubbery mouth.

'He wants to know where he can hide,' Fearless explained.

Phil, who had been staring open-mouthed, couldn't reply straight away and continued to gawp at the talking lizard. He shrugged. 'I didn't bring –' he began at last, but stopped when the lizard suddenly took off at a run. It sped down the wall, crossed the small patch of bare earth, ran on to Phil's shoe and darted up his leg.

'Waah!' Phil could not help crying out at the shocking sensation of the tiny feet pulling at his skin, and this seemed to infuriate the little reptile.

'Tka tka tka tka glk glk glk, fidget, fidget, dok, dok,dok, tik hshshs!'

Nikwata ran over his shoulder, slipped beneath the neck of his shirt and settled himself between Phil's shoulder blades. Phil shuddered as Nikwata clung to his skin.

'Looks like he's made himself at home,' Fearless said. 'Now, Phil, we've got a problem with the satellite phone and Great-Aunt Elizabeth's not happy about you doing anything until she gets it fixed. She says that you're not to arouse suspicion but just try to fit in with everyone else and keep your eyes open.'

With this news Phil was jolted back to remembering what had already happened to him inside Caddington Lodge. 'I've already seen Cynthia Caddington,' he blurted out, 'except she wears a veil so I didn't see her face – but I think it could be *her*.'

'Well, just keep your wits about you.' Fearless frowned before continuing. 'Nikwata will make a thorough search of your room and the residential buildings just to be on the safe side. I'll make sure I'm here from dawn until nine and between dusk and midnight each day if you need me. If you come out at night use Emily's Night-Vision Scanner and carry the Insult Fermenter just in case. I'll tell you what Great-Aunt Elizabeth says as soon as she gets back.'

A bell began to ring in the main building.

'I'd better get going before I'm missed,' Phil said, though he felt reluctant to leave Fearless.

'Just remember,' Fearless called after him, 'you're not to do anything until Great-Aunt Elizabeth gives you instructions.'

Phil stepped out from between the gym and the squash courts, casually kicking a stone as he went, conscious of the tiny reptile that had hitched a ride on his back.

'Right! Are you ready for some action?' Jim Tacker said, bursting into the room.

Just moments before Phil had been standing on a chair, fiddling with the ceiling fan. When he had got back to his room the little lizard had scrambled out from beneath the collar of his shirt and begun scurrying about, criss-crossing the walls and ceiling. He had scampered beneath the beds and behind the cupboards, making a thorough search of the room. When he got to the ceiling fan he stopped still for a minute or two and then became excited.

It had taken several minutes of Nikwata running in

circles round the ceiling, saying, 'Tk tk tk stop tk tk tk hole tk tk tk stop tk tk', before Phil had understood enough to drag over a chair.

'What is it?' Phil asked, scrutinizing the fan.

Nikwata became very agitated and began speaking in Swahili, but in the end Phil saw a tiny hole in the centre of the fan and plugged it with chewing gum. He had just finished doing this when he heard someone coming. He jumped down and dragged the chair away, then Tacker appeared, clapping his hands together. He sent a radiant smile bouncing round the walls like reflected sunshine. 'It's time to get you out on the playing field. Ever thrown a javelin?'

'Where's Mark?' Phil asked, ignoring his question.

'Oh, he's fine. Doc fixed him up nicely. He's already out there. So, how about it?'

Phil reached for his baseball cap.

'Atta boy!' cried Tacker, slapping him playfully on the shoulder before leading him from the room.

In France, Cicely and Barking were helping Kate make a cake for Harold's birthday. Kate beat the eggs, squeezed the juice from three lemons, grated the zest from four and weighed out caster sugar and ground almonds, while Cicely sat beside her cuddling a packet of birthday candles. Every so often she dipped quick little fingers into the bowl and into her mouth. Barking read the recipe aloud and commented on the colour of the yolks and the consistency of the mixture.

Emily and Harold had gone to CERN to run a test on the Time-Space Navigator that Great-Aunt Elizabeth had commissioned Emily to make. Harold's laboratory had more sensitive equipment than they had at home and Emily was anxious to get the device finished. They were supposed to be in a restaurant, celebrating Harold's birthday, while Kate and Barking looked after Cicely, but both were never more happy than when in a laboratory and they were so engrossed that they were hardly aware of time passing.

'If we increase the range we risk compromising the accuracy,' Emily said, taking a sheet of paper from the printer and passing it to Harold.

'A 0.0001 per cent positional error,' remarked Harold. 'How accurate has it got to be?'

'Great-Aunt Elizabeth said that there is no room for error at all. It's got to be 100 per cent accurate – 99.9999 per cent just isn't good enough.'

Harold sat with his chin resting in his palm. He frowned and drummed his fingers on his bottom lip.

'We could,' Emily said slowly, 'keep shortening the range until we get the optimum timescale.'

'Which will be determined by achieving your 100 per cent accuracy on position,' Harold commented.

'Exactly,' Emily replied.

'Alternatively,' Harold mused, 'you could start with no time, no distance, no error, and keep stretching the first two by, say, one-thousandth of a degree per nanosecond, until you identify your error threshold.'

They stared at each other for a full half-minute before Emily smiled.

'I suggest, my darling, that you go over there,' she pointed to the computer suite on the far side of the lab, 'and do it your way, and I'll stay here and do it my way and whoever gets a result first buys dinner.'

'But it's my birthday!' Harold laughed. 'You get to buy whoever wins.'

'You're on!' said Emily settling down to work.

Great-Aunt Elizabeth regretted not having Harold with her to fix things like dodgy satellite phones. She had, after all, bought one that was top of the range and purported to be reliable. She was feeling cross as she drove to Mikumi and she clenched her teeth against the dust that flew up from the road. Suddenly, a streak of vivid turquoise flashed in front of her and she pulled on the brakes. In a tree beside the road she saw a paradise flycatcher. She smiled, remembering that there had been one in the aviary when she was a child. She watched the bird for a while before driving slowly up the road, and sighed as she thought to herself how happy and uncomplicated those long-ago days had been.

Great-Aunt Elizabeth had gone barely 100 metres before something else caught her eye and she stopped again. Perched on a branch in a nearby mango tree was a lilac-breasted roller, resplendent in its extraordinary courtship plumage. In a moment Great-Aunt Elizabeth was standing on the seat of her Harley, binoculars to

her eyes, watching the bird with its wonderful exotic feathers cavorting, the purpose of her journey momentarily forgotten.

Phil joined a group of boys on the field inside the running track. A small Tanzanian man was showing them how to grasp the javelin and draw the arm back, ready to propel it through the air. He turned to Phil and introduced himself. '*Hujambo*. My name is Majenda.'

Apart from his eyes, which were widely spaced and shone as if lit from within, everything about him seemed economical. Although his body was strong and muscular, it was compact, and this gave the impression that he was slightly built.

As Majenda demonstrated the throw, he seemed to defy gravity. His run was graceful and he drew back his arm until his fist was behind his ear, then released the javelin. It flew straight and true and speared the ground beyond the 300-metre mark as if it had a motor and a homing device. Phil watched while the other boys threw their javelins and, despite everything, looked forward to his turn. He had never tried this before and it looked like fun.

As Phil took the javelin from Majenda, something small was speeding towards him. Phil felt the weight of the javelin and tested how it balanced as he moved it slightly. He was oblivious to the tiny body hurtling across the field, looking as though a minute jet of air was being blasted through the AstroTurf . . . Nikwata.

Phil drew his arm back and took the tip of the javelin to a point just beside his eye. At that moment Nikwata was closing in on Phil like a missile, his minuscule legs a blur as the blades of artificial grass parted and closed behind him. Phil began to run, copying Majenda's side-stepping lope, and just as he reached optimum speed Nikwata jumped on to his shoe and ran up his leg. Phil shuddered and the javelin wobbled and juddered as it left his hand. As Nikwata scampered to his hiding place, Phil let the javelin fly with the full force of his strength in an uncontrolled jerk.

The javelin's trajectory was low and a full ninety degrees off course. Beside the discus cage, some twenty metres away to the left of the javelin throwers, Jim Tacker was leading a group of boys in a warm-up session. His back towards Phil, he was interspersing star jumps with a spate of running on the spot and was completely oblivious to the quivering pole that soared towards him. Phil held his breath.

Suddenly Majenda was running after the off-course javelin. 'Look out, Mr Jim!' he shouted.

Alerted by the hint of panic in Majenda's voice, Jim Tacker spun round just as the nose of the javelin was pulled to earth by gravity. He toppled backwards and it speared the grass between his legs.

Nikwata peeped out from Phil's collar and peered over his shoulder. 'Ek, Ek ek ek ek eh heh, heh, hee, hee eeh, ek ek ek!'

Phil watched, dismayed, as Majenda and the other boys ran off to help Jim Tacker. 'It's not funny,' he hissed

at the lizard. 'What do you think you're doing, Nikwata?'

'Tk tk tk, you come see tk tk!' Nikwata whispered in Phil's ear before slipping out of sight down his neck.

'I can't just go off when I feel like it,' Phil murmured through clenched teeth as he watched Majenda helping Jim Tacker to his feet. Nikwata retreated inside Phil's T-shirt and stamped a furious little dance between his shoulder blades.

Jim Tacker brushed aside the huddle of boys that had gathered around him and headed towards Phil. He leant forward as he walked as if something was propelling him faster than he wanted to go. He held his hands in fists and his body language suggested that when he reached Phil he was going to punch him. Phil took a deep breath and placed his feet squarely on the ground, but, as Tacker came closer, Phil was surprised to see that he was still smiling.

Tacker placed his tanned face a few centimetres from Phil's and smiled even wider. 'That's enough javelin for you today,' he said, as if he were an actor giving a bad reading at an audition. 'Do you know how to play squash?'

Phil shook his head and Tacker stood straight and spoke calmly. 'OK. Well, there's not a lot can go wrong with squash. Off you go to the squash courts.'

As Phil set off across the field, Nikwata emerged on to his shoulder and climbed up his neck. He curled round Phil's ear like a discreet phone earpiece.

'Tk tk no no no no no wrong way – you come tk tk with Nikwata tk tk.'

Phil glanced over his shoulder to where Tacker stood with his arms on his hips, watching him. 'I can't,' he replied through his teeth.

A fierce flurry of clicks and grunts came from the lizard as he ran down Phil's back, leapt into the grass and scuttled away. Phil checked himself from calling after him and kept walking.

Jim Tacker had hoped to keep the humiliating episode with the javelin from her, but when he arrived at Cynthia Caddington's office she exploded with crackling laughter.

'That is the first thing I've seen to amuse me in a long time!' she howled.

He was chewing gum with his mouth open. He nodded and smiled while his eyes looked everywhere around the room except at his boss.

'Oh, come on – don't be so grumpy.'

Tacker turned his head sharply to face her and gave her a broad fixed grin.

'And don't be childish.' Cynthia Caddington's mood was now sombre.

Jim Tacker was not going to be manipulated quite that easily and chose attack as his best means of defence. 'That outburst from the Danby lad was witnessed by the new boys,' he countered. 'I thought he was supposed to be finished by the time I got them here.'

Cynthia Caddington glowered at him and even though she wore a swathe of black fabric over her head and across the lower part of her face, her cruel eyes were

enough to express her anger and exert her power over him. 'Don't you dare take that tone with me, sonny Jim.' She spat the words at him in an icy staccato. 'Without me you would still be a low-life petty thief and don't you forget it.'

A weak and subservient smile faltered at the corner of his mouth as Tacker made his reply. 'I don't deny that I'd be nothing without you,' he murmured.

'Quite.' She blinked slowly as she fixed him in a steady gaze. He saw the red glow flare at her throat and was mesmerized.

'So, javelins aside, how are our two new boys getting on? Have you determined which one is my grandson yet?'

Jim Tacker hesitated. He knew which boy was which, he had brought them over from England, but in her present mood he didn't want to risk telling her that the uncooperative and less able one was her relative. And as he thought about it a flicker of doubt took hold in his mind. He remembered that when he had first met the boys at the house he had confused them. And hadn't the mother made a big fuss of the one who wasn't supposed to be her son?

'Well? Hurry up!' Mrs Caddington spat at him.

Jim Tacker decided to play safe. 'Well, I'd say that the boy who can swim a three-and-a-half-minute length is your grandson and the one who can't throw a javelin isn't.'

'Hmm,' Mrs Caddington agreed. 'If he was wearing a heartstone there would be no doubt.'

Tacker frowned. 'The boy has a heartstone?'

'No, I would know if he did, but . . .' She got up from her desk and went and stood in front of him. She was taller than he was, and as she stared into his eyes Tacker felt as if he were shrinking. 'I have a feeling I am being tricked and I don't like it one bit.'

'Maybe he's hiding a heartstone. You want me to confiscate it if I find it?'

Cynthia Caddington's claw-like hand lashed out and grabbed hold of his shoulder. 'No! You mustn't take it under any circumstances – you will destroy it.'

Jim Tacker raised his hands in defence. 'OK, OK, I'm sorry! I was just trying to be helpful, you know.'

Cynthia Caddington released him and returned to her desk. 'Well, you can help me by turning that irresistible charm of yours on your grandmother. Hildy is driving me mad. We agreed that we would do the boys in batches of 200 and she keeps sending more.'

Tacker laughed. 'Why, that's Grandma all over! Every scam we ever pulled Grandma could never quit while we were ahead. She'd go for one last trick and get the law on to us!'

'It's not the law I'm concerned about – you're not the only one with a difficult family member. I have to get finished here before my goody-goody sister arrives and spoils everything.'

Phil had a gruelling hour on the squash court. His opponent was a much older and stronger boy who was

reluctant to answer any of Phil's questions but returned the ball with precision. After an hour of this Phil was panting hard and dripping with sweat. It was a relief when the message came telling him to go to the pool and then on to the gymnasium. As he crossed the grounds beneath the brilliant sunshine, he wondered about the boys he passed. Everywhere he looked he was seeing signs of athletic skill and prowess, as if these boys had been hand-picked for their sportsmanship and stamina. But Phil had seen the brochure and he knew what the boys of Caddington Lodge had in common were wealthy parents and signs of behaviour that were a cause of concern. Preoccupied with his thoughts, Phil was surprised to see Mark hauling himself from the water as he arrived at the pool.

He grinned at Phil and called him over. 'I've just swum a length underwater!' he gasped, and he tapped the pocket on his shorts to show where he had put the keystone and winked.

Phil glanced around but no one was watching them. 'Look, you've got to be careful with that, remember? Anyway, Mark, I don't think it's the stone that's helping you. There's something going on at this place. What happened when you went to the sickbay?'

Mark shook water from his hair and a look of faint surprise passed across his face. 'Oh, yeah, I'd forgotten about that. I think I must have fainted or something but when I came to, Jim said that the doc had fixed me up and I'd be OK. I feel great.'

'Jim?' Phil echoed.

Mark shrugged. 'Oh, he's all right when you get to know him.'

'Look, Mark –'

Phil didn't have a chance to finish as a lifeguard blew a whistle and shouted at him to get changed and into the water.

When Phil returned to their room that evening, after an afternoon of wrestling, badminton and fencing, he felt drained and exhausted. The physical activity had stopped him dwelling on the things that were troubling him. Now he just wanted to lie down, get his thoughts straight and see what information he could extract from Mark. Opening the door, he found Mark on his hands and knees looking under his bed.

'What are you doing?'

'I'm looking for a lizard – I nearly caught it twice. I can't see where it's gone now.'

Nikwata. What with everything else, Phil had forgotten all about him. What was it that had upset him so much earlier on? He joined Mark in the search, but Nikwata was nowhere to be seen.

It wasn't until Phil got into bed an hour later that he discovered where the little lizard had hidden himself. As he nestled his head into the pillow he felt something writhe beneath it. 'Owah!' Phil couldn't help a small cry of disgust as he sprang upright. He disturbed Mark, who had been in bed for over half an hour and was already asleep.

'Whassa matter?' Mark murmured, his voice thick and slow.

Nikwata's arrow-shaped head poked out from beneath the corner of the pillow and he winked at Phil. 'Tk tk tk key key tdk ktdkk kk!' he said in his tiny high voice, and disappeared.

Phil pulled the pillow away and exposed Nikwata lying beside a small brass key.

'Tk tk hik hik – get key – tk tk – come on – tk tk – let's go – tk duk duk tk.'

Phil picked up the key and hurriedly began to dress. As his head came through the neck of his T-shirt he saw Mark's face. He was sitting up in bed, staring at Nikwata, his eyes wide with disbelief. The lizard cocked his head, stuck out his tongue, then made a dash for the door.

Mark looked at Phil. 'It talks,' he said, his voice uncertain. 'The lizard talks.'

Phil told him to go back to sleep and he would explain later. To his surprise, Mark shook his head as if he had water in his ears and obediently lay back down in the bed. Phil picked up the key and hurried after Nikwata. He found him doing an impatient dance at the end of the corridor. As soon as he saw Phil, he took off and turned the corner. Phil stood completely still and listened. He was sure that there was no one close by, but he took a moment to extend his listening beyond the immediate vicinity. Barking and Fearless had taught him to do this as part of his stealth training. Carefully, he followed Nikwata. He kept close to the walls and was practically gliding along in a cautious, silent crouch. Beyond the dormitories and dining hall Phil spotted the lizard making his way to the reception lobby, where at last he came to a halt beside the fish tank. On the floor behind the reception desk there was a trapdoor.

'Tk tk tk down tk tk tk,' Nikwata said, dashing over to the door and springing about on it. 'Tk tk key tk tk.'

While Phil examined the brass keyhole in the floor, Nikwata scuttled over to a small crack where the wall met the floor. He lifted a foot and pointed into the hole with sharp little jabbing movements. 'Tk tk Nikwata down tk tk tk,' he said, and disappeared.

'Wait –' Phil hissed, but Nikwata had gone.

Phil crouched behind the reception desk and wondered what to do. In his mind he could hear Fearless telling him to do nothing, to stay out of trouble. The key felt hot in his hand and he rolled it around in his palm while he looked from the trapdoor to the hole in the wall and back again. He was conscious of the seconds ticking away and his indecisiveness irked him. If he didn't move soon the chance was that Nikwata would reappear and begin some furious reptilian war dance and he'd get caught anyway. Maybe, Phil decided, the way to stay out of trouble was not by doing nothing. Besides, he was now curious to see what was causing Nikwata's excitement.

After checking once more that there was no one around, Phil put the key in the hole and turned it. The lock rolled over easily and the door began to lift as if on a spring. Phil pulled it upwards and had raised it only a

few centimetres when Nikwata appeared beneath it and fired a loud report of clicks and hisses at him before disappearing again. Phil lowered his face to the gap and looked down. He had expected it to be dark, but he could see Nikwata running down the wall beside some rickety-looking wooden steps that led down ten metres to a concrete floor.

'Tk tk tk quick-quick tk tk,' Nikwata called back to him.

Phil hesitated as the sound of Fearless's words echoed once more in his mind: *You're not to arouse suspicion. Just try to fit in with everyone else and keep your eyes open.* He peered after the lizard, unsure what to do. Suddenly he heard a noise behind him and, with no time to consider the consequences, he slipped into the gap and, grabbing a handle on the underside of the door, pulled it closed on top of him. On this side of the trapdoor he saw that the lock mechanism slid a bolt into the wall and held the door shut. He heard footsteps above his head come closer, then fade away. When he was sure it was safe, he pushed the bolt with the heel of his palm and made his way carefully down the steps.

When he reached the floor he spotted Nikwata ahead of him, dancing from foot to foot, running up the wall and springing off. Phil looked around him and saw that he was in a narrow storeroom. Beside him there were stacked crates of soda, a bucket with a mop in it and a shelf of cleaning materials. Ahead of him Nikwata began chattering excitedly and leaping in the air.

Phil went over to him and whispered, 'Look, we're not supposed to do anything until Great-Aunt Elizabeth gets

back. Just show me whatever it is that's upsetting you and then we'd better get out of here. OK?'

Overhead, pipes lagged with tatty grey hessian ran to and from a large metal tank that was softly churning. Nikwata skittered up the wall and pelted across the ceiling and down a narrow passage before suddenly halting. He waited for Phil to catch up and then tapped a foot against the ceiling.

'Tk tk tk glug glug tk tk splash splash tk tk tk,' he said, and then clamped his mouth shut and puffed out his cheeks as if holding his breath.

Phil gazed up and then back the way he'd come towards the steps that had led down from the reception and he understood. 'We're beneath the swimming pool.'

Nikwata dropped from the ceiling on to Phil's head, scampered on to his shoulder and held one little green leg out in front of him, pointing ahead. 'Tk tk tk hup two! Hup two! tk tk tk!' he cried, before leaping from Phil's shoulder and running full pelt along the floor.

Phil began to make sense of where he was. 'So now we're underneath the gym, right?'

It was a bit like the underground network of maintenance tunnels and storage cellars in the basement of his school. He hurried after Nikwata, glancing down another unlit passage that he figured must run beneath the squash courts. Suddenly Nikwata was tearing back towards him, his eyes staring wide and his mouth open as if he were silently screaming. It was a sight that could, under other circumstances and in another place, have been funny. But in the silent grey bowels of the building, with its stale smell and grim shadowy corners, the lizard's panic filled Phil with dread. He stopped dead in his tracks and his stomach seemed to fall from his body. He crouched down close to the wall and placed a steadying hand on a lagged pipe that was sticky with black grease.

Nikwata returned to his shoulder. 'Dk dk dk bad! Bad! Dk dk dk,' he said, and placed his tiny feet with their circular toepads over his eyes.

Phil reached up and touched the lizard for the first time. He felt loose skin roll slightly over sharp little bones and the tiny heart banging behind his ribs. The creature's panic seemed to enter Phil's body and mind through his fingertips. He wished that he had Fearless beside him. He took a few deep breaths and attempted to quell the flow of fear in his body. If he had had the keystone, he would have taken it in his hand and felt its power, and for a brief moment he considered going back. But although he didn't have the stone in his possession, he could remember the feeling of strength and courage it gave him. Gradually he was able reassure himself that although he had not worn the keystone for nearly three years he had retained the strength, knowledge and ability that he had achieved with its help. Then he remembered something that Great-Aunt Elizabeth had once said about the unknown being more fearful than any reality. He swallowed hard and hoped she was right.

Phil stood cautiously and ventured forward in order to see for himself what had distressed Nikwata. As he began to move, the lizard turned and darted down the neck of his shirt and clung to his back, where he could feel him quivering. Phil came to the end of the tunnel and slowly, carefully, leant forward to look round the corner. He placed a hand flat against on the wall as a sickening weight landed in his stomach. In front of him Phil saw the all too familiar sight of a laboratory.

The laboratory benches were the same as the ones in Nevada, where Lorabeth Lampton had developed her Earth-destroying cosmetics, and had adapted a Humanitron to extract the ageing genes from cats and dogs in order to give people eternal youth. Afraid of what he might find, Phil's eyes scoured the room from top to bottom. At least there were no cages of animals here and no sign of a Humanitron. Phil waited a moment longer until he felt sure that there was no one in the lab and then carefully moved in for a closer look. *Just suppose*, he thought suddenly, *I found the Historograph down here. What would I do then?* The whole objective was to recover it and return it to Great-Aunt Elizabeth – but should he risk getting caught? Phil pushed these thoughts from his mind and continued to explore the underground laboratory.

Lining the walls were rows of wooden racks holding glass spheres the size of small goldfish bowls. They contained thick, viscous liquid in varying amounts and of such luminous colours that they reflected Phil's image as he crossed the room, causing him to fear for a moment that he was being watched. He stood still beside a table

in the middle of the room and considered the strange machine that had been placed on it. It looked like an enormous home-made food blender. Phil studied it closely.

It was a strange piece of equipment and Phil was deeply puzzled by it. Rubber tubing led to and from a large tilted bowl. While some of the tubing disappeared into a metal box that had dials, switches and levers on it, one tube led from the back of the bowl and passed between some clamps but went nowhere. The bowl was fixed at such an extreme angle that its lip rested on the edge of the table. Anything that was put into it would immediately pour on to the floor. Beside the table, directly in front of the bowl, was a chair. Nikwata crept from Phil's collar and on to his shoulder. As Phil trailed his hand along the back of the chair, the lizard ran down his arm and jumped on to the seat. Nikwata disappeared beneath it and reappeared dragging a webbing strap. Phil leant forward, took it from him and checked the side closest to him. Along the length of the chair, at thirty-centimetre intervals, buckled straps had been soldered in place and were meant, Phil realized with horror, for restraining someone. Nikwata ran up the back of the chair and gripped the rim of the bowl in his hands. He shook his hammer-shaped head from side to side and let off a volley of distressed clicks that went echoing round the bowl.

Phil frowned and looked back at the racks of glass spheres around the room, then went over to the nearest ones. Each sphere had a boy's name beneath it: Thomas Street,

Matthew Barker, Callum Cheney. Then he saw a few
names that he recognized – Don Church, the distance
swimmer they had met as they arrived; Gideon Mayhew
and Justin Hayton, two of the boys Tacker had mentioned
in assembly. The last rack held three empty spheres. The
first had the name Robert Danby inscribed beneath it and
Phil remembered the boy who had thrown his tray and
shouted in the dining hall; Jim Tacker had called him
Robert, he was sure of it. Phil had to move a small meas-
uring scale before he could see the names beneath the last
two spheres but he knew what he would find. Even so, the
sight of the carefully inscribed names Mark Longbridge
and Philip Reynolds turned his blood to water.

Kidnapped

Kate took a peek at Cicely and leant close to her. She felt Cicely's soft breath against her temple and gently kissed her cheek. Cicely sighed. Kate watched her a little longer before returning to the living room, where Barking was sitting on the sofa staring at the television.

'She's fast asleep.'

'Good. I expect Harold and Emily will be back any minute,' Barking replied, not looking at her.

'Thanks for all your help today,' said Kate with exaggerated sarcasm.

'You're welcome,' Barking replied with a small flick of his tail.

Kate stood and watched the programme for a moment; it was a documentary about a pride of lions. When Emily had phoned in the afternoon to see if Cicely was all right and to ask whether Kate and Barking would mind looking after her a little longer, Kate agreed happily. She didn't really mind that Barking had done little to help. When she thought about it, there wasn't really anything he could do. His games always got Cicely over-excited as the pair

of them chased round and round the apartment, squealing and caterwauling. And he wasn't much use with the practical things either. Obviously cooking was out of the question and if he ran a bath it was either too hot or too cold, as he refused to dip his paw in and test the temperature of the water.

Kate went over to the window and looked out. Parked across the road, beneath a street lamp, was a large black saloon car. She peered closely at it and saw that it was occupied. Perhaps Harold and Emily had got a taxi home, she thought to herself, but while she stared at it the car engine started up and it moved off. As Kate watched the street she wondered how Harold and Emily had spent their day, and she imagined them leaning into soft candlelight in a restaurant or sitting together in a darkened cinema.

In fact, at that moment, Harold and Emily were still in the laboratory. They had been unable to tear themselves away from the search for a solution to Great-Aunt Elizabeth's problem until it at last yielded to the combined effort of their logic and creativity. They did indeed return home by taxi shortly after nine o'clock. They were tired, hungry and dishevelled and had done none of the celebratory things that Kate imagined, but they were, nonetheless, ecstatically happy. In her arms, Emily carried a prototype Time-Space Navigator.

Phil spent a troubled night waiting for dawn, when he would slip out to meet Fearless. He knew that something terrible was going on in the basement beneath the lodge. He was also not sure what to tell Mark about Nikwata. As his thoughts turned to Mark, his concern deepened. He had totally changed since their first morning in Tanzania. He had kicked up such a fuss in Cornwall and had sulked on the journey to Africa, but now he was enthusiastic about the activities on offer and seemed to think the lodge was a fantastic place. He had even changed his opinion of Jim Tacker and was acting as if the man was his best friend. Worse still, Mark was convinced that the keystone was helping him, but Phil knew that it wasn't – it couldn't be.

Phil sat up, flicked on the light and saw that it was five-thirty. The sun would be up at six. There was no gradual lightening of the sky here; instead the dawn arrived suddenly and spectacularly. He looked over towards Mark and, as he did so, the other boy sprang out of bed and stood yawning and scratching his ribs.

'I had a weird dream about a talking lizard,' Mark said.

He then sat down on his bed and began scratching the tops of his feet. He yawned for the second time and Phil studied him closely. He didn't know what the glass spheres were, but there was one for both of them and his conscience told him to warn Mark about what he had seen.

'Er,' he began tentatively, but before he could continue there was a short rap at the door and Jim Tacker came into their bedroom. He smiled broadly to see them both up.

'Great! Early risers. That's what I like to see!'

He carried a clipboard and he removed the top two sheets of paper, passing one to each of them. As Phil took his, he saw Tacker glance up at the ceiling fan. Phil lowered his face over the page and studied it. It was a timetable and, to his dismay, he saw that it accounted for every minute of his day, commencing with a fencing lesson at seven. He checked his watch; he had an hour to go. When he looked up, he saw that Tacker had placed an arm on Mark's shoulder and was turning him away.

'So,' he was saying, 'you feel OK this morning – sure we don't need to take you to see the doc again?'

'He's absolutely fine,' Phil interjected. 'I can't remember when I last saw Mark looking so well.'

'That's just great!' Tacker replied, jabbing a playful punch at Mark's shoulder. 'You're well on the road to perfection, young Mark.' Tacker turned his attention to Phil. 'But I don't think we're getting 100 per cent from you yet, though, are we? Maybe you should come and see doc – get a tonic or something.'

Phil reached for his towel and washbag. 'Thanks, but I'm fine. I'm going to have a shower now.'

As Phil left the room, he felt Tacker's eyes on his back. He was convinced now that something had already happened to Mark and that the same was planned for him. He had to see Fearless and get a message to Great-Aunt Elizabeth – and he had to do it soon, because he and Mark were in danger and if he didn't act quickly who knew what would happen next.

Phil waited patiently but saw no opportunity to get away. Tacker was constantly hovering nearby; he even followed them to the dining hall for breakfast. Phil managed to let a few other boys into the queue between him and Tacker and Mark. Then Mrs Mbeli needed to open another jar of honey and he lingered at the counter. When he got his bowl of porridge at last, Tacker and Mark were sitting at a bench and he was able to make for the table nearest the door. He didn't like leaving Mark but he had to get out. He was just weighing up the risks of slipping outside when he noticed that the door was bolted. He couldn't believe it. Where was Nikwata when he needed him?

Phil ate his porridge hastily, deciding to go out to the rendezvous before the morning sports began. He placed his empty bowl on a trolley and went to leave the dining hall, but Jim Tacker stepped in his way and steered him by the shoulder back to a seat. Tacker still had his doubts about the true identity of the boys and was determined to keep an eye on this one and have him seen by the doc as soon as he could.

'Now then, you're not giving your digestive system a chance if you bolt your food like that, son,' he said, pushing Phil down on to a bench. 'You just sit a while. Let that porridge settle.'

Throughout the day Phil schemed and plotted his getaway but every plan was no sooner made than something happened to scupper it. As he went from pitch to track and from pool to court, he determined that nothing,

nothing at all, would stop him from going out and meeting Fearless that night.

In France, the morning dawned a beautiful warm, hazy blue and Kate took Cicely to the park while Harold and Emily enjoyed birthday cake for breakfast.

'Do you want to come with us?' Kate asked Barking, who was sitting on the balcony rail humming the theme tune to *The Aristocats*.

'No thanks,' he said. 'I have plans.'

'Hmm,' Kate replied. 'Do these plans of yours involve sleep and sunshine by any chance?'

'You are forgetting a small jar of duck pâté, which I must see to before it spoils,' Barking retorted, closing his eyes and beginning to purr.

Kate left the pushchair at the park gate because Cicely preferred to walk. The air was sweet and there was the gentlest of warm breezes. One small brushstroke of white cloud hung in a sky that was a clean and brilliant blue. As they walked beneath the avenue of trees they heard birds twittering among the leaves as if in an absent-minded accompaniment to some absorbing pastime. Kate laughed as she imagined cartoon birds in aprons sweeping out their nests. On the far side of the park a golf course stretched to the horizon. The fairways were like bolts of emerald felt that had been flung out between borders of woodland. Scattered among this luscious green expanse, kidney-shaped bunkers of yellow sand waited to waylay misdirected golf balls. In the distance, on a perfect circle of lighter green, a little red flag fluttered in the breeze. Several small electric golf carts criss-crossed the fairway, carrying golfers and their clubs from hole to hole. Kate held Cicely's hand and let her lead the way through the gardens. They stopped while Cicely watched a dog hurry by. His stump of a tail wagged continuously as he followed a trail of interesting scents that led him in a zigzag across the path.

'His got busy nose,' Cicely observed.

'Yes.' Kate laughed. 'He's enjoying sniffing around, isn't he?'

'Hmm,' replied Cicely seriously. 'His got a happy tail.'

They continued beneath the trees towards the swings and roundabout. Kate lifted her into the swing and gave her a push. Cicely squealed as she rose and fell back to Kate's hands. After a few minutes of this, the little girl kicked her legs and began to wriggle and climb out of the bucket seat.

'Hang on, sweetie – you can't get out while it's going!' Kate said, slowing the swing.

She lifted the child from the seat and no sooner had Cicely's little red shoes touched the ground than she was off at a run towards the roundabout. Kate was circling round the swing in pursuit of Cicely when a shout from behind her made her look back. She could not see anyone but she was sure that she had heard her name. She turned back to the roundabout, but where she had expected to see Cicely clambering aboard there was no one. The roundabout was turning slowly but it was completely empty.

Frowning, Kate moved forward, scanning left and right as she called Cicely's name. She must have fallen out of sight behind the roundabout. That could be the only explanation.

Kate hurried, but as she came close she could see that the toddler was not there. A terrible crushing sensation gripped Kate's chest and drained unpleasantly down her body. Somehow, inexplicably, Cicely had disappeared.

Kate stared around frantically, looking for a clue or a sign. Suddenly a golf cart caught her attention. It was being driven fast and appeared to be leaving the course and heading for the main park gates. With rising panic, Kate began to run.

She was faintly aware of startled gasps from the people she passed. She was sprinting so fast that witnesses were unable to distinguish who or what had just sped by them. She outpaced the spaniel that momentarily joined her and she had to leap over a bench and cut across a flowerbed in order to avoid crashing into a small group of elderly men and women who ambled along the path. Her heart pounded in her chest as she pursued the electric golf buggy and she was gaining on it. She was sure she would catch it. Then she saw the car waiting by the kerb at the park gates. She had seen the car before, but where? To her right there was a gate, too narrow for the golf cart, which would bring her out on to the road closer to the waiting car. She altered her course slightly and, with her chest feeling that it was about to explode, she hurtled towards the gate.

Kate was sprinting up the road towards the car when she saw the golf cart swing out of the park and on to the pavement. Now that it was facing her she could clearly see Cicely bumping around in the front, the driver holding on to her arm with one hand while steering with the other. The buggy reached the car and Kate still had twenty metres to go. She watched in wide-eyed horror as a large stocky man climbed awkwardly from the buggy, pulling Cicely with him. Kate took in his broad shoulders and close-cropped balding hair and recognized him as one of the thugs who had worked for Lorabeth Lampton.

'I know you!' Kate screamed at him as she closed the gap. He glanced at her as he yanked open the rear door of the car and threw Cicely inside as if she were a bag of laundry. *Black Saab, damaged bumper*, thought Kate, as she memorized the numberplate. As she heard the engine start and the door slam shut, she dived forwards and grabbed the handle of the front passenger's door. With her other hand she began banging on the darkened glass. She screamed Cicely's name.

The car pulled away at speed and Kate was momentarily flung out behind it before falling to the ground and being dragged along the road. Her fingers slipped from their hold but she managed to grab the wheel arch with both hands. She held on and shut her eyes. She could feel the bumpy road beneath her hip and legs and could feel that her skin was being torn and grazed but she felt no pain. Suddenly the car turned abruptly to the left and Kate lost her hold and was thrown into

the path of the oncoming traffic. In the split second of flailing flight she opened her eyes and saw, in extraordinary detail, a motorbike and a bus, then she hit the road and screwed her eyes tight shut and rolled herself into a ball. Kate pulled every muscle in her body into a tight contraction and made sure her head was tucked in. She held her breath as she heard the fast approach of screaming brakes. Then everything went black.

An Old Enemy

Phil took the Night-Vision Scanner from his backpack and hung it around his neck like a pair of binoculars. He unscrewed the lid of the Insult Fermenter and whispered into it. He turned the dial on the bottom to four seconds. If he had to use it he would only need to buy enough time to get away. It would not be sensible to leave anyone incapacitated for others to find, whereas anyone on the receiving end of a four-second zap would be fully recovered in minutes – if somewhat confused and unable to say what had happened to them. Just then, Mark stirred in his sleep and Phil froze with his hand on the door handle. After Mark had been still and quiet for a count of ten, Phil opened the door and slipped out into the corridor. On the ceiling above him, Nikwata's head jerked to a new position. He ran a looping course down the wall, jumped on to Phil's shoulder and scurried out of sight down the neck of his T-shirt.

Phil walked to the end of the corridor and listened. At supper he had idled past the door and turned the key to unlock it. As he went to clear his plate he passed the door again and managed to kick the bolt across with his foot.

The guard had been in his usual position talking to Mrs Mbeli and none of the other boys paid him any attention. He hoped the guard hadn't had a sudden call of conscience to do his duty, locking up after they had all gone to bed. Phil *had* to get outside and meet Fearless. He had to tell him about the laboratory. He was about to turn the corner when he heard a voice and simultaneously Nikwata's four small feet clenched his skin. The voice belonged to Jim Tacker.

'Right, young Robert, I think you've been successfully reminded of your goals and duties. You probably feel a bit groggy now, but when you wake up in the morning everything will be just fine.'

'Yes, thank you.'

The reply was softly spoken. Phil held the Insult Fermenter at the ready and crouched by the wall. Cautiously, he placed the canister against the corner and was able to use the shiny metal to see into the next corridor. Jim Tacker was walking away from him, a guiding hand on Robert's shoulder. After they had turned the next corner, Phil straightened and moved to the dining hall in silence. He remembered the glass sphere he had seen with Robert's name beneath it, and the thought occurred to him that it would not be empty any more. He shuddered. As he moved into the dining hall, he wondered about the spheres and the change in Robert and also the change in Mark since he had visited the sickbay. Mark's sphere was next in the line . . .

Phil had to see Fearless before it was too late. He was

halfway across the dining hall and directly opposite the serving hatch when he realized that he was not alone. He froze. Behind the canteen counter a large shadowy figure stood silhouetted before the open fridge door. Phil ducked out of sight and held the Insult Fermenter ready. Just as he felt the flow of shock ebb in his veins he experienced another. A realization came to him that the bulky shape at the fridge, though indistinct, was familiar. Straining to see in the dark, Phil then remembered his Night-Vision Scanner and lifted it to his eyes. His heart leapt in his chest at what he saw. A large man held the fridge door open with one hand, while the other rummaged impatiently through the shelves. He was murmuring to himself, 'What's a guy got to do to get a beer in this hell hole?'

Phil could clearly see the stocky figure, the creased and shiny suit, and the thick neck beneath closely cropped hair. It was his old enemy Bardolph, ferreting through Mrs Mbeli's jars of spices and pickles. The fridge door slammed and Bardolph lumbered out through the kitchen door.

Phil's mind was reeling. There was no longer any doubt at all that Cynthia Caddington had once been the glamorous Lorabeth Lampton and Bardolph's presence discounted any possibility of her being a reformed character. Phil had witnessed the cruel violence that this man was capable of at Lorabeth Lampton's bidding and he gritted his teeth, determined to get to Fearless as fast as he could. The dining-hall door hadn't been locked and Phil slipped out into the night.

Cicadas throbbed a steady rhythm and Phil concentrated

on slowing his racing heart to keep pace with it. He kept to the darkest shadows and made for the gap between the gymnasium and the squash courts. Nikwata emerged from his T-shirt and leapt from his shoulder. Glancing after him through the Night-Vision Scanner as he tore along the ground, Phil saw him flick out his tongue and gobble up any insects that he passed. When Phil reached the fence Fearless was waiting for him, and Phil fell to his knees in the dirt and pushed his fingers through the wire to find comfort in the soft warmth of the dog's fur.

Phil's relief was overwhelming and his fears and the dreadful news of what he had seen poured out of him. He had not taken in the fact that Fearless had been impatiently pacing the fence as he approached. 'I've just seen Bardolph,' he said breathlessly, 'and there's a laboratory in the basement. I don't know what's happening but there are glass spheres with boys' names on them. There's one for me and there's one for Mark –'

'Phil, listen . . .' Fearless tried to interrupt, but Phil continued.

'Ours are still empty but the others contain some kind of liquid – I think we were gassed when we arrived – and Mark's been to the sickbay and I think they did something to him there. Nikwata found an inlet in the ceiling fan in our room, so I plugged it up, but I think they may have drugged us or something – you remember I had a headache too, didn't I?' Phil spoke quickly and desperately and did not give Fearless any room to speak. 'There's this boy called Robert who had a sort of fit and Tacker

said it was malaria. They took him away, but I just saw him and now he's calm and, I don't know, *weird*, like all the other boys here.' Phil's eyes flitted about as he spoke and he barely paused for breath. 'They give you these goals and everyone has to be perfect. And since Mark saw the doc he's been calling Tacker "Jim" and saying how much he likes the lodge –'

'Phil!' Fearless managed to interrupt him at last. 'You were told not to do anything!'

'I couldn't help it,' Phil replied. 'Nikwata led me to the basement and the other stuff just happened.' Nikwata gave a few sharp hisses and clicks before running off into the darkness. 'You've got to tell Great-Aunt Elizabeth – Cynthia Caddington *is* Lorabeth Lampton! And what's more, if Bardolph's here too, then whatever she's doing it'll be bad –'

'Listen to me,' Fearless said sharply. 'Great-Aunt Elizabeth has had to go to France.' He hesitated while Phil struggled to understand what was being said to him. 'She was on her way back from Mikumi when she had a message from Harold. Phil . . . Cicely has been kidnapped.'

Phil had realized from Fearless's tone and his solemn expression that the dog was about to tell him something serious but he was utterly unprepared for such appalling news.

'What! How?'

'I don't know much, Phil. Great-Aunt Elizabeth has gone to be with Harold and Emily. They have to look for

Cicely. And it means you and I are on our own here.'

'Poor little Cicely . . .' Phil murmured, and his voice faltered. 'Was she . . . ? Is everyone . . . ? How . . . ?' Phil struggled to understand.

'I don't know . . . Great-Aunt Elizabeth was only back for a few minutes, then she left for France. She looked into flights but decided it was quicker to take the Harley on turbo-drive north through Africa and use the Mediterranean tunnel –'

'But if Bardolph's *here* . . .' Phil said, thinking aloud.

Fearless tipped his head to one side and considered Phil. 'Maybe you should just get out of there . . . I'll dig under the fence and there's a cave you can wait in with me –'

'But what if Cicely's here now?' Phil interrupted, continuing to voice his line of thought. 'I mean, what if Bardolph took her and brought her here? I can't leave her on her own. And I can't leave Mark.'

Fearless didn't answer him immediately. They stood in shadowy silence either side of the fence and Phil's thoughts rapidly expanded to new possibilities and scenarios.

What about the other one? Bardolph's sidekick, Frimley? Where was he?

The Mystery of the Darkstone

Emily Baker felt as though her anxiety and fear were leaking out in all directions. She reminded herself of a cartoon character who takes a drink after being shot at and water pours out through its punctured body as though it were a colander. It was a sensation so debilitating that she felt she might collapse at any moment. She paced when standing and rocked when sitting and watched the telephone in case it should ring. Barking stayed with her and was grateful when, occasionally, she stroked his head. Kate lay on the sofa by the window and kept her eyes closed because she could not bear to see Emily's distress. She relived the moment when she had lifted Cicely from the swing, and the memory of how it felt to hold her in her arms was agony. At the hospital, the doctors wished to keep Kate under observation and would have done so but for the arrival on the ward of Great-Aunt Elizabeth, who, in fluent French, declared herself medically qualified to care for her great-niece at home. The registrar and staff nurse on duty at the time had attempted to argue with her but Great-Aunt Elizabeth was forthright.

'I have single-handedly nursed back to good health

soldiers who had been left for dead on battlefields and what's more I was doing so before you two were even born!'

She reached between them and snatched up Kate's notes from the end of her bed. 'Contusions and haematoma . . . fracture of the third and fourth metatarsals on the right foot, left rib fracture . . . Yes, all very straight-forward. I can assure you that my great-niece will be better off under my care than here, with all your superbugs and staff changes. My supervision will be constant and thorough.'

As both were nearing the end of long shifts, they were tired and neither could think of a reply. Without much protest they gave in and discharged Kate into the apparently expert care of her elderly great-aunt. Had they thought to ask when and where this formidable woman had acquired her nursing skills, they would have been astonished to hear Great-Aunt Elizabeth's description of the conditions at Agincourt, Poitiers and Crécy. Undoubtedly, they would have kept Kate and attempted to have Great-Aunt Elizabeth admitted to their psychiatric wing.

'What you need, my dear one,' Great-Aunt Elizabeth had whispered into Kate's ear as she carried her down to the Harley, 'is your heartstone. I have it in my pocket and you will recover quickly once you are wearing it again.'

Kate made a small whimper in answer.

'Are you in a lot of pain, my dear?' Great-Aunt Elizabeth asked.

Kate hardly noticed the aches and stiffness in her body

but her last sight of Cicely kept replaying over and over in her mind and caused an agony that she could hardly bear. She was sporadically overwhelmed by a suffocating sense of guilt that she had not been able to protect her. But Great-Aunt Elizabeth was right about the heartstone and once Kate had it around her neck the healing process began. After sleeping she looked less pale, the bruising started to fade and her mind began to clear. At first she recalled only sudden disjointed images: the empty round-about turning, the sniffing spaniel, Cicely's small red shoes. Then, quite suddenly, she got a flash of the car, and just as if she had glimpsed it through a partially opened door, it was enough to trigger her memory. Excitedly, she gave them the description of the black Saab and its number-plate. They didn't have the heart to tell her that it had already been found abandoned a few streets from the park.

Great-Aunt Elizabeth sat stiffly in a straight-backed chair beside Kate and was preoccupied with worries of her own. If her sister, Margot, was responsible for taking Cicely, then why hadn't she had a premonition of danger? Could Caddington Lodge be an elaborate red herring designed to draw her attention away from France? And why Cicely? What possible use could the baby be to her?

Great-Aunt Elizabeth's thinking was interrupted by Kate's voice, heavy and slow with sadness. 'I keep trying to picture where she is. When Phil was kidnapped I got an image immediately.' Tears overwhelmed Kate and she turned her face away. What she didn't tell her great-aunt

was that she was preoccupied with images of Phil even now – as if he were the one in danger.

'Keep trying, my dear,' said Great-Aunt Elizabeth. 'Your heartstone has been diverting all its energy and resources into your recovery. Now that you're feeling better you might just get something.'

Kate sank back into the sofa and tried to relax her mind so that a more complete memory of what had happened could come to her. There was, she felt sure, some other clue that would help them get Cicely back and it was up to her to find it.

When Phil returned to his room, Jim Tacker was sitting beside Mark's bed.

'Where've you been, son?' he asked, as his fingers drummed the arm of the chair.

Phil sat on his bed and hoped that his rucksack, with the Insult Fermenter and Night-Vision Scanner, was well out of sight behind him.

'I didn't feel well so I went to get some fresh air,' he said.

The lower part of Jim Tacker's face was in shadow but Phil could see his eyes and he noticed that they flickered up towards the ceiling fan. Mark's bed was empty.

'Where's Mark?' Phil asked.

Jim Tacker stood up. 'He wasn't feeling too well either. I've taken him to the sickbay. Don't go wandering about at night. Mrs Caddington doesn't like it.'

'Can I see Mark?' Phil asked, his stomach tight with fear.

'Get some sleep,' said Tacker. 'You'll see him in the morning.' And with that he left the room.

As Phil wondered what to do, Nikwata squeezed under the door. Phil was relieved to see him. 'I've got a bad feeling about Mark,' he whispered.

Nikwata tipped his head. 'Tk, dk, tk, Nik no like, Nik no like, tk tk.' He ran across the floor, up the wall and over the ceiling, coming to a stop beside the slowly revolving fan. 'Tk tk tk tk tk tk gone tk tk tk,' he said, scampering in a tight circle.

Phil switched off the fan and dragged over a chair. He climbed on to it and saw that the tiny inlet pipe had been unplugged.

'Nikwata, go and find Mark.'

'Nik do nothing tk tk tk, Fearless gr gr grrrr gr do nothing nik nik, tk tk.'

'I know, but we can't do nothing, can we? Mark is in trouble and I have to know where he is.'

Nikwata's head jerked up and down in a little nodding gesture, then he took off across the ceiling, down the wall, on to the floor and out under the door. Phil put away the fermenter and the scanner and lay down on his bed, determined not to give way to the tears that were stinging his eyes.

In France, Great-Aunt Elizabeth had traced the origin of a receipt she had found in the back of the abandoned Saab. Dated the day before Cicely was snatched, it had come from a department store in Paris and was for a pair of black leather gloves. Great-Aunt Elizabeth and Harold went to the store and spoke to the young sales assistant who had served the large, broad-shouldered man. He was, she reported, an American gentleman with a face like a boxer or a criminal. She particularly remembered him, she told them, because he had been very rude and very ugly and because he smelt so strongly of garlic and tobacco that even the money he paid with had reeked of them.

When they told Kate the news she started up, her eyes wide with shock. 'I remember! I saw him – it was one of Lorabeth Lampton's men. Oh, God, she's taken Cicely.'

Great-Aunt Elizabeth began to pace the floor, as was her habit when she was agitated or needed to think. Her leather jacket creaked softly as she walked and her bun of silver-streaked black hair, haphazardly and hastily pinned to her head, flopped to one side as she reached the end of the room and spun round. 'Yes, I had feared as much. But, tusks and toenails,' she said crossly, 'I do not understand why she would do it. She claims to hate children. She always says she was glad to be rid of Charlotte!'

Emily let out a cry and rushed from the room. Harold dashed after her, throwing Great-Aunt Elizabeth an angry, dismayed look as he went.

Kate shook her head. 'That was a horrible thing to say. Emily is worried sick.'

'Yes, yes, yes, I'm sorry. But we have to get to the bottom of this if we are going to find Cicely and I don't understand what is motivating my sister. It doesn't make any sense!'

Kate tipped her head to one side as she thought. 'Perhaps she plans to hold Cicely to ransom until you give her the keystone. That's what she wanted before.'

'No, dear, that cannot be it. An abandoned heartstone can be claimed by the first person to touch it, which is why we had to get to the keystone first when it was lost. But otherwise a heartstone must be freely given, in love or friendship. She cannot coerce us or trick us into giving it to her. It would have the same effect as if she stole it.'

'What would happen? If she did steal it, I mean?' Kate asked.

'The positive energy would leave the stone instantly. It would become heavy and dark. Much more than that I cannot tell you. There is only one darkstone among the heartstones and my mother and grandmother were very fearful of it. They said that the stone's negative energy was concentrated and locked inside.'

'I don't understand,' Kate said. 'If a darkstone is dangerous, then why did you take our heartstones away from us and let them go dark?'

Great-Aunt Elizabeth stopped pacing and gave Kate a small smile. 'Still working things out, I see. Well, my dear, a stone that has merely been set aside by its owner or willingly put away for safe-keeping is not a darkstone. It is merely dormant, biding its time, waiting to be reclaimed by its rightful wearer. Your heartstone and Phil's keystone were surrendered willingly into my care and they remained yours. Darkstones are altogether different. They are caused by some kind of betrayal or violence. Their power

is not so much dormant as . . . well, for want of a better word, brewing.'

Kate frowned. 'Like a storm?' she asked.

'Yes,' Great-Aunt Elizabeth replied, her face becoming grave. 'I suppose you could say like a storm.'

'So why does she want Cicely?'

'I do not know, dear, I do not know. But that is what we must find out.'

Phil had not expected to sleep, but he woke with a start in the morning when the tannoy crackled into life and called all boys to assemble immediately in the gymnasium. Phil glanced across to Mark's bed. It was still empty.

'Nikwata, are you here?'

There was no answer and Phil was suddenly over-whelmed by a wave of anxiety that paralysed him. He felt alone and frightened. What could he do? Great-Aunt Elizabeth had left. Should he go out to Fearless and leave Mark? Suddenly anger replaced the fear that Phil was feeling and he was able to spring from his bed. As he ripped clothes from his drawer and began to dress, he felt furious with his family, particularly with Great-Aunt Elizabeth. She knew there was danger, yet she had left him unprotected and the others ignorant of his where-abouts. His parents probably did not even know that he was in Africa and, although this was not their fault, the rage he felt extended to them nonetheless.

A second call to assemble crackled through the tannoy and Phil kicked his legs into his trousers and yanked on his

T-shirt. He was furious with Mark because he didn't know where he was, but most of all, it occurred to him, he was mad at Kate. She always knew best: she bossed and advised and overrode his decisions. And she wasn't here. What was he supposed to do?

Phil joined a line of boys as they filed into the gymnasium and he suddenly saw Mark up ahead of him. He slipped forward to join him. He touched Mark's arm and Mark slowly turned his head and blinked.

'Are you OK?' Phil whispered.

Mark did not answer. His eyes were glassy, his pupils huge.

The boys reached empty seats and sat down. Phil suddenly noticed Nikwata on the leg of the chair in front of him. He jerked his head up and down until Phil raised his eyes and took notice of the boy sitting in the chair.

Phil leant forward and whispered, 'Robert, Robert Danby?'

The boy turned his head and looked at Phil but did not answer. Across his forehead there was a deep impression: a ridge of dented skin. Phil was puzzling over what could have caused it when Jim Tacker appeared on the small platform at the front of the hall.

'Boys, good morning!' He smiled heartily around the room. 'On your feet, boys. Mrs Caddington is going to address you.'

Jim Tacker leant backwards and smiled into the wings as the boys stood. There was a long pause, but he kept smiling and the boys waited in silence. Slowly a shadowy figure appeared and walked to the centre of the stage.

Mrs Caddington wore the dark veil over her head and drawn across her face. She stared steadily at the rows of boys, her gaze scanning each face as if she were looking for someone in particular. Phil's first instinct was to lower his eyes but he checked himself and stared straight ahead, as the rest of them were doing. Mrs Caddington stared back. Phil felt a small moment of time swell into something much greater. It was like watching an egg roll off the table and waiting for it to hit the floor and break.

What happened next was so shocking that it took all of Phil's willpower to stay on his feet.

Jim Tacker walked off into the wings, his arms outstretched like a sleepwalker. When he came back he was carrying Cicely. She looked out at them from frightened eyes as she held her small frame stiffly upright and leant away from Jim Tacker's face.

'This is my adopted daughter,' said Mrs Caddington as Tacker came and stood beside her. 'Her name is Gina.'

'It not! It Sisslee!' shouted Cicely, and she stared at Mrs Caddington, her bottom lip pushed out and her chin puckered.

Phil clenched his teeth and his fists and carefully slid a foot forward towards where Nikwata perched on the chair leg. Nikwata dropped on to his shoe and sidled up Phil's leg to his waist, circled round to his back and scurried up to the nape of his neck. Under his breath, Phil whispered urgently, 'Go to her. Go to Cicely,' until he felt Nikwata run down his back and drop to the floor.

*

Fearless paced the fence, occasionally glancing at the sun to confirm the passing of time. He saw groups of boys stroll by, dressed in cricket whites or running shorts, and realized that the day's sports had begun. He wondered what had prevented Phil from meeting him and hoped nothing was wrong. He lingered a little longer and considered what to do. The satellite phone worked intermittently and the reception kept breaking up. He hadn't yet made contact with Great-Aunt Elizabeth and he had no choice but to go down the mountain, where, he hoped, reception would be better.

A lean and hungry-looking dog appeared at his side and Fearless told her to wait for Phil, then, with one last backward glance, he set off. Hoping to be back by nightfall and with the satellite phone slung round his neck, like a St Bernard's barrel of brandy, Fearless ran. Wherever he could, he avoided open ground and kept to tracks made by other animals. Once or twice he stumbled on loose rocks and another time he got caught on acacia, the thorns snatching hold of his fur and yanking him to a halt. It took him several minutes of wriggling backwards to remove the ten-centimetre spikes at exactly the reverse angle that they had gone in. Soon after he took a thorn in the leg and had to pull it with his teeth. It was easy to see why the other dogs looked as they did.

'He has a stone, just like you said he would,' Tacker said. 'You want me to take it from him?'

Mrs Caddington slammed her fist on her desk.

'How many times do I have to tell you? You can't *take* it from him. If you do the energy drains out of it and the stone becomes worthless. The energy flow is incredibly weak already –' She broke off and narrowed her eyes at Tacker. 'Did you try to take it from him before you got here?'

'No!' Jim Tacker was insulted to be asked. 'I didn't know he had it until you told me about it,' he added sulkily.

Cynthia Caddington began drumming her fingers on the desk. 'I want the keystone but he has to give it to me willingly. There was absolutely no point in giving him the preparatory treatment while he has the stone.'

Cicely began to whimper and Cynthia Caddington glowered at her.

Jim Tacker smiled. 'Look, I bet I can get him to give it to you. The boy trusts me. He'll want to give it to you. Why, he'll even think it was all his own idea.'

Mrs Caddington was considering this when Cicely screamed, 'I want Mama!' and large tears began to roll down her cheeks.

Cynthia Caddington clapped her hands over her ears. 'Take her to Bardolph and tell him to get her some ice cream or something.'

Tacker reached for Cicely and lifted her into his arms, holding her at a distance as she arched her back and drummed her fists and feet against his head and chest.

'Steady, pussy cat!' He laughed, turning to leave the room.

Nikwata squeezed through the gap beside the hinge of

the door and followed them. In the opposite corner of the office a man stood quietly and jumped with fright when Mrs Caddington turned towards him.

'Bernhard,' she said, adjusting her veil, 'there are two boys left to be reminded about their potential for perfection.'

'Yes, Mrs Caddington.'

'One of them is in possession of something that is very valuable to me.' She placed a thin arm protectively round the leather bag she carried. 'He must be made to willingly give this to me before the treatment.'

'He is more er, likely to give it to you after the treatment, I think.'

'Well, that's as may be but it must be willingly given and I think the treatment will be tantamount to coercion, in which case the stone will be powerless in my possession.'

'I don't understand this.'

'Well, no,' snapped Cynthia Caddington, 'because you're not as clever as you think you are. Are you able to account for what happened to the Danby boy? Why wasn't his personality properly polished the first time?'

'I don't know yet. I am sorry, Mrs Caddington.'

'Sorry doesn't help us, though, does it, Bernhard? Is your mother's convalescence going well?'

This last and unexpected question threw Bernhard into a state of even greater anxiety. He pressed his lips together in an attempt to stop shaking and his mouth went dry. 'Er, no, sorry, er, yes, thank you.'

'Good. You don't want her having a relapse at her time of life, do you?'

'N-n-no, Mrs Caddington.'

'Better get back to work, then.'

Bernhard had been eyeing the door throughout the interview and he now made a move towards it.

'Oh, and Bernhard –' she caught the sleeve of his lab coat with a wrinkled hook of a finger – 'prepare a sphere for the child. She's a defiant little madam and I can't stand that nonsense a minute longer than I have to.'

Escape from the Lodge

Phil had not seen Nikwata since he had sent the lizard after Cicely. He kept imagining how worried Harold and Emily must be and longed to let them know where she was. It was now evening and he had pursued a punishing timetable that included wrestling, tennis, work on the parallel bars and soccer. And Jim Tacker arriving at regular intervals to offer words of encouragement had ruined any chance of slipping away to meet Fearless. Phil found it impossible to concentrate on what he was doing and time passed agonizingly slowly.

For the last activity of the day he was assigned to the same five-a-side team as Mark and in the changing room after the match he had a chance to speak to him. 'Mark, are you OK?'

'Fine.'

'You didn't look fine this morning.'

'Well, I'm OK now.' Mark shrugged off Phil's enquiry and did not meet his eye.

Phil checked that no one was near enough to overhear before speaking again. 'Look, Mark, there's something

really weird going on here. Tell me what happened to you in the sickbay.'

'You're the one who's weird!' Mark exclaimed, laughing. 'I saw the doctor, he gave me a jab and now I'm fine. What's your problem?' He walked off to the showers and Phil followed him.

'Listen, Mark,' he hissed angrily, 'they kidnapped that baby! We cannot trust anyone here. Not the doctor, not Jim Tacker and certainly not Mrs Caddington.'

'Oh, she's *really* nice,' Mark said, popping his head round the shower and grinning at Phil.

Phil reached in and turned the shower off. 'What did you say?'

'She's nice. She came to see me when I was in the sickbay. She's actually really kind.' He put the shower back on and turned away from Phil.

Before Phil had a chance to think what to do or say next, Tacker's face appeared round the end of the shower block.

'Hurry up, son. Are you waiting for a shower or are you off to get dressed?'

Phil returned to his locker and began dressing slowly, waiting for Mark. But Jim Tacker appeared first. He sat at the end of his bench and talked to him about setting higher goals for the next day. Phil dragged out tying his shoelaces for as long as he could but there was still no sign of Mark. Fully dressed and with Tacker smiling at him, he couldn't delay things any longer and so he went back to their room to wait for Mark. He had just sat

down on the bed when Nikwata squeezed under the door and began dancing from foot to foot, making tiny agitated sounds. Phil thought he had seen the lizard in a state of excitement but this was something else.

'Tk, tk, wap, wap, tszk, weet, weet, tk, tk.'

Nikwata then ran over Phil's shoe and up his leg and arrived on his shoulder.

'Tk, tk, mtoto, tk, haraka! Haraka!'

'Tell me in English,' Phil begged him. 'What's wrong? Have you found Cicely?'

Nikwata did a little stamping dance.

'Tk tk tk tk, you come! Tk tk tk.'

Just then the door opened and Mark stepped into the room. Phil pulled him in and shut the door.

'Mark, you've got to give me the keystone. Now! It's urgent.'

From Phil's shoulder Nikwata stared at Mark, shook his head and hissed. As Mark's mouth fell open in astonishment, Phil raised his hand as if swearing an oath and hid Nikwata from view.

'Mark, give me my heartstone. Now!'

'Wow, you caught the lizard!' Mark said, ignoring his request.

'Mark!' Phil took hold of the boy's arm and shook him roughly. 'Give me the keystone. Remember my Great-Aunt Elizabeth told you to give it to me when I needed it? Well, I need it now, so hand it over!'

Mark pulled away from him and threw his sports bag on his bed. 'I can't. I just told Jim that I would give it to Mrs Caddington.'

'You did what!'

'Yes, Jim's just gone to tell her now.'

Phil reached for his bag and slung it on his back. 'We've got to get out of here.'

He made a grab for Mark's sleeve. Mark considered him for a second, then his face lightened and he lifted one eyebrow. 'Can I have the lizard?' he asked.

Phil was about to explain that the lizard wasn't his to give when Nikwata jumped from his shoulder to Mark's and said, 'Tk tk tk, OK, let's go! Tk tk!'

Mark's mouth fell open and Phil took his chance and bundled him through the door.

Outside the room, Nikwata leapt to the wall, ran down to the floor and tore along it at full pelt. His bursts of speed were punctuated by sudden momentary stillness as Phil hurried behind, dragging Mark along beside him. Beyond the reception area was a curtained-off corridor and Nikwata glanced back at them before disappearing behind it.

'Wait here,' whispered Phil, pushing Mark down behind the reception desk. Mark began to protest and got back on to his feet. Phil took hold of his shoulders and pushed him down. He felt desperate. 'Just stay here!' he growled viciously. Then, controlling his voice, he added, 'Mark, I'll tell you everything, about the keystone, about the lizard, about Great-Aunt Elizabeth and Fearless and everything . . . But please, please just wait here, Mark, please.'

Mark stared at Phil for a moment and then nodded. 'OK, I'll wait five minutes.'

Seconds before he had felt murderous towards Mark

for not handing over the keystone, but now that he was at least cooperating a little Phil was quick to see the advantage of having the keystone quiet and undetectable at Mark's throat. He moved the curtain aside and squinted into the gloomy corridor. He could see Nikwata's silhouette framed in the crack of light by an open door. Phil breathed deeply to calm himself and put his back flat against the wall. He moved silently and peered around the door. Nikwata tipped his head in a little jerking movement and Phil looked in that direction. Cicely was sitting in a large carved chair, her head bent over a mobile phone that she held in both hands on her lap. Phil moved his head slightly so that he could see more of the room. A metre or so away from Cicely, sitting in a chair, his feet up on the desk, was Bardolph. He had his hands behind his head and his eyes were closed. At the sight of him Phil's jaw tensed. Bardolph had aged; his close-cropped hair was grey and his face had sagged. But Phil would have recognized him anywhere. On the desk in front of him was a large half-eaten tub of rum and raisin ice cream.

Nikwata ran up Phil's leg, on to his shoulder and up his neck. He held on to the side of Phil's earlobe and whispered, 'Tk tk. You – little one, tk tk tk, Nik – big one, tk, tk, tk.'

Phil lifted Nikwata down and held him in his cupped hand close to his mouth. 'No, *I'll* stop the big one,' he whispered, remembering how Bardolph had smashed his way into Great-Aunt Elizabeth's house, kidnapped Phil and tried to drag Kate from the Humanitron, with no concern for the pain and damage this would cause her.

He was an ignorant oaf and he was also a violent bully – and Phil didn't see how a mere lizard could stop him.

Phil reached into his bag for the Insult Fermenter and opened it, while Nikwata clung to his index finger by his tiny-suckered feet. Phil explained in a whisper what he was going to do. The fermenter could exaggerate an insult until it was potentially lethal. He raised the canister to his lips but before he could whisper into it Nikwata climbed to the end of his finger, leant his head inside the neck of the canister and jabbered something in his squeaky Swahili. Phil recognized a couple of words as they echoed softly round the inside of the fermenter. '*Nyoka*' meant snake and '*moyo*' meant heart, and he grimaced as his imagination conjured up the possible effect it might have on his old enemy. Phil set the timer on the fermenter for ten seconds and whispered a last instruction to Nikwata. The lizard nodded and ran down to the floor.

Phil watched through the crack as Nikwata walked around the door and stood where Cicely could see him but where he was out of sight of the desk. She was holding the phone close to her face and frowning at it. Every so often she glanced over at Bardolph, who had relaxed into sleep, his mouth open, his chin resting on his chest.

Nikwata reared up and waved his arms frantically at Cicely, but the child was focused in rapt concentration on the phone and did not notice him. Nikwata threw himself in the air and spun round a few times before stopping to check if she had seen him. She hadn't. In an increasingly desperate attempt to get Cicely's attention and lure her from the room, he hopped up and down on the spot for a full minute – but still the toddler was oblivious. He began to sway, rocking his body this way and that, swishing his tail from side to side and rolling his head. Next he raised his feet one after another and then took a few steps to the left and a few to the right. He turned his back on her and spun his tail as if it were a lime-green lasso. Cicely was so totally absorbed in what she was doing, it was as if she was in another world. She remained engrossed with the phone, her head bent over it, her little brown legs stretching out straight in front of her, her red shoes pointing up to the ceiling.

So far Nikwata had managed to stay quiet but now he was desperate. As his movements became increasingly agitated, he made little squeaks, clicks and grunts. He turned writhing somersaults and backflips, so that he appeared to be either suffering electrocution or performing some bizarre reptilian version of breakdancing. At last Cicely looked up.

Nikwata slapped a hand over his mouth and smacked her a kiss before turning and beckoning her to follow him. Cicely wriggled down from the chair and toddled after Nikwata. As she stepped into the shadow of the corridor, Phil reached out and caught hold of her wrist and swept her behind him and out of sight. She gazed up at him and for a second her startled eyes seemed close to tears. Then a smile of recognition spread across her face and she flung her arms around his knees and clung to him, making strange little laughing sobs. Phil patted her hair, which was soft and bouncy beneath his fingers. Then put a finger to his lips. Cicely nodded and popped her thumb in her mouth, while with her other hand she held tight to Phil's leg and leant her face against his knee.

Inside the room, Bardolph snored. Phil unscrewed the fermenter, leant round the door and pointed it at the bulky figure sprawled over the desk. The fermenter began to vibrate gently and a soft curl of smoke escaped from it. Phil glanced down, afraid that it wasn't going to work properly, when suddenly it roared into action and buzzed violently in his hand. Bardolph's eyes opened in alarm but before he could do anything the chair into which he had crammed his body slammed back against the wall and he banged his head. Bardolph rubbed his eyes with a thick hairy hand, before leaning forward and squinting out at the room. Although Phil could see that there was nothing there, Bardolph reacted as if he were living a nightmare. He began desperately trying to push something away from his chest and screamed down at his legs and feet.

With his free hand, Phil found the soft mass of Cicely's curls and slipped the palm of his hand gently over her eyes so that she would not witness his grotesque pantomime.

Bardolph's distress may have been horrifying to watch but it was nothing compared to the hallucination he was seeing. A tangle of snakes slithered towards him, intent on wrapping themselves around him and crushing his bones until his heart shot out of his mouth.

The fermenter stilled and Phil stuffed it back into his

bag and stooped to lift Cicely into his arms. He hugged her. 'It's OK now, Cicely. I'm going to take you home.'

There was a thump as Bardolph collapsed unconscious on to the desk.

Cicely still held the mobile phone that she had pulled from Bardolph's pocket while he slept. 'Phone Mama,' she said, thrusting the phone into Phil's face.

Phil shook his head in amazement, he took the phone and hugged her. 'Oh, you clever girl, Cicely! But we've got to go away from here first.'

Cicely gazed at him with her large brown eyes and nodded. 'Bad lady,' she whispered.

When Phil reappeared in reception with Cicely in his arms and Nikwata clinging to his shoulder, Mark stood up uncertainly from behind the reception desk.

'What are you *doing*?' He stared, aghast, at Cicely.

'Come on!' Phil hissed at him. 'We've got to hurry!'

Phil turned for the door and as Mark lurched forward to follow him, his hip caught the corner of a fish tank. It leant somewhere between thirty and forty degrees and for the briefest moment appeared to stay in equilibrium as if it were undecided whether to right itself or fall.

'I've got to get her away from here. Come on!' Phil pleaded from the doorway.

Mark stood as if petrified, cringing beside the teetering tank. Suddenly the tank crashed to the floor, sending a mini tidal wave of water, weed and fish across the tiles. Without looking back, they ran out through the door and headed for the compound gate.

The gate was chained and padlocked but there was a small gate within it that was open. The guard looked out from his box, where he had been watching a small television, but they had climbed through the gate and sprinted down the road before he had time to stand.

When they reached the bend opposite Caddington Lodge's gymnasium, Phil led them off the road and into the scrub of thorn trees from where Fearless had emerged on the first day. Phil gave a low whistle and called Fearless's name. An answer came in a series of growls and yelps and the slow, menacing approach of the dog pack. A small, thin bitch appeared and bared its teeth until a larger yellow dog snapped at it and the dogs fell back and became silent.

They could still hear the guard shouting in urgent Swahili and Mark, who was catching his breath, said, 'This is stupid. They're bound to catch us – that's if we're not ripped to shreds by a pack of dogs.'

A twig snapped and another, older dog stepped out from behind the boulders.

'This dog will help us.' Phil said confidently, though not entirely sure himself, just placing his trust in Fearless.

'Oh, for God's sake,' Mark scoffed, but his voice wavered with fear. 'It's not Scooby-Doo, you know!'

The dog looked at them, its gaze lingering on Mark. Nikwata jumped from Phil's shoulder, ran over and leapt on to the dog. As Nikwata arrived on its shoulder and began to chatter Swahili in its ear, the dog turned and began to pick a path over the scree of stones and across

the sharp needles of the thorn trees. Putting their trust in Nikwata, they followed.

The night air buzzed with the sound of crickets and as they passed behind a large rock the sound of the alarm being raised at the lodge was muffled.

Cicely grasped Phil's T-shirt and wrapped her legs tight around his waist. 'Phone Mama now? Shall we?' she asked, her voice trembling.

Phil pulled the phone from his bag with his free hand and glanced at it. There was no signal. 'Soon, Cicely – we can't phone her yet. We have to go down the mountain a little way before it will work.'

Cicely gave a small whimper. 'Me want Mama,' she cried softly, and Phil suddenly felt overwhelmed with anxiety. How could he do this? He didn't know how to look after a baby. Sensing his self-doubt, Cicely began to cry.

'Oh, for goodness' sake, don't start crying!' Mark's voice was shrill. 'Shut her up, Phil, or someone'll hear her.'

Cicely turned her head sharply towards the sound of Mark's voice. 'You shut up, you big ugly!' she said, and fell silent.

After several minutes of stumbling after the dog in the darkness, it stopped beside a vertical crevice, glanced back at them and then slipped through the gap in the rock.

'I'm not going in there,' said Mark.

Phil turned to face him. 'Then give me the keystone, Mark. I really need it now.'

Mark shook his head. 'You'll leave me behind if I give it to you.'

'Give me my keystone. You can go back. They'll not bother with you. It's me they're after. I'll get help and be back soon. I can do it if I have the keystone. I know I can.'

Suddenly Cicely leant forward in Phil's arms and thrust her chin in Mark's direction. 'You big ugly!' she repeated, and put her thumb in her mouth.

Mark shook his head. 'I'm keeping the stone. I'm coming with you.'

'OK,' said Phil as frustration tensed every fibre of his body. 'You've got the stone, so you get to check out what's behind the rock.'

Above them the sky was splattered with stars, and a half-moon gave enough light for them to be able to see each other. Nikwata reappeared and stared up at them, perplexed by the delay. Phil watched Mark's face as he weighed his courage against his fear. At last he nodded and bent towards the cleft in the rock into which the dog had disappeared.

'Wait,' said Phil, reaching into his bag. 'Take this.' He passed Mark the Night-Vision Scanner.

A moment later Mark reappeared smiling. 'You're not gonna believe this!' he said.

It was a small cave and Great-Aunt Elizabeth had begun to set it up as a headquarters. It was clean, containing two mattresses, with mosquito nets, several large containers of bottled water and, hanging from the ceiling, a net containing two mangoes, packets of biscuits and four boxes of Great-Aunt Elizabeth's favourite chocolates. In a corner, a series of heavy-duty car batteries was attached to a lamp that Mark had turned on. A number of bugs crawled on the walls and Nikwata dashed about, flicking his tongue into crooks and niches, gobbling them up.

Phil put Cicely down on one of the mattresses and dropped his bag. He opened the net and gave the dog a handful of biscuits. It ate them greedily and watched Phil while he put the mangoes and the chocolates into his bag. Realizing that Phil was not going to give it more biscuits, the dog turned and curled himself up on the mattress beside Cicely.

Mark slumped down on the other mattress. 'No one will find us here,' he said.

'We're not staying,' said Phil. 'See how much water you can carry. Decant some into those smaller bottles.'

'What's the matter with staying?' Mark said. 'We'll be safe here.'

'We've got to go down the mountain to get a signal on the phone. We have to let them know that Cicely's safe.'

Phil scanned the cave, looking for Nikwata, and as he did so the lizard suddenly dropped from the roof to his shoulder.

'Nikwata, you stay here and wait for Fearless – tell him what's happened. OK?'

'Tk tk tk tk tk OK tk tk tk.'

Phil pulled a sheet from the bed and stuffed one of the

mosquito nets into his bag. He folded the sheet in half. The Tanzanian mothers and elder sisters tied young children to their backs with *kangas*, rectangles of brightly dyed cotton. If he could do the same with Cicely, then he'd have both hands free.

'I think they'll look for an hour or so, then they'll wait for the light. We'll rest for a couple of hours, then make a move.'

'What, in the dark?' Mark asked.

'I'll wear the Night-Vision Scanner and you can follow me.'

Having stroked the dog and sucked her thumb, Cicely had let herself slip into a curled position on the mattress and fallen asleep. Phil glanced at her and felt relief flood through him. He still had plenty to worry about but at least while she slept he didn't have to worry about her.

'Try and get some sleep too,' he said to Mark. 'We'll be on the move again soon.'

Phil's Safari

As his mind cleared and the hallucinatory snakes vanished, Bardolph heard an alarm ringing. He screwed up his eyes and managed to focus, and that's when he saw Cynthia Caddington standing over him, her wizened face twisted into a spiteful scowl. He glanced at the chair where the baby had been and found it empty.

'Where's . . .?' he began, then Cynthia Caddington swung her arm out, scooped up the steel-based desktop lamp on the way and slammed it into the side of his head.

'Incompetent idiot!' she hissed.

Bernhard stood in the corner of the room, his face turned to the floor. He jumped when Mrs Caddington spun round and pointed at him. 'Get back to work! What are you doing here?'

'You sent for me —'

'Go and get ready. There is no time, no time. When we get them back I want my stepdaughter to receive an instant reminder. I want her to be loyal to no one but me, do you hear?'

'Er, no, I've been thinking about that little girl, Mrs Caddington. It is very difficult. I must get the proportions right. It is virtually impossible to calculate the capacity of the extraction. A small child might have a big personality and an adult perhaps has next to none.' He glanced nervously to where Bardolph rocked in pain. 'This is what I've learnt. The Danby boy – I've looked again at his case, like you asked, and I think he had something that I was unable to measure. He was unusual. And I think this baby is very unusual . . . She has a powerful personality and I –'

Bernhard's voice trailed away as Cynthia Caddington moved towards him. From the desk, Bardolph cradled his head in his hands and groaned.

Cynthia Caddington stopped with her face close to Bernhard's. 'Go . . . to . . . the . . . basement . . .' She leant even closer as Bernhard recoiled, and screamed in his face, 'I don't care if you extract her whole brain! She just has to like me!'

Bernhard turned and fled, passing Jim Tacker in the doorway. Tacker watched over his shoulder as the doctor disappeared down the corridor, then he addressed Cynthia Caddington.

'Maybe we should just quit while we're ahead. You've got several hundred boys ready to follow you to the ends of the Earth. Just forget those two and the baby.'

Jim Tacker's smile froze on his face as Cynthia Caddington spun round to face him. At her throat her heartstone flared and lit Tacker's face in a red glow. His

dark eyebrows slowly lowered and his eyes glazed over.

'Go. Find those children and bring them back.'

Tacker raised his dark eyebrows and nodded. 'I'll set off at daybreak – they won't have got far.'

Tacker left the lodge at dawn. He began confidently, amused to see their footprints in the red dust, whistling under his breath as he followed the tracks where the boys had left the road opposite the gymnasium. But then after a few hundred metres they had been obliterated by a pack of wild dogs and he lost the trail. Tacker wasted a couple of hours going round in circles before he eventually picked them up again. *Maybe this isn't going to be so easy after all*, he thought, gritting his teeth.

Phil's hand closed round the mobile phone in his pocket. He kept it switched off so as not to waste the battery and resisted the temptation to switch it on again. During the day he had checked it hourly and, though he estimated that they had descended more than 1,000 metres, there had still been no signal when he looked before they made camp in another cave. Phil opened his eyes to darkness and silence. It was cold now but he still felt stifled by the stale air. His right arm felt like dead wood and was damp where Cicely's head nestled, heavy with sleep. With his free hand he felt for her face in the darkness and she sighed softly. He realized then that, in her sleep at least, she felt safe, and a feeling of protectiveness overwhelmed him.

Behind him Mark stirred and whispered, 'Are you awake? What shall we do now? I was thinking that maybe we could go back and try to apologize. We could say she ran away and we found her and brought her back. What do you think? Do you think they'd believe us?'

Phil's heart sank. Somehow Mark was making everything more difficult. But there was no denying that they would need a plan before daybreak. He gently moved the crook of his elbow from beneath Cicely's head and quietly lifted himself to a crouching position before creeping away to the mouth of the cave. Outside, the air thrummed with the sound of insects and the rock face still radiated some heat from the day. Mark came out and stood beside him.

'Oh, gross! I've been lying in something disgusting,' he complained, brushing at his trousers.

Phil could just make out the repulsed expression on his face. 'Bat guano probably –'

'Oh, yeuch.'

'We'll climb down to the water and follow the animal trails beside the river. We'll follow the current and move towards the coast.' Phil pointed down to the valley below them.

'But we're bound to be seen if we're out in the open.'

'Not necessarily. You'll have to carry Cicely too, take turns with me. She's too young to manage and I can't carry her all the time.'

'She doesn't like me.'

'Well, make her like you. Be nice to her – she's only a baby.'

'OK,' Mark muttered.

On the long walk he had been remembering the old days before his family had moved to Cornwall. Phil had always looked up to him then and he had been the one to make the plans and decisions. Well, the tables had turned, but nonetheless Mark found himself feeling nostalgic for those times. He had been happy back then, he realized suddenly. He hadn't been rich, he hadn't lived in a big house, but he had had a friend. Mark studied Phil's profile and resolved that he would try to be more worthy of his friendship from that moment on.

Phil looked at the sky and decided that they should make a move straight away. A bat returned to the cave and he guessed that it would soon be dawn. They should make a start before the heat of the day. Phil returned to the cave, put his bag on his back and felt for Cicely in the dark. Her little body shuddered as he pulled her into his arms. She had cried so much before sleeping that she was exhausted and he hoped that she would continue to sleep in his arms. He let her head loll on his shoulder while, leaning backwards, he flung the fabric round her and tied it behind his back. He carried her from the cave and Mark followed him.

The path down to the valley led them between thorny plants and at times large boulders blocked their way, forcing them to make a detour. It was difficult and they made slow progress. Mark did not complain, although Phil could tell from his breathing that he was uncom-

fortable. As they reached the water's edge dawn suddenly broke in a blaze of red across the sky, and the river appeared purple and mauve. Cicely, her hair lit like copper wire, lifted her head from Phil's shoulder and called, 'Mama!' in her confusion.

'Mama's not here, Cicely, I'm going to take you to Mama, and Papa too . . . and Kate and Barking. We're going to find everyone. I'm going to take you home.'

Cicely began to wriggle in his arms and Phil had to loosen the cloth and put her down.

'How do we know where to go?' Mark asked.

Phil's jaw tensed. He had studied the map that Fearless had given him and he knew how to navigate by the sun and the stars and had remembered what his dad had told him about finding north in the southern hemisphere. He reasoned that a river would be flowing towards the east coast. But the weight of the responsibility was wearing away at his confidence.

'I just know – OK?' he snapped.

'Him a big ugly, big ugly, big ugly, big ugly . . .' chanted Cicely from the water's edge, where she had squatted to pee. With her left arm she hugged her knees while her right arm was thrust out with a finger pointing at Mark.

Suddenly the shallow water beside Cicely churned violently and a large crocodile launched itself through the water. It was as if the beast had been catapulted from the murky shallows, its head, body and tail writhing in sections of solid muscular propulsion. Phil grabbed Cicely's wrist and flung his arm up and away, snatching her thin, dangling legs out of the reach of the snapping jaws. As suddenly as it had come, the crocodile sank back into the water and disappeared beneath the surface, empty-jawed. It all happened so fast that Mark had not moved a muscle and now could not completely grasp what he had seen. He began to swear and Cicely began to cry. Phil's heart hammered behind his ribs and he held Cicely tight in his arms.

'Now will you give me the keystone?' he said at last.

Cicely lifted her head from Phil's shoulder and howled, 'I want Mama!'

Instinctively, Phil pulled the phone from his pocket and switched it on with his thumb. He was still staring at Mark, waiting for his reaction, positive that he would now hand over the keystone. Couldn't he see the danger he was putting them all in?

Suddenly the phone rang. Phil stared down at the display and read the name Frimley.

'Oh, my God,' screamed Mark. 'Quick, answer it!'

Cicely tried to grab the phone from Phil and he held it above his head. 'Wait, wait,' he said, 'wait! Wait till it stops. It's Bardolph's buddy. We mustn't answer it.'

At last the repetitive jingle stopped and Phil turned to Cicely, who had slid from his arms and was now hopping up and down beside him. 'Phone Mama! Phone Mama!'

'What's Mama's number, Cicely? Do you know Mama's number?'

'Let's just ring my mum,' Mark said, reaching out for the phone.

Cicely looked crestfallen.

'Kate!' Phil cried. 'It's all right, Cicely. We'll ring Kate – she's with Mama!'

Phil dialled Kate's number and held his breath as he listened to the space between the digits registering and then a longer moment of silence before he at last heard Kate's phone ringing. Beside him, Cicely, her face still wet with tears, laughed and hopped up and down and pulled at Phil's T-shirt. Mark and Phil stared at each other and Phil was just about to redial when he heard Kate's voice.

'Hello?' she asked. 'Who is this?'

Phil grinned. 'Kate! It's me, Phil – and I've got Cicely! Cicely's safe! Tell everyone she's safe. OK, OK, yeah, she's here . . . yes, OK . . .'

Phil crouched down and held the phone to Cicely's ear. 'Mama, 'ere am, Mama!' She began to laugh and cry simultaneously and tears flew from her eyes.

Behind him Mark continuously tried to interrupt. 'Phil . . . Phil . . . Phil . . .' His voice was flat and persistent, and Phil couldn't believe that he wouldn't wait one second. Irritation raced through his body and he spun round.

'Can't you wait for just –' and there he stopped, because standing next to Mark, his hand on Mark's shoulder, was Jim Tacker.

'Give me the phone, pussy cat,' Tacker said as he bent down and beamed his warmest smile at Cicely. Gently he took the phone out of her hands and switched it off.

A Harley and a Cessna to the Rescue

The only people who had her number were her friends and her family, and when they called their name was displayed. Kate looked at the unknown number – no doubt a wrong number – and nearly didn't answer it. When she heard Phil's voice and what he was saying, she jumped up and stumbled from the room, looking for Emily. She found her sitting in a corner of Cicely's bedroom, her back against the wall.

By the time the call was finished, Great-Aunt Elizabeth, Harold and Barking had joined them, alerted by Kate running to the stairs and shouting. They didn't need to hear what she was saying to know that it was good news. By the time they reached Cicely's bedroom the call was over and Emily was sobbing in Kate's arms. Emily had dropped the phone and Kate turned to the door as they entered.

'It was Phil and he was with Cicely and they're safe, but we got cut off.'

'There was someone else there – I heard a man's voice,' Emily wailed.

Harold picked the phone up from the floor and redialled the last number. He heard a charming and articulate

woman's voice 'You have reached the voicemail of –' before a gruff and deep American accent butted in with 'Floyd Bardolph the Fourth'. He pressed '2' to replay and passed the phone to Great-Aunt Elizabeth. Harold watched her face while she listened and saw the flicker of a twitch beneath her left eye.

'Where are they? Where's Phil?' Harold asked.

'He's in Cornwall,' Kate answered for her.

'Are they in Cornwall, Aunt E?' Harold asked.

Great-Aunt Elizabeth's face turned red, then purple.

'Africa!' she bellowed, and their faces registered shock, disbelief and dismay. 'They're in Africa. We must go immediately. Harold, we need the super turbo-boost and supplies of rocket fuel. Any provisions you have in the house – we'll take. Come on!'

Suddenly everyone was rushing from the room and no one noticed that Barking was speaking.

'Hang on . . .' he said. 'Listen, shouldn't we . . . ?' He raised his voice but there was so much commotion that still no one paid him any attention. 'Will you just hold on a . . .'

Barking leapt on to a nearby table, filled his lungs with air and emitted the loudest caterwaul of his twenty-three-year life as a cat. Everyone stopped in their tracks and looked at him. He cleared his throat and composed his human voice. 'I think we should call Charlotte and Michael – they're in Africa already and they could get there before us.'

As Great-Aunt Elizabeth pulled her own phone from her pocket it began to ring. 'Fearless! We've just had a

call from Phil. Yes, Cicely . . . I know. Why aren't you with them, Fearless?'

She paused and listened while the others watched her anxiously. 'The line keeps breaking up,' she said to them.

'Can you hear me? Go to Phil. He's with Cicely – blasted bog-berries, we got cut off. That satellite phone is so unreliable, Harold,' she said crossly. 'Do you have another we can take with us?'

Emily jumped as if she had been stung. The shock of losing Cicely had left her thin face looking tense but devoid of emotion. Suddenly her eyes became large behind her glasses as they flashed with anger. 'Unreliable? *Unreliable!*' Emily's voice faltered at first, then became strong. 'Just look what you have done! My baby has been kidnapped!'

Kate hurried over to Emily and put her arms around her.

'I'm so sorry, my dear,' Great-Aunt Elizabeth said sadly. 'Truly, I am very sorry. But we will get her back – I promise. Now, come on, quick as you can, everyone. There's no time to lose.'

'OK,' said Harold as he packed up, 'but you must tell us everything you know. I mean absolutely everything. No more secrets, Aunt E.'

Fearless had devised a method of holding a stick between his teeth to press the buttons on the phone. After getting disconnected he switched it off and spat the stick on to the ground. He nosed the strap over his head and looked back up the mountain and then glanced at the sky to judge the time from the position of the sun. It was several

hours since he had last found water and he would have to find some before retracing his steps. He could see a baobab tree to his left no more than a kilometre away and he should find water there. He set off towards it.

Charlotte and Michael were eating lobster on the waterfront in Stonetown when Charlotte's phone rang. She felt her nerves jangle as she lifted it to her ear, her dread of bad news heightened by the fact that she had been enjoying herself and had not thought about the children all morning. She and Michael had wandered the streets and trailed through the House of Wonders and the Fordhani Gardens. Michael watched her face, his fork poised midway to his mouth. Suddenly Charlotte was on her feet and piling Tanzanian shillings from her purse on to the table and dragging Michael from the restaurant.

'What is it? If you tell me that that mad aunt of yours has put Kate or Phil in danger I swear I'll run her over with her own motorbike!' Michael hissed as Charlotte ran into the road and flagged down the first car that drove towards them. She flung a fistful of shilling notes at the driver and shouted, 'Emergency! Airport . . . take us to the airport!'

'I knew it!' Michael cried. '"A holiday, a treat," she said. Why on earth you trust her, I'll never know. What's happened? Is it the children?'

'It's Cicely, Michael – little Cicely!'

After Cicely had managed to land a surprisingly powerful punch in his left eye, Tacker allowed Phil to take her.

He carried her on his back and she pressed her hot face against his neck and left ear. She was quiet and did not cry but every so often she gave a deep juddering sigh that made Phil feel desperately sad. He led the way and Mark followed and Tacker brought up the rear.

'I'm not at all sure what Mrs Caddington'll be saying about this when we get back,' he said as if he were wondering aloud. 'I mean, we see some difficult boys here, boys with real problems, boys whose families have long since given up knowing what to do with them. But we ain't never, ever had a situation like this one. Seems to me that you boys are gonna have to think of a way of making things up to Mrs Caddington.' He nudged Mark in the back with a loose fist. 'Now, you could set everything right if you just handed over that stone she wants.'

Phil stiffened and he was ready to fight Mark if he had to, but Mark walked on with his head down and refused to speak. After a couple of hours they reached the mountain road and Tacker called the lodge and asked them to send a driver to meet them.

Charlotte ran to the check-in desk and asked for times of flights to Dar es Salaam. The woman at the desk smiled apologetically and said that due to illness among the crew they had had to ground four planes and all the remaining flights were full. There were none until tomorrow. Charlotte moved away from the desk with Michael at her shoulder.

'What do we do? Get the boat to Dar and hire a car?'

he asked, following her through the exit and as she walked round the side of the building and surveyed the airstrip. She squinted out into the sun and did not answer him.

'Charlotte?'

'Come on, quickly,' she replied. 'We'll take that Cessna – it'll be the easiest to land on rough ground.' And she strode off across the airfield towards a small plane.

Michael glanced around him and saw that there was no one nearby before following her with a peculiar straight-legged run that he thought would make him inconspicuous. 'Charlotte, what are you doing?' he asked gruffly, and made a grab for her arm.

She shook him off. 'This is serious, Michael. See if you can find extra fuel.'

Charlotte reached the Cessna and unclipped wires beneath the wings that held it fast to two concrete blocks. She tried the door. It wasn't locked and in another second she was inside. She slipped her hand into the overhead storage compartment, and there were the keys, just where she would have left them. She did a fast pre-flight check before pulling on her headset and starting the engine.

Michael, who had disappeared behind a hangar, re-appeared carrying two jerry cans and stood with his mouth open for a moment before breaking into a run. Charlotte turned the plane towards him and pulled up alongside. The sound of the engine was deafening and Michael was ashen-faced as he clambered into the cockpit beside her and stowed the cans of spare fuel behind him. Charlotte passed him his headset and indicated that he should do up his seat belt. A couple of airfield crew emerged from another hangar and stared at them, shading their eyes with their hands. Charlotte taxied into position before opening up the throttle and gathering speed for take-off.

Nikwata stayed in the cave for a day and a night. He occupied himself during his wait by constantly running over the entire surface of the interior of the cave, feasting on flies and cockroaches until his yellow belly ballooned on his skinny body. Full and tired, he began to wonder how long he should wait for Fearless and whether the cave was the best place to wait, especially now that he had emptied the larder, as it were. Eventually he decided to go back to the lodge and wait where the gymnasium wall met the fence, and he had first met Phil. At the entrance to the cave, he was distracted from his purpose by the discovery of a column of bull ants and it was late afternoon by the time he slipped through the fence and climbed the wall. Exhausted, he closed his eyes and fell into a state of inertia, deeper than mere sleep, where his heart slowed and his body temperature dropped and he was oblivious to the world around him. Little wonder, then, that he did not see Phil, Mark and Cicely's return to the lodge, firmly escorted by Jim Tacker.

Phil sat on the bed in his room, which, since Tacker had left him there and turned the key in the lock, had become a prison cell. Cicely had been taken from him and her screams still rang in his ears.

At the last minute as Phil entered the room, Tacker had placed his hand on Mark's shoulder and stopped him from going inside. 'Come along with me, son. Let's see if you can't restore Mrs Caddington's faith in you with that lucky charm of yours, eh?' Then he had closed the door and locked it.

Alone and feeling powerless and afraid, Phil tried to think clearly. He had spoken to Kate, so they knew that Cicely was with him and so Great-Aunt Elizabeth would be on her way back to Africa. He looked at his watch. He had phoned Kate eight hours ago – he wondered how quickly they could get flights and organize transport to Caddington Lodge. Phil knew that his family would do everything they could to reach him, so all he could do now was wait.

Even as Phil sat and considered how long it would take them to fly from France to Dar es Salaam and then make the drive inland towards Mikumi, Great-Aunt Elizabeth's turbo-charged Harley, running on triple-concentrated rocket fuel, had already crossed from Libya into Sudan. Earlier she had broken her own road speed record driving into Switzerland and down through Italy to Bari, where a sub-Mediterranean tunnel took them to Shahhat on the northern shore of Africa. Once off road and in the desert, the Harley's wheels left the ground as it sped across the barren uninhabited terrain at speeds of over 240kph.

In the sidecar Kate followed their route south on a map. She sat beside Emily and now and again she squeezed her hand and said something to reassure her. 'We're going to

find Cicely,' Kate told Emily in a firm voice. 'And Phil will be looking after her. We will get to them soon, I know we will.' And being positive helped Kate too; she could feel her heartstone thrum with energy at her throat.

Emily shook her head and sighed. 'I just don't understand why she did this,' she murmured, staring out at Great-Aunt Elizabeth's speed-flattened profile. 'Why didn't she warn us? What made her think that she had the right?'

Harold had now been fully briefed by Great-Aunt Elizabeth and was online, investigating Caddington Lodge. He looked up from the screen, his expression grim. 'I have to agree, Aunt E is way out of line this time. This Caddington Lodge has Lorabeth Lampton – Penelope Parton, what's her ugly face – written all over it. I can't imagine why Aunt E didn't tell us about it. Listen to this.'

Harold double-clicked a file and a video began playing in a new window. To the accompaniment of sweeping strings, an aerial view of the lodge, its swimming pool shimmering in sunlight, came into view. Barking jumped on to Harold's lap for a closer look and Kate and Emily leant nearer in order to hear the voice-over.

'Are you one of those lucky people who have it all? Are you someone who has striven to achieve the ultimate in perfection? Do you have the perfect home and the perfect lifestyle? Have you spent money on products and cosmetic surgery, achieving the perfect face and body, only to be let down by the one thing that is beyond your control . . . your child?'

The music changed abruptly to a heavy-metal guitar solo that sounded as though an entire farmyard was being put to death by electrocution. On the screen, a dour-faced boy barged his way through a door and let it slam into the face of the elderly woman behind him. The music faded and the soothing voice continued.

'They say that money can't buy you everything – and once upon a time that was true. No matter what you did in pursuit of perfection your efforts could be destroyed in a moment by the flawed personality of your offspring. But why should your hope of a perfect life be crushed by a disappointing performance at school or any of the numerous irritations caused by a child's wilfulness and bad temper?

Well, here at last at Caddington Lodge it is now possible to purchase the perfect life.'

Trumpets played a triumphant and uplifting march while, on the screen, smiling boys won races, opened doors for their elders, waved certificates and generally looked handsome in suits.

'Our Polished Performance Plan will remind your child how to be perfect and provide you with the perfect life. Caddington Lodge is currently taking boys aged between ten and fifteen and admission to the lodge is by strict invitation only, subject to interview. Prices on application. Plans for a girls' summer camp await further funding. All donations gratefully received.'

Kate was the first to speak. 'So she sent Phil because he's a boy.'

'And it's in Africa,' said Barking. 'I'm sure she thought it was far enough away not to put anyone at risk in England or France.'

'I guess she thought she was covering herself, having Michael and Charlotte nearby,' said Harold flatly.

'No,' said Emily. 'There's no excuse. She should have told us. She was worried that day she came back and asked me to design the Time-Space Navigator – that's why she was behaving oddly. I bet she knew even then that Cicely was in danger.' Emily began to cry.

Struggling to keep his own emotions in check, Harold took hold of his wife's small hand in his large, long-fingered one and held it tight, as if that would stem the flow of her tears. The tips of Emily's fingers became crimson, then waxy-white between his brown knuckles.

Just then, a mail alert appeared on the monitor. Letting go of Emily's hand, Harold jumped into action. 'It's a message from Michael,' he said. 'I've got their location details. They're looking for somewhere to land.'

Harold began to rummage beneath his seat and a few moments later he pulled out a UHF radio and transmitter and busied himself wiring up. 'We're not in range yet but Michael's given me a wavelength that we can communicate on.'

Kate checked the time, their speed and the compass, and found their new position on the map. 'We're in Uganda,' she told them. 'We could be there in four to five hours at this rate.'

Evacuation

Tacker brought Mark back to the room and told them to go to sleep, as Mrs Caddington wanted to see them both in the morning.

'Do you still have it?' Phil asked as soon as Tacker had left them alone.

'Yeah, he asked me about it, what it did and stuff, but he didn't ask me to give it to him.'

'What did you tell him?' Phil asked, his voice fearful and shaky.

'Nothing. I don't know anything, do I?' Mark answered unhappily.

Phil studied Mark closely for a moment or two and almost felt sorry for him. It wasn't like Mark to admit to not knowing things. 'Mark, there's something evil here. Mrs Caddington is able to make everyone do what she says. I think you were hypnotized or drugged. You remember that boy Robert on our first day? Something terrible happened to him in the basement. I saw the marks on his head. They're going to do the same to you and me. You've got to give me the keystone – it's our only hope. You will give it to me, won't you?'

When Mark didn't reply immediately it took all of Phil's willpower not to rush at him. Eventually Mark said, 'Will you tell me everything – about the keystone and that lizard? Where is he anyway? Have you seen him?'

'I don't know.' Phil sighed, suddenly deflated. 'Look, Mark, if I tell you – you'll give me the keystone?'

Mark nodded. 'Yes. I promise.'

They got ready for bed in silence and then, after switching off the light, Phil told Mark his story, beginning with the start of the summer holidays three years earlier, when Great-Aunt Elizabeth had taken them to New York. As he listened, Mark took the keystone from his neck and held it in his hand. It had never surged with power the way Phil described. He opened his hand and peeped under the covers. It gave off a faint glow from a streak of light down one side. It had never 'buzzed with light and energy', the way Phil claimed it had for him, and nor had he felt 'as though anything he wanted to do were possible'. Listening to his friend, he became drowsy and found it difficult not to let his mind drift. And Phil, despite his anxiety and desire to have his keystone returned to him, found his voice turning to treacle in his mouth and his sentences slowing down, so that he forgot what he was saying. The boys were exhausted after their ordeal on the mountain and night in the bush. The room was cool and the beds comfortable. Both intended to stay awake and alert but soon both were asleep.

Just as a starving man will dream he is at a banquet, dining on delicious delicacies, Phil dreamt that he and

Cicely were safely home and his evil grandmother was in prison, where she belonged. Briefly he almost rose to consciousness when a noise in the room disturbed him. He held his breath and listened and thought he heard a small click, like a key turning in the lock. But his drowsiness and the temptation to sink back into the depths proved too strong.

While Phil and Mark slept, Cynthia Caddington was harrying an exhausted Bernhard in the basement. 'Get on with it! I have other things to deal with!' she hissed at him.

Bernhard took an empty glass sphere from the rack and brought it over to where Mrs Caddington stood beside the table. Neither of them noticed Nikwata run across the ceiling and come to a halt above their heads, where he cocked his head and watched them.

Next to Cynthia Caddington, in a padded seat like a dentist's chair and propped up on cushions, lay Cicely. Her head rested in a ceramic bowl, her halo of curls tangling around her small face. Her eyes were closed and her mouth was open a little. Every so often her lips and tongue moved rhythmically, as if she were sucking an invisible dummy. Her hands lay limply at her side and her little red shoes dangled from her feet. Around Cicely's brow a tight narrow band held a series of wires and plastic tubing in place. The wires travelled under her hair and criss-crossed her scalp until they met at the nape of her neck, where they passed through the back of the

ceramic bowl and joined a circular plug. As Bernhard lowered the glass sphere towards the plug he trembled so violently that it banged against the bowl. Cynthia Caddington swore and snatched hold of his hands and guided the sphere into place. A small hole lined with a rubber seal fitted snugly over the plug.

At that moment Cynthia started, as if she had suddenly remembered something important.

'Is something wrong, Mrs Caddington? Bernhard asked.

A red glow crept up Cynthia Caddington's neck and she held her throat in her hands.

'Is everything all right?' Bernhard repeated.

'Damn it! No, it is not. Hurry up and finish this, then destroy everything –'

'Everything?' Bernhard asked horrified.

'Smash the spheres and break up the Reminder. We have to leave here as soon as we can.'

And with that she ran from the basement.

When Phil woke it was morning and Mark was frantically searching his bed.

'Where is it? Have you got it?'

'What?' Phil asked him.

'The keystone. It's not here.'

'What!'

Phil rushed over and helped strip the sheets from the bed and then lay down and peered underneath it. He reached for Mark's tennis shoes and turned them over and shook them.

'Why weren't you wearing it?'

Mark sat on the bed and put his head in his hands. 'I was going to give it back to you. I'd taken it off ready to give to you. I was holding it in my hand when I fell asleep.'

A key turned in the lock and Jim Tacker stood in the open doorway. 'Well, I hope you boys are feeling remorseful this morning,' he said, and for once his smile was small and cold. 'You'll be pleased to hear that the little lady has recovered from her ordeal – although Dr Bernhard said it was touch and go for a while.'

'There wasn't anything wrong with her!' Phil interjected, alarmed for Cicely's safety.

Jim Tacker raised an eyebrow but didn't respond. 'You're to come to the assembly in the gym immediately. Mrs Caddington wants to address all the boys.'

Phil pulled on jeans over his boxers and dragged a T-shirt over his head. As he pulled the covers up his bed, he saw that his rucksack was missing. He froze. He glanced up in alarm at the sound of Jim Tacker's voice.

'Lost something?'

But Jim Tacker was talking to Mark, who had resumed looking through his bedding. Mark stopped reluctantly and shuffled into his clothes.

Tacker escorted the boys to the gymnasium. Phil was in despair, certain that Jim Tacker had taken the keystone. Mark had been on the point of giving it back. That willingness on his part meant that the keystone was there for the taking. Phil's only hope was that his family were on

their way and he willed them to hurry. *And little Cicely*, he thought with rising panic, *please, please let her be all right*.

The boys of Caddington Lodge were already assembled and standing quietly in rows as Tacker ushered them to a space at the front of the hall, where they stood alone. After a moment or two Mrs Caddington stepped out from the wings on to the stage. She wore a long, black, shapeless dress that hung from her shoulders as if from a coat hanger. She was as thin as a stick beneath it and her collarbones could be clearly seen, protruding through the fabric. A worn leather strap hung diagonally across her body and secured a large bag to her back. She wore a thin black shawl around her head and across the lower half of her face and this exaggerated the enormity of her deep-set eyes. She stood perfectly still and looked slowly around the gym, and Phil took care not to meet her eyes when they passed across his face.

When Cynthia Caddington spoke her voice boomed around the vast gymnasium walls. 'In the short but successful career of Caddington Lodge there has never —' she paused and repeated with violent emphasis — '*never* been such a vile, cowardly and despicable act of malice as the one perpetrated by these two boys.' She stretched out her thin arm, uncurled a bony finger and pointed towards Phil and Mark. 'But it was not their act of rebellion and defiance that sickens me with disgust, but their wanton cruelty. These boys kidnapped my daughter and exposed her to near-death in the bush.' She blinked slowly and precisely. 'They will be punished.'

She turned and held out her hand towards Jim Tacker, gesturing for him to join her on the stage. 'This man,' she said as he came and stood beside her, 'was once a scoundrel, a liar and a cheat. A hypocrite, a braggart and a philanderer.'

Jim Tacker's smile stretched with self-satisfied ease across his face, while he rolled his head on his shoulders as if he were hearing praise that modesty made it hard for him to accept.

'But he was never a coward!' Mrs Caddington's voice rose in pitch and volume, so that she was now shrieking, and her body quivered with anger.

Phil glanced at Mark and tried to imagine what their punishment would be. He was unprepared for what Cynthia Caddington said next and the shock had him reeling.

'I believe that one of these two boys is innocent and one of them is here to spy on me and to trick me!'

Jim Tacker jumped down from the stage and approached Phil and Mark.

'Philip Reynolds thought he could fool me. He thought I would not recognize him – as if I wouldn't recognize my own flesh and blood.' She flung a crazed look around the gym. 'Yes, boys! Even a member of *my* family can lack perfection and need reminding. Take him to my office, Jim. I want to give him a chance to redeem himself.'

Phil tensed every muscle in his body. Jim Tacker would have to drag him; he wasn't going to go without a fight. Desperately, he tried to think what to do. Should he run?

Were Nikwata or Fearless nearby? Had Kate heard enough on the phone to be able to locate them? He'd seen that in enough movies for him to believe it might be possible. He glanced at the door in case help were about to burst through it.

Tacker had crossed the floor and stood before them. His lips were drawn back in a broad smile as he reached out and clamped his hand firmly on Mark's shoulder.

'Hang on a minute –' Mark cried, trying to duck away from Tacker's grip. 'I'm not Phil Reynolds – he is!'

'Still he lies!' Cynthia Caddington screamed as Tacker led Mark from the hall.

Phil remained frozen. Part of him thought he should stop them and confess who he was, but he quickly assessed the situation and realized that there might be advantages to Mrs Caddington's mistake.

Just then a small figure appeared in the wings and walked slowly towards the centre of the stage. It was Cicely and Phil craned his neck forward to get a better look at her. She reached Mrs Caddington's side and the woman bent down and lifted her up to her hip.

Cicely stared round the gymnasium at the boys as Mrs Caddington had done and then she spoke. 'You are big uglies. You will do what we say!'

Cynthia Caddington threw back her head and roared with delighted laughter.

As Cicely's words swam in Phil's mind she turned her head and stared directly at him and he barely recognized her. The smiling dimples and cheeky grin that

came to mind when he heard her name had vanished. Her beautiful face was haughty and unmoving, as if it had been finely chiselled from stone. Phil felt his own bones become heavy as granite.

Jim Tacker returned without Mark and ran up the steps to the stage.

'Prepare for evacuation – we are leaving here immediately,' Cynthia Caddington flung at him before she swept from the stage, Cicely still in her arms.

Numb from shock, Phil watched them disappear into the darkness of the wings, Cicely's big blank eyes gazing at him from over her shoulder.

As Phil left Caddington Lodge for the second time, this time through the open gate, he stole a glance along the road to where the pack of dogs had previously lain in the shade. He hoped to see Fearless, but was disappointed to find that none of the dogs were there and the dirt road looked bleak and empty. He bitterly regretted telling Nikwata to stay in the cave – and how typical of the contrary lizard to do as he'd been told for once. A few metres ahead of him, at the front of the line, Cynthia Caddington carried Cicely in her arms. Behind her Jim Tacker escorted Mark and behind Phil the remaining 400 boys of Caddington Lodge evacuated the camp in silent, straight lines. They left the road soon after the first bend and joined a dirt track that led between thorn trees.

Phil almost stepped on a giant millipede that dashed across the path, its needle-like legs moving in a Mexican wave along its body. Around them the air throbbed with the sound of insects. From the distance the call of a wild pigeon met his ears and the pattern and rhythm were so similar to that of an English wood pigeon and yet so strange in tone and with a mournful quality that he yearned for home and things familiar. And it wasn't his parents who first sprang to mind, but Kate. All of a sudden he could hear her voice and see her face as clearly as if she were there beside him. Then, with a jolt, it occurred to him that Kate would be wearing her heartstone now and that she would be looking for Cicely. When Phil had been kidnapped Kate had known where to look for him – so maybe she could find Cicely too. Phil leant his head slightly and studied Cicely's straight back where she held herself up tall in Cynthia Caddington's arms and he willed Kate to see through his eyes. 'Here she is Kate,' he whispered. 'Here she is.'

The Ravine

The Cessna cast a shadow on the plain below. Charlotte was flying low enough for them to be able to see a large herd of water buffalo move through the long grasses in Mikumi National Park and smaller groups of zebra and giraffe run startled from a drinking hole. Not far ahead, they could see the mountain location of Caddington Lodge, and Charlotte asked Michael to try getting the others on the radio as she looked for a suitable landing place. It was late afternoon and Charlotte knew they could not make a safe landing in the dark. She would need to bring the plane down quickly. She could see the road that had been cut up the side of the mountain and banked left to follow the line of it. As they flew over a high peak to their right they suddenly saw the lodge beneath them, the swimming pool, a small rectangle of blue, signalling its whereabouts. Charlotte shouted to Michael and pointed.

They climbed to gain enough height to get over the ridge and immediately to their right was a shallow crater. The diameter looked large enough to bring down the

Cessna and Charlotte circled the area and descended to 500 feet.

'Do you think you can land here?' Michael asked.

'It'll be a bit steep and rough but I'm bringing her in.'

With barely any warning, night fell on the sidecar as it climbed into the Udzungwa mountains. For the last hour the occupants had been shaken and rattled and rolled about and Kate felt as if her teeth where being dislodged.

'That was Michael,' said Harold, flicking the switch on the radio. 'The Cessna's down and I've got their coordinates. They're on foot now and are going to make their way to the road.'

Kate was anxious about Phil and Cicely. She had been holding her heartstone and she sensed that they were together and that with every juddering kilometre they were getting closer to them. But she also knew, as if Phil was whispering in her ear, that something was terribly wrong and she bit her lip to stop herself communicating her anxiety to the others.

Charlotte and Michael had climbed the sides of the crater and were gazing down on the road from the ridge above when they saw the column of children being led by a tall, lean figure carrying a baby. To their left they could see the single headlight of the Harley snaking its way steadily up the mountain.

'There,' Michael pointed. 'They're going to meet on that stretch of road beside the mine shaft!'

He took Charlotte's hand and together they began to scramble down to the road below.

The destination was inaccessible to vehicles and so they had set off on foot. The march was long and Cynthia Caddington had been impatient every time they stopped for water. Before leaving the lodge she had dismissed the staff – they were no longer needed; they would not be coming back. Silently she led the procession through steep gorges that had been blasted by the miners.

As darkness fell the path became treacherous, stones rolled underfoot and the vast sweep of stars above his head made Phil giddy. He considered leaving the line, slipping away into the blackness of the night, but he couldn't do it. Ahead of him, Jim Tacker held Mark's arm and despite everything he felt responsible for his erstwhile friend. Besides, he was afraid to leave Cicely. Phil stared at the back of Cicely's head until she disappeared in the darkness of the night and then kept his gaze on the place where he imagined her to be. He held the image of her face in his mind. He willed Kate to find them and imagined her heartstone glowing at her throat.

Suddenly the procession stopped and Cynthia Caddington shouted for silence.

'Silence!' Jim Tacker echoed, but the instruction was unnecessary as there had not been the slightest murmur from any of the 400 boys since they had left the lodge.

Phil stood and listened. He could see the shadowed shape of the boys around him and sensed the presence of the ranks behind him. He could hear the ever-present buzz of cicadas and, in the distance, the intermittent call of a night bird. Suddenly he heard something else – something so wonderfully familiar he nearly cried out. Up ahead the narrow path curved around the wall of a steep crater and from behind it a thin beam of light swung across the sky. It traced the far wall of the steep ravine on their right in a sweeping arc until, accompanied by the deep roar of an engine, the light found the road they were on and shone directly at the column of boys.

The Harley came to a halt some 300 metres in front of the line and Great-Aunt Elizabeth dismounted and began to walk towards them – covering the ground quickly in great long strides. The dome of the sidecar rolled back and first Kate and Barking, then Emily and Harold climbed out and began hurrying along the road after her.

Cynthia Caddington raised her hand and screamed at them. 'Stop there! Don't come any closer!'

In the beam of yellow light, Phil saw Great-Aunt Elizabeth stand squarely on the path with Harold and Emily beside her. Then his sister stepped out from behind them with Barking at her heels, and Phil could see her scanning the rows and rows of boys on the path ahead of her.

Phil longed to run to her, but instead he sidled past the boys nearest to him and carefully, silently, he began making

his way towards his family. The words '*I'm here, Kate, I'm here*' kept repeating in his mind and in his head he could hear Kate's answer. '*I know, you dweeb. What's keeping you? Get over here!*'

But he knew he had to be cautious. He had to get past Tacker, who was three heads away from him now and holding on to Mark – who had begun struggling the moment he recognized Great-Aunt Elizabeth. Phil could see Cynthia Caddington's back as she walked ahead of the halted line. She had lowered Cicely to the ground and held her hand. She began to laugh and beside her Cicely's tiny figure was lit in the beam of the headlight, her mass of curls forming a golden glow around her head. She stared up at Cynthia Caddington with an expression of gleeful admiration.

Great-Aunt Elizabeth's voice boomed out in the night air. 'Margot! I absolutely forbid this. Let the child go.'

Emily pushed past Great-Aunt Elizabeth and hurried forward until she stumbled. She stayed where she fell, two metres in front of her daughter, as Harold ran to her side to help her up.

Cynthia Caddington dropped her hold on Cicely's hand and, jabbing a bony finger in the nape of her neck, pushed the child forward. 'Go on, *Cicely* – go to Mummy and Daddy!'

Emily was crouching now, her face level with Cicely's. She held out her arms and pleaded softly. 'You're safe now, sweetheart. Come to Mama.'

Cicely screwed up her nose and lifted her chin as if

encountering something disgusting. 'Me not Sis-lee, me called Gina. You not Mama, you big ugly!'

Emily cried out and collapsed into the dirt, with Harold struggling to hold her. Her hands reached out towards Cicely and from where Phil stood it seemed as though she was begging Cicely to come to her with every part of her body. From somewhere deep within her a great cry came wailing out of her mouth and she began to sob. Harold crouched at Emily's side, at a loss how to comfort her; his own heart was breaking and he could hardly bear it. Cicely stood for a moment gazing at her parents and then she turned her back on them. She returned to Cynthia Caddington, her little hands held up, waiting to be lifted.

Emily's scream shattered the night. And that was when Phil moved into action. He had no plan; he simply could not bear to hear Emily cry out as if she were losing her life, and he never ever wanted to see Cicely back in the arms of that monster.

Phil rushed forward, dodging past Jim Tacker, and leapt on to Cynthia Caddington's back. He wrapped his arms and legs round her and clung on tight. Her back was so hard that Phil felt his ribs bruise. And then he realized that it was not, in fact, Cynthia Caddington's bony body that he could feel beneath his chest but the Historograph in its leather bag – and he was instantly fired with a new purpose. As Cynthia Caddington swung around, trying to throw him off, Phil fought to stay on. He managed to twist his wrists inside the leather straps where they crossed her shoulders and, as she flung herself about, he held fast to the bag. If she dislodged him she would lose the Historograph as well.

Phil was vaguely aware of some commotion around them, people coming in close, then dodging away as they struggled. Cynthia Caddington missed her footing and staggered forward, so that Phil's feet found the ground. He held on and, without thinking what it was he was doing, began manoeuvring her towards the edge of the ravine.

Cynthia Caddington let out a roar of fury and twisted her head so that her profile almost touched his face, and he saw the anger and hatred in her eye. She continued to twist and struggle but Phil gritted his teeth and held on. As she writhed about, the veil slipped from her face and she was lit in the beam of the Harley's headlight. Her face, so close to his own, imprinted itself on Phil's mind like a motif from a recurring nightmare. It was deeply lined, but not in the soft, wrinkled way that Great-Aunt Elizabeth's skin had aged and weathered. This skin was scaly and sagging and besplattered with weeping sores and pustules. Blue veins coursed across her cheeks like the runnels in a piece of Stilton cheese and her snarling lips, as she twisted her face towards him, were drawn back over long yellow teeth and swollen purple gums. But far from causing Phil to falter or loosen his grip, the sight of her hag's face gave Phil the last bit of strength he needed. He dug in his heels and, with one mighty effort, drove her over the edge. Bound as he was by the straps on the Historograph's bag, over he went with her.

As they flew out into the night air, he heard Kate scream his name. Then he felt the fall. Air was rushing past his body and he could hear stones bouncing off the walls of the ravine and branches snapping as they crashed through them. There was a tearing sound and the bag suddenly felt lighter. He heard several thuds below him and realized that Cynthia Caddington was no longer attached to the bag. He wrapped his arms tightly round the leather and hugged the Historograph to his chest. He felt a swell of triumph – he had it! He had the Historograph! And then he hit the ground.

He heard a terriying crack. He was engulfed in sickening pain. He fell on to his back. He saw the stars in the slit of sky at the top of the chasm; he felt the stones beneath him. One was large and sharp and digging into his hip. He tried to turn over and crawl away from it, but he no longer had any control over his body. The pain was excruciating . . . He lost consciousness.

Harold ran forward and snatched Cicely up into his arms and dragged Emily to her feet.

Jim Tacker pushed his way past the boys and he stared over the edge. 'Mrs Caddington! Oh, my God, Cynthia!' he shouted into the black chasm.

Great-Aunt Elizabeth came to his side and put an arm around his shoulders. He made to resist, but as he turned to face her something in him changed and he allowed himself to be guided back to the path. He could not take his eyes from the red light that shone at her throat.

'That's right,' said Great-Aunt Elizabeth, sensing his submission, 'Listen to me, young man. You are in charge here now. You are accompanying these boys on a night walk and your employer has had an accident – missed her footing in the dark. You had better get the children back to the lodge and call out the rescue services. There will be an inquiry and I will vouch for you. Your immediate concern is for the safety of the remaining boys in your care. You will be commended for your conduct. Do you understand?'

Jim Tacker leant towards Great-Aunt Elizabeth as if drawn to a magnet and his face picked up a pink glow from her heartstone. He listened intently to her words, nodding softly. When she finished speaking, he hesitated for the briefest moment before becoming perfectly composed and detaching himself from her reassuring arm. He called to the boys to about-turn. The ranks silently shuffled around and Tacker gave Great-Aunt Elizabeth a curt nod.

'I'll call the emergency services as soon as i reach the lodge. This was an unfortunate accident. It's my job to think of these boys, you know!'

He hurried off to the front of the line, barked out a command and then began the long march back to the lodge.

Charlotte and Michael had seen the fall as they scrambled down the scree and, as Tacker and the boys moved off, they came stumbling on to the path close to the Harley. They hurried to the edge of the ravine and

ran backwards and forwards, desperately shouting Phil's name into the black void.

As Great-Aunt Elizabeth joined them, Charlotte rushed to her side, her eyes wild and her voice a hysterical sob. 'Barking and Kate have gone down to him. Kate has climbed down twenty metres or so already but she can't see him!' Charlotte pulled frantically at Great-Aunt Elizabeth's sleeve. 'Oh, my God, Aunt E. Phil – will he be all right? Please say he's going to be all right!'

Great-Aunt Elizabeth pushed her back, almost roughly. 'I'll climb down myself and get him. Now, you go and find the Longbridge boy – he must have the keystone.'

Charlotte eyes widened in horror. 'Phil isn't wearing his keystone?' she gasped.

Great-Aunt Elizabeth took her by the shoulders and shook her, then turned her round and began to push her along the path. 'Hurry, Charlotte, bring the boy.' Her voice was forceful and without emotion and it did the trick. Charlotte ran after the retreating column of boys – but Michael, who had been standing behind her, stayed where he was, rooted to the spot with rage. He stared at Great-Aunt Elizabeth as she began her descent over the edge.

Best-laid Plans

Harold and Emily had taken Cicely to the sidecar and were trying to calm her. She struggled from Harold's arms and pushed and slapped Emily away every time she tried to get close.

'What has happened to you?' cried Emily, looking at Harold for help.

'She has been brainwashed,' Harold said. 'We'll have to be patient. She's bound to come round in the end.' He spoke as much to convince himself as to console his distraught wife as, in fact, he had no idea what had happened to their tiny daughter and whether it was reversible or not.

Cicely had crawled to the furthest seat and stared at them with angry eyes. 'You go away, bad lady!' she said, pointing a finger at Emily, then putting her thumb firmly in her mouth.

'Keep talking to her,' said Harold, placing his hand on Emily's shoulder. 'Try and get her to remember. Tell her about the park. Keep telling her how much we love her.' His voice caught in his throat and he turned to leave. 'I'm going to see what's happening outside.'

*

Great-Aunt Elizabeth overtook Kate's more careful descent as she slid and tumbled and jumped down the ravine. Barking had reached Phil first and called to her from his side, guiding her to where his body lay. Crouching beside him, Great-Aunt Elizabeth took a torch from her jacket pocket and shone it on his face and then down his body. His right leg stuck out at an alarming angle from his hip and the knuckles of both his hands were raw and bleeding. He was still clutching the rim of the Historograph through the leather bag and held it hugged tight against his body.

Barking stood beside Phil's head and watched Great-Aunt Elizabeth as she examined Phil's battered body. 'Can we move him?'

Great-Aunt Elizabeth ignored Barking's question and began to prise Phil's damaged hands from the Historograph.

Barking's tail flicked wildly. 'How are we going to lift him?' he asked anxiously, settling on to his haunches, his face beside Phil's ear.

At that moment a scurry of falling stones announced Kate's arrival. 'Oh no . . .' Her voice crumpled. 'Oh, he's not . . . ?'

Kate fell to her knees beside her brother and placed the palm of her hand against his mouth and nose. The gentle warmth of his breath brought relief, then anger.

'What are you doing? Help him!' She glared at Great-Aunt Elizabeth, who now had hold of the Historograph and was pulling it from its bag. 'You horrible woman! I hate you – you're just as mean and selfish as she is!' Kate spat the words. 'No, you're not. You're worse. You pretend

to care for us but all the while all you care about is your-self and the heartstones –' Kate swung her arm and struck Great-Aunt Elizabeth on her shoulder. 'And your precious Historograph!'

Crying now, Kate leant over Phil and touched his face. 'Phil, hey, come on, bro, wake up. Phil . . . Phil . . . come on . . .'

Great-Aunt Elizabeth spoke calmly as she began to get to her feet. 'Stay with them, Barking. I'll be back directly.' She turned her attention to Kate. 'I know you don't want to hear this from me right now but you must trust me. I am going to do everything I can to help him.'

Kate did not answer but stroked Phil's hair back from his forehead and waited for Great-Aunt Elizabeth to go. 'Phil . . . wake up . . . Phil . . . come on, wake up . . . Phil, Phil, Phil . . .'

It was strange, Phil thought, that he had not noticed before how comfortable his bed was. He guessed he had always taken it for granted but now, for some reason, he was aware of it and it filled him with pleasure. He lay there luxuriating in the softness of the duvet and the supreme comfort of the mattress. He felt safe and cosy and warm. From somewhere nearby Kate was calling him, but he didn't want to wake up so he stopped himself from listen-ing to her. No, he wouldn't get up yet. This was too deli-cious a feeling to resist – he'd just drift back to sleep a little longer.

*

Meanwhile, Fearless was making his way back to Caddington Lodge and although he was less than five kilometres from where Phil lay unconscious, he was separated from him by a mountainous wall of rock. Fearless, too, was injured. The pain was relentless and he had no hope of respite. He had to press on and get back to Phil and to Cicely. Maybe the diversion to find water had been a mistake. Besides, it had been less than an hour ago and he felt thirstier now than ever. After his water stop he had chosen a more direct but difficult route back to the lodge, hoping that it would be quicker than retracing his steps. But the shorter distance was the only thing his chosen route had going for it. The way was steep and treacherous – he had disturbed a snake and had his ears bitten by insects. The pads of his paws were burning and sore, and a dull ache had begun in the leg that had been speared by the thorn. Fearless gritted his teeth and pressed on, images of the family he loved driving him. It was just like, he thought wryly, *The Incredible Journey*.

For an elderly woman of such immense proportions Great-Aunt Elizabeth's ascent was an extraordinary display of strength and agility. As soon as she reached the path, she began pulling things from beneath the seat of her motorbike and in moments she had assembled a makeshift stretcher. She grabbed a first-aid kit and gave instructions to Harold to fetch a winding block from the back of the sidecar. As they glanced over towards it, they could see Emily inside, struggling to hold Cicely, who was wriggling in her arms and raining blows on her mother's head with her little fists. Great-Aunt Elizabeth continued to bustle around and Michael followed her, firing curt questions: 'Did you find him? How is he?'

'Where's Charlotte? Does she have the keystone?' Great-Aunt Elizabeth snapped, scanning the path ahead for her niece. When he didn't reply she glanced at Michael's face for the first time and saw that he was seething with anger. She shook her head impatiently. 'Hell's teeth, Michael! I need the keystone so that I can help Phil. He's going to be all right. Trust –'

Michael interrupted her with an explosive outburst of pent-up fury. 'Do *not* ask me to trust you. I'll do what you tell me – not because I trust you but because I have no choice. And you had better get us all out of this mess, and when you do I don't want you coming near any of my family ever again. Understood?'

He turned his back on her as Charlotte came hurrying along the path and stumbled, out of breath, into Great-Aunt Elizabeth's arms.

'He doesn't have it – Mark – he says they lost it. He says he was going to give it back to Phil this morning but when he woke up it had gone.'

'What!' Great-Aunt Elizabeth cried in dismay, and a small twitch began to pulse beneath her right eye. 'We need it, Charlotte – we have to have it. It's the only way to help Phil and Cicely.'

'Tell me what you're planning . . . Tell me what to do!' Charlotte pleaded.

Great-Aunt Elizabeth tightened her grip on the Historograph. 'I have the Historograph and with the keystone I can send Phil back to before the accident,' she said matter-of-factly. 'Where is Mark? There must be something, some detail that he's forgotten, that will provide a clue to where the keystone is.'

'He's coming,' said Charlotte, looking back over her shoulder. 'I told his teacher that we needed him to help us – I hurried ahead. How is Phil? Is he badly hurt?'

Mark appeared in the shadows behind them and Great-Aunt Elizabeth took hold of his arm. 'I need your help to make Phil and the baby better. Go inside the sidecar and tell Emily everything you can remember about the lodge and try to recall when you last had the keystone.'

While Michael and Harold roped up the stretcher, Great-Aunt Elizabeth drove the Harley closer to the edge and directed the beam of the headlight into the ravine. As the men began to lower the stretcher down to Kate, Great-Aunt Elizabeth climbed swiftly down. Just before she disappeared over the edge she looked up at Charlotte and Michael.

'Prepare yourselves – he looks pretty bad.'

18

The Time-Space Navigator

Charlotte, Michael and Harold waited anxiously. No matter how long or how hard they stared into the black chasm they could see no further than a few metres. Above them, the darker peaks of the mountains were silhouetted against the blue-black of the sky and the stars appeared to be close enough to touch from the highest summit. Overhead the Milky Way seemed clearer and closer than they had ever seen it.

Charlotte took hold of Michael's arm. 'Great-Aunt Elizabeth wants to send Phil back in time –' Michael pulled away from her but she caught hold of him once more. 'No, you must listen to me, Michael. I vowed to myself that I wouldn't keep secrets from you ever again. I know you think it's crazy, but time travel *is* possible with the Historograph and the keystone. Whatever state Phil is in now, we only need to send him back a couple of hours to before the accident and he will be fine.'

They turned their heads and peered into the sidecar, where Mark was sitting with Emily, telling her everything he could remember. Cicely had struggled herself to exhaustion and lay sleeping on one of the large cushions.

'I think I'm beginning to understand something here,' Harold said suddenly, and he went to the sidecar and signalled to Emily to come out.

Emily's face was red and puffy from crying when she emerged.

'Did you bring the Time-Space Navigator?'

'It's inside. Why?'

'I'll explain in a sec. Will you get it, please?'

Emily turned from him and went back to the sidecar, only to return a moment later looking confused.

'I stowed it under the bench seat, I know I did. But –'

'It isn't there.' Harold finished her sentence for her.

Just then, a tug on the rope signalled that the stretcher was ready to be hauled back up the ravine. They stood in silence, watching the block winch back the length of rope, until, peering into the abyss, they suddenly saw the stretcher emerging from the darkness with Phil lying on it. Michael and Harold caught the ends and swung it on to the path.

Barking, his fur puffed up, was crouched beside Phil and he leapt off as it was being lowered. 'He was unconscious when I got to him and hasn't regained consciousness. His pulse is stable,' Barking said.

Charlotte gasped in horror at the sight of Phil's twisted leg.

Great-Aunt Elizabeth clambered on to the path, reached down behind her and hauled Kate up.

Harold turned to her. 'Aunt E, you're planning on going back in time, aren't you?'

She looked at him, her face drawn and tired. She shook her head. 'I had hoped – if we had the keystone, then I could send Phil back to before the accident.'

'But there is a way of doing it without the keystone, isn't there?' Harold said.

Everyone looked at Harold, apart from Emily, who was rapt in thought.

Great-Aunt Elizabeth spoke first. 'There is a way – I've done it once or twice before. I can return briefly to a place I've been in the not-too-distant past. My mother told me it was permissible to use the elastic-time technique to retrieve something important that had been forgotten during a time move.'

'Elastic time?' Michael interjected, fascinated by what he was hearing despite everything. 'What do you mean? Like a bungee jump into last week?'

'Exactly so. But Phil can't go,' continued Great-Aunt Elizabeth. 'In any case, it wouldn't help him. He would have to return and his body would still be damaged. No. I'm afraid that it can only be done using my heartstone and my past, and what use is that?'

Suddenly Emily clapped her hands together. 'Oh, Harold, you are a genius!'

Charlotte and Kate had been kneeling beside Phil and his eyes began to flicker. 'He's coming to,' Charlotte called.

Emily's revelation was forgotten for a moment as everyone huddled round the stretcher.

Phil's face was pale and, as he turned his head to look at them all, he grimaced from the pain that racked his

broken body. 'I thought I was dreaming,' he murmured. 'What happened? I can't feel my legs.'

Charlotte tucked a blanket around him. 'It's OK now, my darling. You're going to be fine,' she said.

Harold pulled Great-Aunt Elizabeth away from the group and towards the sidecar, and Emily followed them, relieved to be doing something constructive at last.

'Do you remember when you visited and asked Emily to make the Insult Fermenter and a Night-Vision Scanner?'

'Yes, Harold. Goats' cheeks and pigs' jowls! Of course I remember.'

'Well, the next day you came back and asked me to make a Time-Space Navigator,' Emily said.

Great-Aunt Elizabeth's head jerked up as if she had just received an electric shock. 'I asked you to make a what?'

Emily nodded keenly at Great-Aunt Elizabeth. 'You asked me to make a Time-Space Navigator.'

'And did you make one?' the older woman demanded, immediately regaining her authoritative tone.

Emily nodded. 'You gave me a sheet of paper with some specifications on it. That's how I got started. Only . . . I know I made it, but somehow it all seems . . . vague . . . like it happened in a dream.'

Michael had been standing nearby, listening, and he moved closer. 'Did you call it a navigator?'

'A Time-Space Navigator – a Time-Space Navigator with 100 per cent accuracy,' replied Emily. 'That was your brief, Aunt E.'

'But I don't know anything about these specifications you say I gave you,' Great-Aunt Elizabeth murmured.

Suddenly Michael began to speak, the words tumbling fast and urgently from his mouth. 'At any one moment the positions of the stars are unique. If you can instantaneously identify stars and correlate that to time and position viewed from Earth, then it should be possible to locate time and space accurately. I have been working on a star identification program.'

'And I have invented a teleporter,' Harold said. 'If Michael and I combine our knowledge –'

'Oh!' Emily interjected excitedly. 'I think I understand! The navigator isn't in the sidecar and Aunt E doesn't remember coming back to see me because those things have not happened yet. I'm finding it more and more difficult to remember what the navigator looked like, let alone how it was made –'

'What the blazes are you talking about?' Great-Aunt Elizabeth asked impatiently.

It was Harold who answered her. 'We must be approaching a crucial point in time – *this* time, the one we are all experiencing now – very soon. Aunt E, you must use the elastic-time technique to go back and ask Emily to make the navigator. If we miss the moment, then not only will the navigator have disappeared, but Emily and I will have no recollection of having made it. Because it won't have happened.

'Then what are we wasting time for!' Great-Aunt Elizabeth cried. 'I must prepare the Historograph.

Michael! Hurry and write down the information that Emily and Harold need!'

But Michael had already rushed to the sidecar and was bent over a sheet of paper, scribbling furiously.

Phil had fallen unconscious once more. Kate sat on the ground beside him, one arm circling her knees, her free hand resting on his forearm. As soon as she touched him a surge of power flooded her heartstone and it occurred to her that, as her heartstone had recently experienced and aided her own recovery, it would 'know' how to help him too. She instinctively sensed that this was possible and the next thought that occurred to her was that, in future, she wouldn't need to worry about trying to understand the power of her heartstone. She would simply learn its capabilities as different situations presented themselves. And while she could no more predict the full potential of the heartstone than see into the future, she felt sure it would always help her. It was a comforting thought and her sense that Phil would become stronger as she focused on him magnified. *I must always remember*, Kate thought, *to trust my heartstone.* Then she felt a twinge of remorse as she remembered her angry outburst.

Great-Aunt Elizabeth spoke from the shadows behind her. 'How is he?'

'I'm not sure. I'm just hoping . . . Great-Aunt Elizabeth? I'm sorry that I lashed out at you before.'

'No, dear, you were right to be angry.' She raised her voice so that the others could hear. 'And Emily too, you

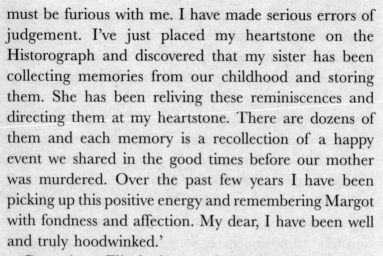

must be furious with me. I have made serious errors of judgement. I've just placed my heartstone on the Historograph and discovered that my sister has been collecting memories from our childhood and storing them. She has been reliving these reminiscences and directing them at my heartstone. There are dozens of them and each memory is a recollection of a happy event we shared in the good times before our mother was murdered. Over the past few years I have been picking up this positive energy and remembering Margot with fondness and affection. My dear, I have been well and truly hoodwinked.'

Great-Aunt Elizabeth moved to where Harold and Michael were waiting for her and placed the Historograph on a flat rock beside the path. Harold passed her a soldering iron and she touched it against her heartstone and as it fell into her hands she lowered it on to the plate. A strong beam of red light flared and lit the mountainside and path. Michael gave her a sheet of paper – calculations that he had drawn up to help Emily make the Time-Space Navigator. Great-Aunt Elizabeth rotated her heartstone and, as it clicked softly into place, a mist clouded their view of the Historograph's surface. Great-Aunt Elizabeth leant forward as the mist cleared and Emily, who had not seen the Historograph before, gasped to find herself gazing down upon her apartment in France. Suddenly a strange hum came from the Historograph and seemed to engulf them as it increased in volume. Great-Aunt Elizabeth stood up tall, and her shoulders

rose as she took a deep breath, then she moved slowly towards the Historograph and vanished.

Great-Aunt Elizabeth pressed the buzzer for Emily and Harold's apartment and took the stairs four at a time just as soon as Emily had let her into the lobby. She arrived at the door so quickly that Emily jumped when she opened it and found her there.

'Goodness, that was quick! Come in.'

'No, my dear, I'll not stop. Can you make this for me? It's very important.'

Emily took the piece of paper that Great-Aunt Elizabeth thrust into her hand and studied it. Behind her, an excited Cicely pulled herself up on the gate of her play area and called to her. 'Date Darn Liz-bet! Date Darn Liz-bet!'

Emily laughed and started to repeat the invitation to come inside, but as she looked up from the page she saw Great-Aunt Elizabeth's face. She was staring beyond her towards Cicely and she was frowning. She recovered quickly and smiled at Emily. 'My dear I really do have to be off!'

With that she turned and rushed down the stairs.

In Great-Aunt Elizabeth's absence Emily returned to the sidecar to check on her sleeping daughter. She nodded to Mark and sat beside Cicely, who was deeply asleep, her little mouth held in a defiant pout.

'Is Phil going to be OK?' Mark asked in a quiet voice,

studying Emily's face for signs in case any reassurance she might give lacked conviction.

'Yes, we think so,' she replied.

Emily gently stroked Cicely's forehead, lifting the curls from her brow.

'You see those marks there,' Mark said, coming closer and pointing to tiny dents on Cicely's temples. 'They did something to her in the basement of the lodge.'

Emily's hand froze and she looked at Mark in horror, then back at Cicely, and peered closely at the small, shallow depressions beneath her hairline.

'What do you mean?' she whispered.

'You'll have to ask Phil, he knows more than me. He went down there. But he told me he thought that Cynthia Caddington was doing something weird to change people's personalities and behaviour and everything –'

Emily rushed from the sidecar and threw herself down beside Kate and Charlotte. 'Is he awake? I have to ask him something,' she said.

But Phil was unconscious again and they could not rouse him.

They spent twenty anxious minutes watching Great-Aunt Elizabeth's heartstone glow and the smaller stones flicker in the Historograph. Suddenly a thin circle of mist began to curl over the rim of the plate and a low hum swelled to a roar in the night air. All at once Great-Aunt Elizabeth was there, or at least a suggestion of her. For several seconds she appeared to have no substance, as if she were

merely an image projected on to a transparent screen. Then gradually she seemed to solidify and at last she stepped forward and stood beside them.

'Well, is it there?' she shouted as the roar from the Historograph subsided.

Emily had returned to the sidecar as soon as Great-Aunt Elizabeth's form took shape. Her hands trembled as she knelt before the bench and lifted the hinged lid. Carefully she removed the Time-Space Navigator and carried it out to where the others were waiting.

The Glass Sphere

Jim Tacker and the boys of Caddington Lodge returned to a deserted building. After sending them to their dormitories, he went straight to Cynthia Caddington's office and used her phone to report the accident to the police. Bardolph had been given instructions to help Dr Bernhard destroy the Reminder and remove all evidence of personality polishing from the basement. After seeing that the boys were settled, Tacker made his way to the basement to see for himself that nothing incriminating had been left behind.

As he descended the steps and walked the corridor to the lab, he was shocked to find Dr Bernhard, the thin lab professor, still at work. The machinery was in place and, indeed, looked as if it had been elaborated on, and the racks of glass spheres, each of them still labelled with a boy's name, were now lined up on the bench where Bernhard was working.

'What's going on?' he asked. 'I thought you were supposed to be –' Tacker stopped dead as he approached Bernhard. Lying slumped against the wall behind him was Bardolph. He was staring sightlessly from round

protruding eyes and a swollen blue tongue hung from his open mouth.

'Good God, is he . . . ?' Tacker gasped, moving forward.

Bernhard raised a hand in which he held a piece of equipment that Tacker did not recognize. 'Do not come any closer. 'e may be dead. I do not know. But as I 'ave now discovered that he is the man who is responsible for putting my mother in hospital, I do not care what happens to him.'

Tacker grinned at Bernhard and took a step forward. 'Now, you need to calm –'

But Jim Tacker did not finish his sentence and nor did he see what caused him to lose consciousness.

Michael carried the now conscious Phil into the shade of an ancient baobab tree where Harold and Emily had positioned the navigator and were checking the settings. Great-Aunt Elizabeth joined them and cupped her hand beneath Phil's chin.

'How are you feeling?' she asked.

Phil remembered the last time they had met at night beside the apple tree in the Longbridges' garden. It seemed like a thousand years ago. 'I'm OK,' he said, 'but Mark lost the keystone.'

'Don't worry about that. I'm going to help you get it back. Now listen carefully, Phil. Can you tell me everything you remember about what that vile sister of mine is doing in the basement? Cicely has marks on her forehead. Do you know how they got there?'

Phil gulped and nodded. Charlotte brought some water to his lips and after quenching his thirst Phil described what he had seen in the basement of the lodge. Great-Aunt Elizabeth listened gravely and when he had finished she remained quiet for several minutes.

'I'm going to ask you to do something very brave, Phil. Harold, Emily and your father have constructed a device to send you back in time, back to last night, when you and Mark were locked in your room and he still had the keystone. Now, the Time-Space Navigator can get you there but it won't bring you back. You will have to use the Historograph. Listen carefully, Phil, I have much to tell you and we must hurry.'

Great-Aunt Elizabeth nodded to Michael and he gently lowered Phil so that he could see the Historograph, which she had placed on the ground beside them. Great-Aunt Elizabeth began to point at the stones embedded in its beaten surface.

'The Historograph has seventeen heartstones and each one has a corresponding separate heartstone. Your keystone will lock on to one of the central five.' She waved her hand to indicate the stones she referred to.

'This one is mine and this, my sister's. One of the other three is yours. Obviously when you come to place the keystone, it will depend how you have orientated the Historograph – so I cannot show you precisely. You'll have to do it by trial and error.'

'How will I know when I've got the right one?' Phil asked.

'Position your keystone on top of another heartstone and slowly turn it. If it is the partner stone, then it will lock into place.'

Phil nodded to show that he understood.

'Good,' Great-Aunt Elizabeth whispered. 'Now, as soon as the keystone is in place, you need to envisage where you want to be. You should come back to the mountainside but not too close – you don't want to materialize in the middle of everything happening.' She looked around and pointed to the ridge that overlooked the path. 'I suggest you imagine yourself looking down on the scene from up there. Do you think you can do that?'

Phil considered for a moment. The ridge would give him a vantage point and he imagined what he would be able to see if he were looking back from it now. He nodded and Great-Aunt Elizabeth continued. 'Once you are there, make your way to the lodge. You should arrive at daybreak and by this time we will be there to meet you.'

'Don't I need more heartstones?' Phil interjected. 'I remember that you once told Kate and me that you needed to collaborate –'

Great-Aunt Elizabeth interrupted him. 'Potentially devastating negative energy forces are released if the heartstones become separated in time. But it is only one day and you will be reuniting the stones, so do not worry. Now remember, as soon as you are in possession of the keystone, its energy will alert Cynthia Caddington, so you will have to move quickly.'

Barking stepped forward.

'Remember to employ virtual invisibility and make strong visualizations. Repeat in your head, "You are silent as falling snow, faster than light, stronger than steel. Your enemies are weak and frail and will look right through you. Believe these things and it will be so."'

Barking stood up against Michael's leg and nudged Phil's hand with his head. 'Good luck,' he said, then turned and jumped into Kate's arms.

'Go straight to the basement,' said Great-Aunt Elizabeth. 'Take the sphere that belongs to Cicely and bring it back to us. Under no circumstances must you change the events of that night apart from removing the sphere. Everything must happen as it did today – do you understand?'

Phil nodded.

'It's ready?' Harold asked.

Great-Aunt Elizabeth looked at Michael and Charlotte, who was trying not to cry and failing. Charlotte hugged Phil, pressing her face against his, and part of her wanted to resist. She wanted to shout out 'Stop!' and forbid this mad experiment. Phil needn't go, she thought, his leg would heal – and far better a damaged Phil than no Phil at all. What if it didn't work? What if he disappeared into some eternal limbo? But lifting her head slightly, Charlotte saw Emily's ruined face. This was Cicely's only chance. It was the only way to undo what had happened to her and all the boys in that terrible place.

Great-Aunt Elizabeth placed her hand on Charlotte's back. 'It's time for him to go.'

Michael turned towards the baobab and lowered Phil to the ground, propping him up against the trunk. Phil winced as a rush of pain passed through his leg and up his spine. His face paled.

'Are you OK? Can you do this?' Michael asked as Great-Aunt Elizabeth placed the Historograph back in its bag and hung it from Phil's neck.

Kate held Barking tight and knew that it was more for her own comfort than his. She automatically raised her hand to her throat and took hold of her heartstone. She could imagine Phil's pain and she focused on helping him to bear it.

Phil swallowed and smiled weakly. Too many questions clouded his thinking and the pain in his hip and leg made him stupid. Supposing it didn't work and he found himself in some strange time and place? And even if it did work, how could he make sure he got his keystone back?

Suddenly Phil remembered the previous night, when he and Mark had been locked in their room. He had been roused by the sound of a soft click. Suppose that what he had heard had been the door closing and the key turning in the lock? Just suppose that it hadn't been his imagination or his tired mind playing tricks on him but his future self come back to recover the keystone. And then he realized with a grin that it would work. It had to work. It had already happened.

'Yes,' he said, laughing softly despite everything. 'I'm OK. I can do it.'

Emily set the navigator while Harold and Michael looked on and nodded approvingly.

'And you're sure that it's accurate?' Michael asked.

'One hundred per cent,' Harold replied.

'OK, Phil,' said Emily. 'As soon as you're ready raise your hand and I'll hit the switch.'

'Good luck, Phil!' Kate called, and Charlotte went back and kissed his cheek one more time. 'See you soon, sweetheart,' she said.

His family moved away and stood in a close circle and watched him. Phil stared steadily at them, his face calm and determined. Then he raised his hand.

Cynthia Caddington opened her eyes. It was pitch black and she had no idea where she was. She tried to get to her feet but a pain in her back made it impossible. Then she remembered that the wretched boy had pushed her off the path. Gritting her teeth, she hauled herself on her hands and knees and began to feel around her for the Historograph. Slowly, she began to crawl along the dry riverbed, and with each painful movement her anger raged within her. As she made slow progress, her knees and palms getting torn on the rough ground, she made herself a promise. She would survive this. She had survived before and she would do so again, and Elizabeth would pay. Yes, Elizabeth would pay dearly this time.

Gazing out at his family, Phil heard a crackle of energy and saw them raise their arms to shield their eyes from the glare that he could feel, rather than see, flaring around him. He placed his hands flat against the gnarled bark of the baobab and felt reassured by its solidity. For a couple of seconds he watched the silhouettes of his family, as if he were looking at a photographic negative, then they disappeared into inky blackness. Phil heard a roar of air rushing past him and felt his body jolt and shudder as if he were on a roller-coaster. He closed his eyes and held his breath. Suddenly there was silence and as he took a new breath he noticed that the air around him was cool and moving gently. Slowly, he opened his eyes. It was dark and overhead he could see a million stars. His palms were still pressed flat against the hard surface behind him, but he immediately knew that it was no longer the baobab tree. He moved his hands about and identified a concrete wall. Phil blinked and as his eyes became used to the dark he realized where he was. To his left was the wire fence where he had met with Fearless and behind him was the wall of the gymnasium where he had first set eyes on Nikwata. The next thing he noticed was that he was no longer in pain and his leg now hung straight from his hip. Cautiously, he put some weight on it. As he straightened up and moved slowly away from the wall, something writhed behind his neck and made him jump. He flung his arm up and back, swatting his hand behind his shoulder, and sent a small animal flying to the ground. Phil had materialized on top of Nikwata, pinning him to the wall and squashing the breath from his tiny lungs.

Phil crouched down and reached for where Nikwata

lay stunned in the dust. His eyes were rolling in their sockets and he emitted a tiny drawn-out wheeze.

'Nik! . . . Nik!' Phil whispered, lifting him on to his hand. 'Are you OK?'

'Eeeeeyeaaargh! Tk tk phifff!'

Nikwata lay on his back and twitched and shivered. At last he raised his head, cleared his throat and spat in Phil's eye before springing to his feet and sounding off a volley of furious Swahili.

'Tk tk tk! *Mpumbavu*! Tk tk!'

'I'm sorry!' Phil said, and carried Nikwata to the end of the alley so that he could look out towards the lodge and make a plan for getting inside.

'Have you seen Fearless?' Phil asked.

'Tk tk tk tk no, not come back tk tk.'

As Phil stole back towards the lodge, Nikwata took his place on his shoulder and Phil told him that he needed the key to his room. 'Can you get it for me and meet me outside the door?'

Nikwata nodded and the two of them made their way round the building until they reached the dining hall. Phil held his breath as he tried the door handle, but it opened easily and he slipped inside and sank to the floor. Once again a narrow strip of light shone from the open fridge in the kitchen and Phil recognized Bardolph's gruff voice. This time he wasn't talking to himself and, as Nikwata leapt from his shoulder and hurtled off towards the exit, Phil crept along the floor until he was able to see into the kitchen.

Bardolph stood before the open fridge, helping himself to handfuls of vegetable curry, some of which fell through his fingers and dropped to the floor before reaching his mouth. In his other hand he held a satellite phone to his large cauliflower ear.

'. . . Yeah, a table lamp I tell yer . . . are you listening to me? . . . Course not, you idiot, nearly cracked me skull open, that's all . . . Oh, it's a nice hotel, is it? Well, that's swell, Frimley. I hope you're having a ball . . . Listen, Frimley, I've had enough. I'm getting outta here . . . Yeah, I'll try and get a flight tomorrow . . . No, we've not been paid yet but I've gotta plan. You say that Hildy's there? Well, she can pay us, can't she? . . . Tell me where to fly to again. What? . . . I can't hear you . . . What? . . . Spell it . . . B-O-G-O . . . Where the hell's Bogo? . . . Whaddya mean "ta" . . . What's ta? . . . Huh? Oh, Bogotá . . . Why the hell didn't you say so?'

Phil crawled across the dining hall and out into the corridor, where he stood with his back flat against the wall. He took a second to focus his mind and let his thoughts move to things small and stealth-like before creeping along in the shadows towards his bedroom. When he got there, Nikwata was arriving from the direction of the reception area. He was wriggling along backwards and dragging the key behind him.

Phil stooped to pick it up. 'Thanks, Nik. Now go down to the basement. I'll meet you there in a few minutes.'

Nikwata gave a couple of clicks and hisses and ran off along the corridor.

Phil placed the key carefully in the lock so that it barely touched the sides. He turned the key and handle simultaneously and, with a last quick glance up and down the corridor, stepped inside and silently closed the door behind him.

He hadn't had time to consider how it would feel to see himself as others saw him and was unprepared for the strange uncomfortable sensation he now experienced. He became curiously self-conscious, as if he had found himself in an embarrassing situation in a public place. It was, he imagined, a bit like seeing oneself unexpectedly on television: a strange mixture of something incredibly familiar being seen from a unique and surprising viewpoint. He could not dwell on it and averted his eyes as he passed his own bed and stood beside Mark's.

Mark's face was softly relaxed in a dreamless sleep. He lay on his side with his knees drawn up and his feet crossed and tucked up behind him. One arm was folded back behind his head and he used his forearm as a pillow. His other arm lay beside his chest, his hand curled around the keystone, where it had fallen from his grasp and now lay on the sheet. Phil reached down and gently picked it up. The keystone pulsed with an intense light that lit the room and Phil quickly slipped the chain around his neck and dropped the stone out of sight inside his T-shirt, where it buzzed with energy. Phil immediately felt the difference that it made to him as he turned and left the room with effortless speed and stealth. As he passed his own bed, he stole one last look at himself and noticed

his rucksack stuffed down the back of his pillow. He reached out and carefully lifted it free. Then he left the room, silently locking the door behind him.

As Phil hurried towards the lobby and the trapdoor to the basement he suddenly felt his keystone flare with power and he recognized it to be a warning of imminent danger. He reached for the nearest door and tried the handle. It opened and he disappeared inside a small cupboard and closed the door just as Cynthia Caddington turned into the far end of the corridor and let out a yell.

'Bardolph!' she shouted. 'Get here this minute! Bardolph! Jim, where are you?'

She has sensed the keystone, Phil thought, while desperately trying to tame his thumping heart. In order to stop his keystone's energy betraying him Phil practised the virtual-invisibility technique taught to him by Barking. He closed his eyes and imagined wrapping the keystone in black velvet and then placing it in a steel box so that it was completely hidden. Then he imagined himself and the box in a dark and empty landscape. He barely breathed and his heartbeat became slow and all but silent. He heard Cynthia Caddington pass the door and waited a few seconds before continuing on his way.

When he got to the lobby there was no sign of Nikwata but he saw that, in her haste, Cynthia Caddington had left the trapdoor open. He climbed down the steps and made his way in a loping sprint to the laboratory. His tread was light and soundless. When he reached the lab he kept to one side and peered round the corner. At the

far end he could see a man in a white coat. Phil observed him for a moment while he thought about what to do next.

Suddenly Nikwata dropped from the ceiling and landed on Bernhard's head, causing him to jump backwards in alarm. With his hands flapping about his head as if he were trying to bat out flames, Bernhard attempted to remove the lizard. But Nikwata worked his little suckered feet through Bernhard's hair and gripped tightly. No amount of swatting or tipping his head over and shaking it could dislodge him. Doubting that this was the best distraction that Nikwata could have come up with, Phil made his approach. As he reached the end of the bench, he saw something that had him reeling in shock.

Cicely's small body was strapped in the chair and her head was clamped to the bowl that was attached by wires and rubber tubing to a glass sphere. The sphere was a third full of turquoise liquid.

Horrorstruck, Phil cried out without thinking. 'Stop it! What are you doing to her?' He pushed Bernhard aside and began lifting the wires, trying to see how to detach them.

'No! Please . . . Do not touch this! . . . You will hurt her!' Bernhard cried, grabbing Phil by the shoulder.

Phil spun round to face him. '*I'll hurt her?* You're the one who is hurting her!' And then he added incredulously, 'She's a *baby*, for pity's sake!'

Phil watched Bernhard's face crumple. Nikwata jumped from his head on to Phil's shoulder.

'I told Mrs Caddington it would not be good to attempt perfection with this little child,' Bernhard whispered, 'but she is very persistent, very persistent.'

Phil gazed down at Cicely's face and gently touched her cheek with a finger.

Phil had travelled back in time knowing that something terrible had happened to Cicely in the basement and his plan was to retrieve the sphere so that Harold and Emily could transform her back to her old self. He had not expected to see her suffering.

'It is too late,' Bernhard was saying. 'You cannot interrupt the process or you may kill her.'

'Can you reverse it?' Phil asked. 'Once it's finished, can you change her back?'

Nikwata climbed down Phil's back on to the bench and began running around the grisly machine, as if trying to see how it worked.

'Yes, perhaps, but I have been told to destroy it all,' Bernhard continued, his voice hushed and shaky. 'As soon as I finish with her I am to smash all the spheres and dismantle the Reminder.'

'The Reminder?' Phil queried.

Bernhard nodded sadly. 'It was never meant to be a bad thing. It merely sifts through the chemical manifestations of behaviour, separating what is desirable from the undesirable. It was supposed to give people better personalities.'

'So when Cynthia Caddington or Jim Tacker talked about reminding us how to behave, this is what they

meant – literally emptying out someone's personality and storing the bits they didn't like in a glass bowl?' Phil asked incredulously.

He stared down at Cicely in dismay and gently touched the sphere behind her head. So that's where the Cicely they knew and loved had gone – suspended in liquid. Phil took hold of his keystone and begged for the resolve to make the right decision. As much as he wanted to lift Cicely up in his arms and take her away from this horrible place, he knew that anything he did tonight must not alter the events of the next day. The lodge must still be evacuated and Cicely and Emily must meet on the path. But this man had to be stopped from destroying the machine they would need to get Cicely back.

'Give me Cicely's sphere – that's the least you can do. I can see you don't really want to hurt anyone.'

'Mrs Caddington will kill me,' Bernhard said. His eyes were small in his pale, narrow face. He held his hand in a fist and he pressed it into the palm of his other hand as he gazed sadly at Phil.

'You could leave here,' Phil said gently. 'You don't have to do what she says.' He hesitated a moment before continuing, unsure how much he could tell this man. 'Look, suppose I told you that right now people are on their way to stop Mrs Caddington and shut the lodge down.'

Nikwata peered out from behind the bowl that cradled Cicely's head and began to click and hiss. 'Tk tk tk tk look! Look! Tk tk tk.'

Phil checked the glass sphere, which was now four-

fifths full. He appealed to Bernhard, who was staring at Nikwata.

'It is finished,' Bernhard said. 'I will give it to you.'

Phil smiled at Bernhard and nodded his approval. 'Please hurry. I have to go before she gets back.'

With shaking hands and clumsy fingers, Bernhard removed the strap from Cicely's head and undid the wires, while giving occasional glances at Nikwata and Phil out of the corner of his eye.

'This lizard,' he said. 'How come he is talking?'

'Cynthia Caddington – I think you know that is not her real name – has had many disguises and masterminded many terrible crimes,' Phil said. 'Messing about with animals is just one of the things she used to do before she got into sucking the brains out of the back of people's heads.'

Bernhard blushed as he pulled the bung from the sphere, quickly tipping it up to prevent any liquid spilling out. He stopped up the hole with a rubber seal and then held it out to Phil. 'I am sorry for what I have done,' he said. 'I hope you can help the little one.'

Phil took the sphere carefully in both hands as Nikwata leapt on to his arm and scurried up to his shoulder.

'You're doing the right thing,' Phil said. He pushed the bag with the bulky Historograph further behind him and slipped the rucksack from his shoulder and gave it to Bernhard. 'And if you decide to stand up to Mrs Caddington there's something that may help you in here,' he added before sprinting from the room.

Essence of Cicely

Fearless ran the last thirty kilometres of road back to the lodge. The pads of his feet were swollen and raw and his body ached but he did not dare rest in case he couldn't get moving again. He went first of all to the cave and found the old dog waiting at the entrance for him. She spoke to him in a low whine, communicating, as a few clever dogs can, in a language that is able to denote objects and places but is devoid of any sense of the order of events. Fearless gleaned that two boys and a baby had been in the cave. A lizard ate insects. They had gone down the mountain. A man had gone down the mountain. They had gone to the buildings. Fearless gazed around the cave and saw what was missing and judged this to be evidence of the supplies Phil would have taken. He stood up on his hind legs and knocked the dog biscuits down for the old dog to eat, then he decided to go to the fence and see if Phil had left Nikwata there with a message from him.

Phil hurried beneath the starry sky and across the playing field towards the gymnasium. He cradled Cicely's sphere

in his hands and felt the liquid gently lap against the inside. He felt his palms warming on the glass. This was the essence of Cicely's personality – every bit as precious as if he were carrying Cicely herself. He would not drop it. He reached the alley between the gym and the squash courts and ran into the pitch black where no starlight penetrated. He could sense the distance of the wall on either side of him and trod lightly on the uneven ground so as not to jolt the sphere. Nikwata hitched a ride on his back, nestled between his shoulder blades.

As Phil reached the end of the alley Fearless scrambled up the bank on the other side of the fence.

'Fearless,' Phil cried. 'Oh, Fearless.'

'What's happening?' Fearless asked. 'Thank goodness you're OK. How's Cicely? Good grief, you got the Historograph? And what's that other thing you've got there?'

Phil cradled the sphere in the crook of his arm and knelt down in order to place the Historograph on the ground. He poked the fingers of his free hand through the wire fence and rubbed Fearless's chin with his knuckles. Phil carefully lowered the sphere and, resting it in the dirt beside the Historograph, he kept one hand on it so that it could not roll. Nikwata emerged from the neck of his T-shirt, ran down his arm and on to the ground, where he scurried beneath the curve of the sphere and propped it up with his hands, like a miniature Atlas holding up the world.

'Fearless, we have to get away from here,' Phil whispered

urgently. 'I have my keystone and Great-Aunt Elizabeth has shown me how to use it.'

'What? Is she here?' Fearless raised his big head and scanned the length of the alley.

'Fearless, this is going to sound weird but I've come back from tomorrow. There's another me – the real me . . . No, I'm the real me – well, I'm here with you, but I'm also still asleep in the lodge and know nothing about this because it hasn't happened yet.'

Fearless raised an injured paw and deep folds furrowed his brow as he listened. 'Go on,' he said simply.

As he spoke, Phil removed his keystone and began to turn it over in his hand on top of the stones in the centre of the Historograph. 'I came back to get the sphere so that Harold and Emily can help Cicely.' He glanced up at Fearless. 'That's what's been happening here – Cynthia Caddington has a machine called a Reminder and she gives people a "perfect personality" by doing something to their brain. You should see Cicely – she doesn't know any of us and she's . . . well, she's . . . well, she's just like a baby version of Cynthia Caddington. The lodge will be evacuated early tomorrow morning, probably because the power from my keystone will have warned Cynthia Caddington that we're close by. Great-Aunt Elizabeth told me how to use the Historograph to get back, or rather go forward to meet them –' He broke off and frowned down at the instrument. He had tried each of the stones in turn and was now back at the first one, but none of them seemed to connect in any way.

Fearless indicated a stone with a jab of his nose. 'Turn it round. That one over there is Great-Aunt Elizabeth's. Look, hang on a sec, I'm coming inside.'

Cynthia Caddington clawed her way along the ground at the base of the cliff until she reached a place where a cataract formed annually after the big rains. Now dry, the surface was rugged and broken and she was able to haul herself up and climb hand over hand, finding crevices for her feet and clasping hold of tree roots and boulders that jutted out above her. As she climbed, dark unhappy memories from her childhood filled her mind and a bitter hatred oozed from her heart. For three years it had taken all her willpower to resist these memories and instead revisit, over and over again, the few fragments of happy days that she could remember. Now she wallowed in the bad times, the injustice, the loneliness and the dreadful knowledge that their mother had loved Elizabeth more than her. As far as she was concerned, everyone they had ever met or known had preferred Elizabeth, and her sister had done everything possible to encourage this prejudice. Elizabeth the *eldest*, the *cleverest*, the *favourite* child – talking privately with their mother, always knowing best and always leaving her out. The memories came thick and fast and her anger gave her the strength and determination to climb. There they were, Elizabeth and Margot – as she had been called back then – Elizabeth carrying plates to the table while she lay underneath it and kicked out at the dog. Elizabeth and their mother laughing while she scowled

from the shadows. Elizabeth being praised and admired while Margot stood alone, awkward and ignored by everyone. Margot was not part of the family and no longer cared to be. She had tried, once, to have something of her own, but Elizabeth had spoiled that too and taken Gina away from her and changed her name to Charlotte. She would get her revenge. A bit more climbing and she would reach her and Elizabeth would finally get what she deserved.

After Phil had slowly dissolved in front of their eyes, what remained of the Reynolds and Baker families wandered slowly back to the sidecar, where they had left Mark watching over Cicely. Mark had fallen asleep and was lying beside Cicely, his arm wrapped protectively around her.

Great-Aunt Elizabeth called Charlotte over. 'Harold and Emily must go to Caddington Lodge so that Cicely's recovery can begin. Can you fit everyone in the Cessna?' she asked.

Charlotte nodded. 'Yes. But, aren't you coming with us?'

'There's something I have to do here first.'

Charlotte shivered. It was just before dawn and the coldest part of the night, but it was fear, not the cold, that made her tremble.

Great-Aunt Elizabeth wrapped her arms around her niece and hugged her. 'This is the last time, my dear. She will not trouble us again.'

'Be careful,' Charlotte whispered, and she breathed

deeply, taking in the familiar scent of leather and chocolate as Great-Aunt Elizabeth patted her back.

'Come on, now, you had better get going.'

Charlotte assembled the others and they climbed the slope to the ridge and the crater beyond, where she and Michael had left the Cessna. Michael led the way, followed by Kate and Barking. Emily carried Cicely, who was still sleeping peacefully, and Mark walked between Harold and Charlotte. Great-Aunt Elizabeth watched them until all she could see were dim shadows moving against the mountainside, then she turned to the ravine and walked to the edge. She stood with her hands on her hips and stared down into the darkness and waited for her sister.

Hate Between Sisters

Fearless turned the Historograph round with his paw and sniffed at the heartstone that partnered Great-Aunt Elizabeth's. Phil placed the keystone over the stone two away from hers and began turning it over and round. Just when he was about to give up and move on to the next one, it flared and his keystone clicked into place.

Fearless raised his chin. 'Take my heartstone from my collar and place it there. I'm coming with you.'

The large retriever leant against him, the breeze gently ruffling his fur, and Phil did as he was asked. Then he picked up Cicely's sphere and Nikwata ran on to his shoulder. Phil held the sphere close to him, cradling it in his arms as he leant over the Historograph. The heart-stones began to pulse with light and a low hum lifted from the surface and engulfed them. Phil closed his eyes and imagined himself into the next night. He saw the column of boys marching along the mountain path beneath the starry sky. At the front of the procession he saw Cynthia Caddington and in her arms he recognized Cicely from her mass of golden corkscrew curls.

Phil felt a brief, alarming sensation, as if they had been

suddenly tipped upside down and righted again. He clutched the sphere close to his chest and felt Fearless's body jolt beside him and heard him whimper. Phil opened his eyes and found himself kneeling before the Historograph on rocky ground. The heartstones were no longer pulsing with light but glowed steadily. Beside him Fearless stood and began to wag his tail in slow, cautious sweeps and Phil followed his gaze down the mountain to the path below. He saw his family gathered behind Great-Aunt Elizabeth, who stood on the path as if she were holding up the traffic. Kneeling a few metres in front of her was Emily, her arms outstretched towards the tiny figure standing close to Cynthia Caddington.

As Phil watched from the ridge above the path he saw himself break free of the group and run at Cynthia Caddington and leap on to her back. But from his new perspective of the scene Phil saw something that he had not known before. As he ran forward, Jim Tacker's arm flew out and made a swiping grab for him and would have caught him if something hadn't held him back. As Phil had made his dash, Mark threw himself against Jim Tacker, knocking him off balance and allowing Phil to pass.

'Tk tk tk hx hx hx tk!' Nikwata jabbered excitedly from his shoulder as Phil and Cynthia Caddington struggled and stumbled towards the ravine. Then, suddenly, in one clean jerk, they disappeared over the edge.

'Phil!' Kate's scream reached their ears and echoed round the mountain. At Phil's side Fearless turned agitated circles and whined.

'It's all right, it's all right,' Phil reassured him, although the sight had shocked him too, and the memory of the fall sickened him. 'We know what happens next. Let's go.'

They turned and followed the ridge until it rose steeply to a summit and stopped to rest. A hundred metres below them they caught a brief glimpse of the retreating army of boys from the lodge, before the ridge and the path diverged. To their right the shallow escarpment fell gently to a crater below.

'We can go this way,' Fearless said, and limped ahead down the slope.

Just after the Cessna took off dawn broke and, as the plane climbed steeply to make it over the ridge and skirt the adjacent summit that concealed Caddington Lodge from view, Cicely woke up. One moment she was asleep in Emily's arms, the next she was kicking her legs and shouting over the noise of the engine and the wind that roared outside.

'You are big ugly baddies!' she yelled, and swung a fist that caught Emily on the side of the head.

Stunned, Emily lost her hold on the child and Cicely was off in a flash. She clambered about the plane's interior, wriggling from everyone's grasp and reaching for the doors and windows. Lurching forward, she grabbed hold of Charlotte's hair and gave it a vicious yank.

'Yeow!' screamed Charlotte, and as her head jolted involuntarily upwards, the Cessna was thrown into an unexpected climb that pinned its occupants to their seats.

'Get hold of her!' yelled Michael over the din of the engine.

As Cicely crawled across Mark's lap to escape Emily and reach the window, Mark seized her and folded his arms across her chest and held her to him. Cicely filled her lungs and emitted an ear-piercing scream that flattened Barking's ears and puffed up his fur so that he more than doubled in size.

'Hang on to her, for heaven's sake!' Barking cried when he had recovered enough to speak.

'You'd better all hang on,' shouted Charlotte. 'We're about to land.'

Ahead of them, Caddington Lodge's swimming pool sparkled in the sunshine as Charlotte brought the plane into a fast, steep descent, aiming for the playing fields beyond.

Exhausted and hungry, Phil walked beside Fearless. Just before daybreak they had heard the Cessna overhead and this had spurred them on. They were close now and began to hurry, and when they finally clambered on to the road that approached the lodge they broke into a run. Phil held Cicely's sphere in his hands as if he were running with a rugby ball for a touchdown. The liquid slopped against the sides as he ran. They passed through the gate and immediately saw the Cessna sitting on the field where Majenda had taught Phil how to throw a javelin. It was less than a week ago but it seemed like a lifetime. Phil's heart leapt into his mouth as first Harold and then his

father stepped from the plane. Suddenly more people tumbled through the aircraft door and, as Phil squinted into the brilliant African sunlight, he saw a small figure break away from the group.

'Quickly!' Phil yelled at Fearless. 'Stop her!'

Cicely was running fast on her little legs. Fearless bounded towards her and, being careful not to hurt her, he knocked her over with a gentle push of his paws. He lifted her in his mouth and carried her by the seat of her pants back to the others, with Cicely kicking and screaming and drumming her fists in the air all the way.

Kate, Charlotte and Michael were the first to greet Phil but, as they ran towards him, he held Cicely's sphere up high for them to see and they stopped before they reached him.

Smiling at his family, he walked past them and held the glass sphere out to Harold. 'Here she is,' he said. 'This is the real Cicely, in here.'

With a rush of clicks and squeaks, Nikwata emerged from the neck of Phil's T-shirt and took up his place on his shoulder.

'Oh, this is Nikwata,' said Phil, as Kate peered curiously at the little reptile. 'I couldn't have coped without him. He saw the Reminder, so he can help us.'

'Help, yes yes yes tk tk tk.'

Kate laughed when she heard his tinny voice and Nikwata turned his head sharply towards her and stuck out his tongue.

'Are you really all right?' Charlotte asked Phil, hugging

him close, then ruffling his hair as she released him so that they could walk towards the lodge. 'I can hardly believe it. Your poor leg was completely mashed up.'

'Yes, I'm fine, but I think you should take a look at Fearless's paws, Mum.' He stopped, suddenly looking around. 'Where's Great-Aunt Elizabeth?'

Charlotte sighed. 'She stayed behind to deal with Cynthia Caddington. She'll be along soon.'

Suddenly they heard the sound of a helicopter and, as they turned to look for it, an army truck swung through the gates, followed by the chopper rising over the nearest peak.

'Oh, Lord,' muttered Charlotte. 'Hurry down to the basement, all of you. I'll send them to the ravine.'

Great-Aunt Elizabeth sensed that her sister was nearby and coming closer, and she waited patiently on the path beside her Harley. The sun had been up for half an hour and was already warming her skin, though the air temperature remained cool. Suddenly she heard the sound of a small flurry of falling stones and expected to see her sister emerge over the edge of the cliff and arrive on the path beside her. But the noise was followed by silence and nothing happened. Great-Aunt Elizabeth took a step towards the edge and listened carefully.

'Scorpion stings! I know you're there, Margot!' she bellowed, taking a chocolate from her pocket which she absent-mindedly unwrapped and popped into her mouth.

Suddenly, with an immense surge of effort, Cynthia

Caddington threw an arm and a leg on to the path and struggled to her feet. The long black garment that she wore was filthy and torn, she had a gash on her brow and she glared out from large eyes that appeared to have sunk into her hideous face.

Great-Aunt Elizabeth gasped. 'Margot, what has happened to you?' she whispered.

Cynthia Caddington slowly turned her head about as if she were looking for something to strike her sister with. At last her eyes rested on Great-Aunt Elizabeth and she spoke.

'Do you really want to know? I am what you have made me, Elizabeth. After you destroyed the Lampton Laboratory and deprived me of my beauty products, my skin began to age. I sat before the mirror and watched sixty years pass by in five minutes.'

Great-Aunt Elizabeth recovered and frowned. 'Well, we all have to get old, Margot. It is no excuse for your appalling behaviour.'

Cynthia Caddington lowered her head for a moment and when she raised it her heartstone was blazing at her throat, throwing a brilliant crimson reflection on to her face. She looked like a medieval devil.

Great-Aunt Elizabeth took a step back as the force of her sister's hatred hit her.

'Now listen, Margot, you're to stop this at once. You know you cannot harm me without harming yourself.'

'Well, what if I don't care?' Margot spat, taking a step closer. 'You have taken away everything I ever had or

dreamt of having. You always ruin everything. Maybe I've had enough. Maybe I don't care if I destroy us both.'

And without further warning, she flung herself at Great-Aunt Elizabeth and grabbed hold of her heartstone. Instantly they were thrown on to their backs as if by magnetic repulsion and an acrid smell filled the air. Gasping for breath, Great-Aunt Elizabeth was the first to get to her feet.

'Margot!' she shouted, 'You will kill us both.'

Margot scrambled up and launched herself at Elizabeth once more. A loud crack resounded around the mountain and the two women were thrown to the ground on their backs. The force was considerably stronger this time and neither of them moved for several moments.

At last Great-Aunt Elizabeth managed to get up on to her knees. 'What do you want, Margot? There must be something.'

With a determined effort she was able to stand up. Several metres from her, Margot staggered to her feet and stared wild-eyed at her sister.

'I . . . wanted . . . that . . .'

She grimaced with anger and frustration, and Great-Aunt Elizabeth braced herself for another attack.

'I wanted . . . that . . . that baby.'

Great-Aunt Elizabeth was breathing heavily and her grey curls sprang about her head like Medusa's snakes. Her motorcycle leathers were dusty from the red ground and her face was smeared with dirt. She stared at Margot until she had regained her breath enough to speak. 'I

promised our mother that I would look after you.'

Margot laughed and spat at the ground. 'Don't give me that rubbish!' she hissed.

Elizabeth began to move slowly away from her, towards the Harley, while Margot eyed her suspiciously. 'What are you doing, Elizabeth? Stay where I can see you.'

Elizabeth stopped beside her motorbike. In order to shine the headlight all night she had left the engine running and the exhaust was still hot. Before Margot could move to stop her, Elizabeth fell upon the Harley and held her heartstone against its exhaust pipe. For a second she feared that the heat was not intense enough. But as Margot screamed and rushed forward, Elizabeth's heartstone dropped from her neck and she flung it into a thorn bush at the side of the road. Margot launched herself on to her sister's back before she could stand straight. Elizabeth tried to throw her off and they staggered and stumbled towards the edge of the path and the precipitous drop to the dry riverbed below. In her desperation, Elizabeth managed to swing the screaming Margot round and they fell to the ground. Without her heartstone Elizabeth should have been at a disadvantage but she was powered by rage and it was Margot who succumbed in the struggle. Elizabeth held her by the neck, dragged her to the Harley and pushed her throat towards the burning exhaust pipe. There was a clunk as Margot's heartstone hit the pipe and fell into the dirt. Elizabeth reached down and snatched it up.

Margot screamed. 'You can't take my heartstone from

me without destroying your own!' she wailed.

Elizabeth pushed her away. 'Well, Margot, if that's the only way to stop your madness, then so be it.'

She stood tall and began to brush the grime from her sleeves. Margot's heartstone dangled from her fingers. The red light flared once, then flickered and sputtered and became dim as its energy waned. In another moment it had faded to black. There was a brief, sinister gurgling sound and Elizabeth almost dropped it as it became suddenly heavy. In a matter of moments its transformation was complete. It had become a darkstone.

Suddenly, from behind her, Margot rushed at her and would have knocked her over the edge but Elizabeth sensed the movement and stepped aside just in time. Margot screamed as she hurtled out into space. She was momentarily displayed against the blue sky and Elizabeth memorized the last sight she would have of her sister; her arms flailing, her black cloak billowing round her legs. Then she fell like a rock and her scream, like her heartstone's power, gradually diminished until it ceased altogether and became nothing.

A Return to Normal

With Bernhard's help they brought the Reminder to the dining hall and set it up there. Cicely had become strangely calm when she saw Bernhard and had allowed him to wire her in while Harold fixed the glass sphere to the back of the machine.

'What does it do exactly?' Kate asked. She had pulled up a couple of chairs and now she and Phil watched the men at work, their expressions intent and sombre.

Bernhard's pale face coloured. 'The Reminder reads and interprets the mind's electrical energy before converting it into chemical energy, when it is possible to alter the proportions. With the boys, Mrs Caddington wanted me to remove all traces of independent decision-making and defiance but to increase motivation with regard to physical activity.' He paused. 'But with this little girl she wanted something more.'

'What?' Emily asked in an anxious whisper. 'What did she want?'

'She wanted her to be obedient, yes, and loyal, yes, but Mrs Caddington, she wanted the little girl to be like her, to think like her. She want the little girl to love her.'

'Love her?' echoed Kate with disgust. 'Poor Cicely!'

Phil remembered the sight of Cynthia Caddington's spiteful face with its rotten flesh and shuddered.

When it was over and her sphere was empty, Harold lifted Cicely's unconscious body and passed her to Emily. 'I'm going to stay and help Bernhard with the boys,' he said, gently kissing her forehead.

Emily took her daughter outside, where Kate and Phil had carried three chairs into the shade of a tree. While Kate sat quietly listening to Phil telling her everything that had happened to him, Emily cradled Cicely in her arms and waited for her to wake with equal measures of hope and fear in her heart.

Inside the dining hall, the boys, who had been organized by Charlotte and Michael, sat in orderly rows on the benches and waited for their turn to sit in Bernhard's chair and undergo a reversal of the personality perfection process. Unlike Cicely, the boys regained consciousness immediately and Harold was glad that Emily was not there to see it. The anxiety was difficult enough for him to bear but at least he had work to do.

When the boys climbed back out of the chair, their spheres empty once more, they were restless and complained of hunger. After an hour, over half the boys had been restored and the far end of the hall soon became untidy and chaotic as boys helped themselves to the fruit, bread and boiled eggs that Charlotte constantly replenished from the kitchen. Meanwhile, at the other end of the room, the Reminded boys sat quietly and waited their turn.

When they had finished eating Michael encouraged them to play outside, and soon the swimming pool echoed with laughter and shouts and a large unruly game of football was in progress on the playing field.

His story told, Phil left his sister with Emily and Cicely and walked to the lodge gate with Barking and Fearless to watch the road for Great-Aunt Elizabeth. Cat and dog chatted quietly but Phil was soon lost in his own thoughts. It was quite something, he realized, to have experienced time travel at just twelve years of age, not to mention all the other extraordinary things he had been through. And something told him that it wasn't over yet.

After only a few minutes Kate joined him again and disturbed his reverie with a kind of running hug. 'Cicely is awake and she's fine!' she announced happily. 'She's *so* sweet. She keeps kissing Emily and saying that she wants pancakes!'

'That's a relief.' Phil sighed, smiling at the news. 'But . . . it's just . . . something still doesn't feel right.'

Fearless took a few steps forward and stopped just outside the gate but he didn't speak.

'I know, I feel it too,' said Kate. 'I expect we will be fine when Great-Aunt Elizabeth gets here.'

'She's coming now,' said Barking, suddenly leaping on to the gatepost for a better view.

Slowly, Fearless began to wag his tail.

Kate and Phil scanned the road, but they could not see or hear any sign of the Harley.

'Are you sure?' Phil had no sooner asked the question than they heard the low rumble of the motorbike and soon after it appeared round the bend.

The moment Great-Aunt Elizabeth pulled up beside them, Barking leapt on to her lap. She had left the dome of the sidecar open and Fearless jumped inside.

Great-Aunt Elizabeth was grubby and dishevelled and looked tired. 'Great-Aunt Elizabeth, are you . . . ?' Kate asked.

Great-Aunt Elizabeth looked at Kate and then at Phil and her eyes glistened. For a shocking second they thought she was going to cry. 'It is over. My sister has gone. The emergency rescue team arrived and I showed them where she went over the edge, but I doubt very much that they will find her body.'

Kate and Phil looked at each other, then Kate said, 'Great-Aunt Elizabeth, are you all right?'

She smiled at them. 'Come along. In you get and let's go to the others. There's something I have to tell you.'

The last of the boys had left the dining hall and Harold was helping Bernhard dismantle the Reminder while Nikwata looked on, hissing and clicking. Charlotte and Emily had cleared the last of the dishes and plates and Mark was playing a game of peek-a-boo chase with Cicely round and round the benches.

'She likes me now,' he said happily, glancing up at Phil as he entered the room with the others.

And it was perfectly obvious to Phil that Mark was

genuinely happy, but only Mark knew that it was the first time that he had truly been so in a long, long time. The wonderful good fortune that had made his family rich beyond their wildest dreams had suddenly and completely severed Mark from a life that he loved. Almost overnight, expensive toys, the latest, most up-to-date gadgets and a luxurious lifestyle that included exotic holidays, fast cars and a private education replaced the world in which he'd spent the first nine years of his life and had flourished. Mark had been a confident child who had enjoyed the security of a happy home and school life and a close friendship with Phil Reynolds. All of this was lost in a flurry of packing and spending that made for a life where he felt curiously deprived. Somehow, through the difficulties and hardship of his recent adventure, Mark had rediscovered the value of friendship and was feeling more like his old self. And it felt good.

He jumped up from behind a table beside Cicely, who had been expecting him to come the other way, and she screamed with delighted terror and ran at Kate, throwing herself at her legs. Kate picked her up and kissed her, while Great-Aunt Elizabeth reached out a big hand and patted her cheek. 'Welcome back, little one,' she said softly.

Cicely looked up at her with enormous eyes and said sweetly, 'You got choc-lot date dart Lizbeth? Have you?'

Great-Aunt Elizabeth laughed and passed a handful of chocolates to Kate before approaching the table where the Reminder lay in pieces. She picked up an empty sphere and frowned at it.

'How are things here?' she asked, looking around the room. 'Everything appears to be fine.'

'Everything's fine apart from the two bodies in the basement,' Michael said drily.

Great-Aunt Elizabeth raised her eyebrows and Charlotte added, 'It's OK. They're unconscious, not dead.'

'Our friend here,' said Harold, patting Bernhard's shoulder, 'got a bit carried away with the Insult Fermenter, didn't you, eh?'

Great-Aunt Elizabeth turned to Fearless. 'Go and check on them for me, then take them to the sidecar when they're conscious and watch over them.'

Fearless spoke to Nikwata as he passed him and the lizard hopped on to his back and they left the room.

'We shall have to decide what to do with them,' Great-Aunt Elizabeth continued.

Bernhard glanced over at her and tried unsuccessfully to clear his throat.

'Bardolph was going to meet Frimley in Bogotá,' Phil said. 'I heard him on the phone. Frimley was going to wait for him at the airport and that woman you mentioned, Great-Aunt Elizabeth – Hildy Martin – she's there too.'

'Well done, Phil, that is very helpful. I think perhaps the best thing to do is to let them catch a plane to Bogotá and get them picked up at the other end – misappropriation of funds and fraud should do nicely. And of course we must contact parents and arrange to get all the boys sent home too.'

Bernhard shuffled about anxiously and Great-Aunt Elizabeth turned to look at him.

'I 'ave done many bad things for this evil woman,' Bernhard mumbled, his face reddening.

'I dare say you are ashamed and repentant for your part in all this,' Great-Aunt Elizabeth replied.

Harold and Emily exchanged glances and looked uncomfortable. They too had worked for the evil woman Bernhard described. In her guise as Lorabeth Lampton she had used Emily to make a device that reversed the energy flow in Great-Aunt Elizabeth's heartstone. And at a time when she had called herself Penelope Parton she had coerced Harold to invent the Humanitron.

'Go home, Bernhard,' said Great-Aunt Elizabeth. 'It was brave of you to stay and help us restore these boys to their natural states.'

At that moment a football smashed through the dining-room window, followed, a few moments later, by Robert Danby, who stuck his head through the broken glass and said, to no one in particular, 'Oi! Gissus our ball back, will ya?'

Mark retrieved the ball and crunched his way through the broken glass to hand it back.

Bernhard continued to stare at Great-Aunt Elizabeth. 'If I go 'ome she will find me and kill me. She 'as said so many times.'

'Well, you have nothing to fear now,' Great-Aunt Elizabeth told him, 'because Cynthia Caddington is dead.'

Charlotte's hand flew to her mouth. 'How?' she began,

but Great-Aunt Elizabeth raised her arm and silenced her.

'Harold and Emily, my dears, would you mind leaving us alone for a moment? I would like to speak to Charlotte and her family first, if I may.'

Emily lifted Cicely from Kate's arms and she, Harold, Mark and Bernhard left the room. The uneasy feeling that Phil had had all morning returned and sat heavily in his gut. He glanced at Kate and recognized the same tension reflected in her face. Great-Aunt Elizabeth beckoned for them all to be seated at a table while she paced the floor in front of them. Barking jumped on to a table and watched her closely, his thick tail swishing wildly behind him.

Great-Aunt Elizabeth spoke plainly and without any introductory preamble. 'My dears, I must give up this life I have lived.'

'No!' Charlotte burst out. 'What are you saying? You can't do that. It's not possible.'

'I have removed my heartstone and I cannot wear it again. After removing my own I forced Margot's stone from her neck. When she fell from the cliff the second time she had no protection and she will not have survived.'

Charlotte gaped wide-eyed at her aunt, while the rest of the Reynolds family sat still and failed to understand the full significance of what had happened.

'Perhaps Charlotte can help me to explain what this means to the rest of you, because we must come to a decision together about what becomes of the heartstones.'

Great-Aunt Elizabeth paced a few lengths of the room in silence and, when she did not resume talking, Charlotte spoke. 'By forcibly removing Margot's heartstone, Great-Aunt Elizabeth has caused it to be in a state of negative energy.'

Great-Aunt Elizabeth picked up a knife from the nearest table and came over to them. 'Had I been wearing my own heartstone at the time it would have suffered the same fate. But I removed it first and so it will merely become dormant.'

'Can't you just pick it up and reactivate it now?' Kate asked.

Great-Aunt Elizabeth took a deep breath and sighed. 'No, my dearheart, sadly not. If I touch my heartstone it will revert instantly to negative energy. I was able to protect my heartstone by removing it – but I cannot deceive it.'

She opened her jacket and pushed the knife into an inside pocket, hooked up the chain and pulled her heartstone out. The light energy that usually emanated from it had dimmed and it appeared to be fading even now as they stared at it.

'I take it a heartstone with negative energy – like your sister's heartstone – it is a bad thing,' Michael said.

Barking's tail flicked violently.

'Yes, Michael,' Great-Aunt Elizabeth said. 'It is now called a darkstone and, though the full nature of such a stone is not known, it is clear that there is a lurking menace locked within it.'

Great-Aunt Elizabeth pushed the knife into her other

pocket and lifted her sister's heartstone by its chain. It was much darker than Elizabeth's heartstone – a deep, dark purple that was almost black – and was so heavy that it bent the knife.

'Kindly bring me the Historograph,' Great-Aunt Elizabeth said, dragging over a nearby table and perching on it so that she could be close to them.

Phil did as she asked, opening the bag that held it. Great-Aunt Elizabeth passed him a second, smaller bag that she had brought with her from the Harley. 'Open it up, Phil. The rest of the heartstones are in there – lesser stones – Minnyons and Sakers. Add my heartstone to them, then place them in the bigger bag with the Historograph, there's a good lad.'

'But what will happen to you – if you haven't got a heartstone, I mean?' Kate asked.

'Well,' said Great-Aunt Elizabeth, 'that rather depends on what we decide to do next.'

'And our choices are?' said Michael.

Great-Aunt Elizabeth looked at each of them in turn. 'We have two choices. The children can come to live with me and I will teach them everything I know – everything my mother taught me. I will show them the full archive of memories stored on the Historograph and explain the uses of the lesser stones.'

'Or?' Michael asked.

Great-Aunt Elizabeth took a deep breath and blinked slowly. She reached inside her pocket for a chocolate, but finding none there she folded her arms across her chest

and sighed. 'Or,' she said carefully, 'I shall take all the heartstones – Kate's and Phil's, Barking's and Fearless's, the whole kit and caboodle – and I shall put them, together with the Historograph, somewhere where no one is going to find them. Well, not for a very long time anyway.'

Charlotte, Kate and Phil were appalled by this suggestion, but Michael tipped his head to one side and looked as though he considered it to be the best option.

'My great-grandmother stumbled across the Historograph and the stones clutched in the arms of a skeleton and that is how our family's strange legacy began. Perhaps it is destined that it should end here, in Africa.'

'How long do we have to decide?' Charlotte asked.

'Let us finish our business here – get these boys back to their parents,' replied Great-Aunt Elizabeth, 'then you can let me know what you want me to do. In the meantime, Charlotte, will you keep the Historograph and heartstones safe for me, please?'

Charlotte reached out and placed her hand on top of her aunt's larger one. 'Of course I will.'

23

The Future is Decided

There was no getting away from it, Phil thought with a heavy heart. Mrs Parker's roof was no longer a thrilling place to be. He sighed, and a pigeon that had been sleeping nearby opened one eye and fidgeted a little. Phil sat crouched in the darkness, hugging his knees and gazing out across the rooftops at the night sky. He would have counted the stars – if he could have been bothered. Another week and school would start and what then? This was completely different from the last time, when Great-Aunt Elizabeth had their heartstones. Back then there had always been the possibility of her turning up and that had made even the most ordinary day special. This time it was possible that he and Kate would never see their heartstones again.

Before they had left Tanzania, Charlotte and Michael had spent hours in deep discussion with Great-Aunt Elizabeth. No decision had been reached by the time they were ready to fly home and so Charlotte gave the leather bag containing the Historograph and all the heartstones to Fearless. He wore the bag strapped across his back,

their designated guard until their fate was decided. Great-Aunt Elizabeth would either leave them in Africa or bring them to England, depending on the decision they came to.

On the journey home, their parents let Kate and Phil know what they were thinking. Charlotte tried to explain the situation as best she could to her children. 'If you were to take up wearing your heartstones now that Great-Aunt Elizabeth can no longer wear hers, you would carry the burden of responsibility to fight crime and combat evil wherever you encountered it.'

'You could never live a normal, ordinary life,' Michael added. 'You would always be exposed to risks and dangers.'

Phil glanced at Kate, but she was looking away from him out of the window.

'It's not as if you haven't already benefited from having worn the stones this far. You'll always have that strength, that ability,' Michael had said.

'If you were to wear your heartstones,' Charlotte ventured, causing Michael to raise his eyebrows, 'you would have to live with Great-Aunt Elizabeth and study very hard. Your lives wouldn't be your own.'

They hadn't really talked about it, but when they left Africa both Kate and Phil had felt their chances of keeping their heartstones were very slim.

As they waited for their luggage in the baggage reclaim, Phil was aware of Mark standing close beside him. He shuffled about uncomfortably and appeared to have some-

thing on his mind. Eventually he said, 'Phil, listen, I'm sorry. I'm really sorry that I took your heartstone.'

Phil couldn't remember Mark ever having apologized to him before and he looked at his friend and smiled. 'It's OK. You know, that was the best thing you could have done as it turned out. Anyway, I've been meaning to thank you.'

Mark flushed and his face was a mixture of pleasure and surprise. 'Thank *me*? Why?'

Phil glanced around, but no one was paying them any attention. 'When I pushed her off the cliff, you held him back – Jim Tacker, I mean. He would have stopped me if it hadn't been for you.'

'You can't thank me for that. You nearly died,' said Mark.

'You were on my side, not his. That means a lot to me.'

Heathrow airport was busy with anxious parents and eager press expecting traumatized boys who had witnessed the principal of Caddington Lodge fall from a mountain path. The body had not been recovered and Cynthia Caddington was officially declared missing, presumed dead. To everyone's surprise, the boys did not appear to have suffered at all from their ordeal. They were lively and glowing with health and vitality – every boy returning fitter and stronger than when he had left home.

Phil's last sight of Mark was him disappearing into the arms of Sally and Darren Longbridge as they rushed

forward from the crowd. He and Mark were friends again, and Phil appreciated how lucky he was to have someone who knew what he had been through and at least partly understood what it meant to have a heartstone. But, if that was it, if all his adventures were now behind him, then it was a small consolation.

Since the family's return home Michael and Charlotte had continued speaking to Great-Aunt Elizabeth each day and sometimes for several hours at a time. Consequently brother and sister had less and less sense of how the adults were thinking. Phil didn't know what to make of it at all – sometimes he despaired and sometimes he felt positive. Sometimes he felt both at once and it was an exhausting combination. Surely, he thought, if the decision was for them to give up the heartstones then that would have been decided quickly. He concluded that all this deliberation and delay had to be a good thing and for several hours he would feel optimistic. Then doubt would set in again and he would be sure that the more they considered the risks and dangers, the more likely they were to decide against him and Kate keeping the stones.

Phil sat silently, still and lost in thought, and didn't notice that Kate had joined him on the roof. So he was surprised when she spoke. 'Penny for your thoughts?'

'I didn't hear you coming,' Phil said.

'I should hope not,' Kate replied. 'Even if we lose everything else, we've still got the skills and training we've had so far. I'm never going to let them slip.'

'No, me neither, but we're going to have to find something more challenging than the roof.'

They sat together in silence for a while until Phil asked, 'We're not going to get them back, are we?'

Kate shook her head. 'One minute I think that they can't possibly expect us to give it all up and then I think of Cicely. It was terrible what Cicely went through – and even though she's fine now, how do we know there won't be any after-effects? Emily is going to be worried sick every time her little girl is ill or has a bad dream. I can see why Dad thinks we should just get rid of the heartstones and stay well out of it – especially now . . . you know . . . now that *she's* gone.'

'That's not what you want, though, is it?' Phil asked. 'You don't want to give up your heartstone forever, do you?'

Kate thought for a moment. 'Can you imagine it? If we go to America to study with Great-Aunt Elizabeth it will mean giving everything else up – school and friends – and I'll be sorry to do that.' She sighed. 'But you're right. I don't think I can bear to be without my heartstone forever.'

'Shall I tell you what I think?' said Phil after they had sat in silence for a minute.

'What?'

'I think that pigeon is going to have a heart attack next time it wakes up.'

Barking had arrived on Phil's other side and sure enough a couple of seconds after Phil spoke the bird

opened one eye and was instantly airborne in a furious flapping of panicky wings.

Barking watched the pigeon disappear before speaking. 'Thought you'd want to know that Great-Aunt Elizabeth is on her way. She'll be here tomorrow.'

'Good,' said Kate. 'I'm sick of not knowing.'

She got up and climbed swiftly and silently down from the roof and Barking left too, picking his way daintily along the guttering. Phil stayed where he was and watched them go, suddenly unsure that he wanted to hear the decision after all. Having longed anxiously to know what his destiny would be, right now ignorance seemed preferable.

Great-Aunt Elizabeth held the leather sack in her arms and climbed steadily up the mountain. When she reached the boarded-up mine entrance she paused and looked back to where Fearless stood beside the Harley, watching her. She raised her hand to him and saw his tail begin to wag from side to side. Turning her back on him, she struggled with the urge to slacken the string on the bag and take one last look at the Historograph and the heartstones. After prising away the wood that sealed the entrance to the mine, Great-Aunt Elizabeth took a torch from her pocket and stepped inside. Slowly, she made her way along a narrow, low-ceilinged tunnel. She shone the torch on the rough ground ahead of her and, after a few twists and turns, the tunnel opened out into a large chamber at least 100 metres into the heart of the

mountain. The torchlight illuminated the tops of ladders that descended into vertical shafts sunk into the rock. The air was stale and musty. Great-Aunt Elizabeth approached the nearest shaft and shone her torch into it but the beam of light penetrated ten metres of darkness and no more. Looking around, she saw a small rock which she picked up and dropped into the hole. It was many seconds before a dull and faint thud echoed back from the bottom of the shaft.

With a heavy heart, Great-Aunt Elizabeth lifted the leather bag high and held it out over the shaft.

'Ooh! Here comes that extraordinary lady on her enormous motorbike!' exclaimed Mrs Parker, who, like the Reynolds family, had heard the distant roar of the approaching Harley and had come out into her front garden. As the Harley swerved to a halt, Barking ran to greet it, but Great-Aunt Elizabeth seemed to be in no mood for a leisurely reunion. She dismounted and, with Fearless and Barking at her heels, marched briskly into the house.

Kate and Phil exchanged glances. So this was it. The wait was finally over. Soon they would know which they would be – an ordinary family receiving a visit from an elderly relative or an extraordinary family with an amazing secret legacy.

Great-Aunt Elizabeth stood tall and gazed steadily at them, one hand resting on Fearless's gigantic head, the

other fumbling around in her pocket for chocolate. The family were assembled in the Reynolds' back room and the atmosphere was tense. No one felt like sitting down even though Charlotte suggested it.

At last Great-Aunt Elizabeth began to speak. 'As you know, children, your parents and I have discussed your future for many days. And I think that you should know that I have tried very hard to convince your father that the legacy of the heartstones must now pass to you.' She paused and stared directly at her niece's husband before continuing to address Kate and Phil. 'Michael fears for your safety and he questions my ability to keep you from harm. He quite rightly points out that I made serious errors of judgement while I was still in possession of my heartstone and so how, he wonders, will I protect you now that I am without it?'

Great-Aunt Elizabeth sighed and at last pulled her hand from her pocket, bringing out three small chocolates wrapped in gold and purple cellophane. As Fearless raised his head in order to watch her closely, Phil bent forward to stroke him, pushing his hand through the dense curls of warm fur beneath his chin. Barking wound his sleek black body round and through Kate's legs before jumping into Charlotte's arms just as she suggested, for the second time, that they might perhaps all take a seat.

No one moved and Michael Reynolds coughed to clear his throat before speaking. 'I think the children will appreciate it if you just come out with it and tell them, Aunt Elizabeth.'

Phil glanced up at his dad. He had always worried about them. Why, even before Great-Aunt Elizabeth had come into their lives he was always telling them to be careful. It had been crazy to think that he would choose differently.

Great-Aunt Elizabeth replied slowly, 'Why don't you tell them, Michael?'

Michael nodded. 'This summer, in a few brief weeks, in fact, you have been exposed to the most dreadful, horrifying events. Cicely was kidnapped and had her brain modified, Kate has been thrown from a moving car and Phil survived a day and a night in the bush, a fall into a ravine and an episode of time travel – tell me if I've forgotten something, won't you?' Michael shook his head before taking a deep breath and continuing. 'And you survived. That's the thing – you did survive. You weren't even wearing your heartstones when you were most in danger and you still survived. So, what I'm saying is – if you want to, and you don't have to, you can accept the legacy. It's up to you.'

They hadn't noticed Charlotte slip from the room, but now she returned carrying the leather bag containing the Historograph and the heartstones in her arms.

'So?' she said, holding the bag out towards her daughter and son. 'Do you accept?'

Phil grinned at his sister over the top of Barking's head. 'Yes,' they said, 'we accept!'

Phil took the bag from his mum and untied the drawstring, hurriedly loosening the gathered neck of the bag and peering inside. Immediately, his face was lit in a brilliant red glow as the heartstones surged with power. He put his hand in, pulled out Kate's heartstone and passed it to her, dangling by its chain from his finger. Next he reached in and passed Barking's and Fearless's stones to Charlotte, who began reattaching them to their collars. Lastly, he pulled out the keystone. Phil smiled at his dad as he closed his fist tight around the stone. He could feel it buzzing in his grasp and rays of red light shone out from between his fingers. He looked at Great-Aunt Elizabeth and grinned as relief flooded him. He would not let her down. He would learn; all there was to learn; he would work hard and study the Historograph. As Phil pulled the drawstring closed, he noticed the larger of the two darkstones skulking at the bottom of the bag and he hesitated. There was something menacing about it that threatened to spoil his mood.

Just then, Fearless's nose nudged at Phil's hand, bringing his attention back to the room where his family were discussing which restaurant should accommodate their celebrations that evening. 'I would prefer a takeaway myself,' Barking was saying.

Phil placed the bag of stones on the table and put his keystone round his neck. As he waited for Great-Aunt Elizabeth to seal it for him, his eyes met Kate's and their stones flared and sent shards of light sparking round the room.

'How about Indian?' Kate suggested at the same moment as Phil said, 'I'd love a pizza!'

Suddenly everyone was speaking at once. Fearless paced excitedly between them and Barking walked his front paws up Charlotte's legs. Michael moved off to the kitchen, to the drawer where they kept the best of the takeaway leaflets that fell through the letter box. Still arguing, the family followed Michael through the door and the room was quiet.

The leather pouch lay on the table where Phil had left it. From the musty darkness deep inside the bag came a small, barely perceptible sound: a faint groan that might easily be mistaken for the creaking sigh of settling floor-boards.

Homeward bound in the golden glow of the late afternoon sun a young *Maasai* boy saw a bundle of sticks in a shadowy hollow at the base of the mountain. Leaving his brother and cousin to drive the cattle, he ran off to collect it. As he approached he saw that what he had taken to be sticks of firewood were thin, sinewy arms and legs. The boy stopped and glanced after the others. They were steadily moving away from him, trailing long shadows across the red earth. He checked his instinct to shout after them. *Would they think him frightened? Would they tell the village that they had found the body instead?* Keen to show his courage, the boy moved closer and received another shock. This was a *mzungu* – an elderly white woman. Leaning forward, peering into the gloom, he took another step closer. A wall of flies lifted into the dusty air, only to resettle immediately on the rags and

bones of the ancient body. The boy strained to see. The face was twisted towards him and was hideous. The skin was scarred and wrinkled and lay against the contours of the skull. The boy squatted in the dust and crept closer. A large fly walked in circles across the corpse's desiccated lips and then paused beside a nostril, rubbing its back legs together. He held out the stick he used to prod reluctant cattle and pushed it into the body. Suddenly, with a speed that caused the boy to topple backwards on to the ground, a claw-like hand flew up and snatched hold of the stick. The cracked lips parted, the sunken eyes opened and a rasping voice gasped the words, 'Water – *maji!*'

Back in the Reynolds' house, while the family sat chatting at the kitchen table, the first minute spark of energy fizzed softly between the darkstones.